W9-CKG-937

A CATERED
TEA PARTY

Center Point
Large Print

Also by Isis Crawford and available from
Center Point Large Print:

A Catered Fourth of July
A Catered Mother's Day

**This Large Print Book carries the
Seal of Approval of N.A.V.H.**

A Mystery with Recipes

A CATERED
TEA PARTY

ISIS CRAWFORD

CENTER POINT LARGE PRINT
THORNDIKE, MAINE

Library of Congress Cataloging-in-Publication Data

Names: Crawford, Isis, author.
Title: A catered tea party : a mystery with recipes / Isis Crawford.
Description: Center Point Large Print edition. | Thorndike, Maine :
Center Point Large Print, 2016.
Identifiers: LCCN 2016028934 | ISBN 9781683241447
    (hardcover : alk. paper)
Subjects: LCSH: Simmons, Bernie (Fictitious character : Crawford)—
Fiction. | Simmons, Libby (Fictitious character)—Fiction. | Caterers and
catering—Fiction. | Murder—Investigation—Fiction. | Large type books.
| GSAFD: Mystery fiction.
Classification: LCC PS3603.R396 C37237 2016 | DDC 813/.6—dc23
LC record available at https://lccn.loc.gov/2016028934

To Betsy Scheu for giving me the idea.

Prologue

One hour before the play

Ludvoc Zalinsky looked at his creation and saw that it was good. It had taken him seven months to create The Blue House instead of seven days, but then God hadn't had to contend with the Longely Planning Commission or the unions. Zalinsky smiled as he rearranged his top hat on his head. The thing was heavier than he thought it would be, but the costumer he'd bought it from had assured him that this hat was the one that had been used in the 2008 off-off Broadway production of *Alice in Wonderland*.

He gave the hat another tap, then readjusted the lapels of his waistcoat. Yes, indeedy. This was going to be the opening to end all openings, the gala to end all galas, the art event of the year. The Blue House was going to become The Place to Be. People would come from the city to experience the art exhibitions, the plays, the concerts, and he would be remembered as the man who created it. Zalinsky frowned briefly as he remembered what that twit had said to him after he'd won the bidding for the Yixing stoneware teapot.

So what if he'd paid two million dollars for it? For heaven's sake, what was the point of living the life if you couldn't get what you wanted? He had wanted the teapot for his collection, and he'd acquired it. Simple as that. He'd wanted it to be showcased in his production of *Alice in Wonderland*, and it was. Who cared what that idiot Cumberbatch, his director, said? So what if it didn't fit in with the set design? It fit in with his plans, plans Cumberbatch knew nothing about.

Zalinsky made a rude noise as he remembered the conversation. Set design! What kind of garbage excuse was that? Ridiculous. Where was it written that you couldn't set the table with Chinese pottery and English sterling silver? Nowhere, that's where. The whole idea of this production was to showcase the damned teapot. To let everyone admire it. And it was a draw. A big draw.

People were coming to see it. I mean how often did a two-million-dollar teapot turn up in a play? Never. That's how often. This was a first. Why else would people be coming? It certainly wasn't to see *Alice in Wonderland*, for God's sake, and to insure that nothing happened to the Yixing he'd hired two guards to keep an eye on it for the evening, which added to the drama. Zalinsky smiled when he thought about what was going to happen, the thing that only he and one other person knew about—and that person wasn't Casper Cumberbatch. Cumberbatch. A man with ideas above his station. He'd only hired him because he was cheap.

Alice in Wonderland as a live play. It was brilliant. The actors would be drinking tea and eating onstage. Then the audience would have their meal and have a chance to interact with the cast, an event he was looking forward to since he'd cast himself as the Mad Hatter. After all, he'd written the play. Or should he say rewritten the play? No, he'd improved the play, giving it a more modern feel, so why shouldn't he be in it as well?

And he was pretty good as the Mad Hatter, if he did say so himself. He was a regular . . . what was that fancy French word . . . *auteur*. He'd recreated himself. He'd gone from starving in Moscow to major success in America. America, the land of opportunity. And how had he done it? By being smarter than everyone else, that's how. Look how he'd financed The Blue House. He rubbed his hands together, thinking of what was coming next. The pinnacle of his career, really.

It just went to show that appearance was everything. It was the appearance of wealth that mattered, not the actuality. People thought he was a billionaire, so he was, even if he wasn't. Why? Because he was confident. Because he behaved the way a billionaire would behave. Because he dressed the part.

Art, writing, acting—they weren't so hard. He didn't know what all the fuss was about. From what he could see, anyone could do those things.

All you had to do was make stuff up. It wasn't like juggling all the balls in the air the way he was doing. If he made a mistake, he'd go to jail. Not that that would happen because he had that eventuality covered as well.

All this criticism from the cast and crew. All this negativity. Those people were giving him a headache. He wished they'd just shut up and do what he told them to, which, come to think of it, they were! After all, everyone, and that included that idiot of a director, was in the play because he told them they were going to be. Except for the Simmons sisters. Them he'd had to pay. Unfortunately. Because they were impossible.

They just went on and on and on about the cohesion of menu choices, but he was damned if he wasn't going to have the kind of food he wanted served. So what if he'd kept on changing the menu around? Wasn't that the sign of a great mind? Anyway, the sisters were being paid enough to deal with it. More than they were worth, actually.

Zalinsky consulted his watch. Six-thirty. One hour before the theater doors to the house opened and the audience trooped in. It was time to adjourn to the backstage lounge, the lounge he'd been kind enough to build, and give the cast members a pep talk before the play began. But before that he had to find his damned gloves. He knew where he'd put them, but they weren't there now. Which was aggravating because he absolutely needed them. He took a deep breath to calm himself down. It wouldn't hurt if he practiced his welcoming speech one more time either. He wanted it to be perfect. After all, there was a chance it might be quoted in Sunday's *New York Times*.

And it was, though not in the way Zalinsky had in mind.

Chapter 1

Sean Simmons, Bernie and Libby's father, was sitting front row center in The Blue House theater watching the amateur theater production of *Alice in Wonderland*. It was twenty minutes into act one, and Sean was not a happy camper. Of course, the fact that he hadn't wanted to be here in the first place, that he was just doing this as a favor to his daughters, might have something to do with his reaction to the play, but judging from the whispering he heard going on around him, the rest of the audience felt the same way he did. If he were a reviewer he'd give the play a minus zero.

For the last ten minutes, Sean had watched Alice chase the March Hare and the Queen of Hearts around a table set for tea, and the only reason Sean could see for that piece of stagecraft was that it highlighted Zalinsky's teapot. Why anyone would pay two million dollars for that thing was beyond him, but then he wasn't a billionaire.

While Sean was thinking about what he would do if he was a billionaire, he watched the two rent-a-cops who had been guarding the doors to the house march down the aisles and take up new positions on the top steps that led up to the stage. Now they stood facing the audience, arms crossed over their bulletproof vests, at the ready to deter anyone from doing a run-and-grab with the teapot. Like that was going to happen.

In Sean's professional opinion, the whole security drama being enacted was ludicrous, but he supposed that the thing about being a billionaire was that you could do whatever you wanted, hence the pierogies being distributed to the audience. The pierogies! Good God, he'd heard about them for the last two weeks. He'd heard about how bad serving them would make his daughters look, about what a jerk Zalinsky was, about what a bad recipe Zalinksy's mother had used. And then there'd been the tastings. Endless. If he never saw another one of those damned dumplings again, it wouldn't be a moment too soon.

Sean sighed and looked at his watch. He was just thinking that maybe he could find an excuse to leave after act one when Ellen Crestfield turned and whispered in his ear how much she was enjoying the play. Then she squeezed his hand. He mustered up a smile, but he didn't squeeze Ellen Crestfield's hand back. Instead, he freed it and began studying the playbill.

It wasn't that he didn't like Ellen Crestfield. Ellen Crestfield was a very nice woman, but she was, as the saying goes, dull as dishwater, and he had no intention of entering into a relationship with her. He wouldn't have even cared about going to the gala with her if Libby hadn't arranged it to get him away from Michelle. Sean knew that Libby thought she was being clever. She thought he didn't know what she and Bernie were up to; she thought he didn't know what they thought of Michelle, but she was wrong on all counts.

Sean knew alright. His daughters didn't like Michelle—not even a little bit—but Sean was damned if he could figure out why. He would have thought that all of them being in the same business would have given Michelle and his daughters something to talk about. Michelle said his daughters were just jealous. Maybe they were. Maybe Michelle was right, although he didn't think so, but what did he know? He fanned himself with the playbill. He'd admit it: when it came to women he didn't know a lot. He'd been married to Rose for almost thirty years, and he hadn't understood her any better on the day she'd died than on the day they'd gotten married. He'd loved her, but he hadn't understood her.

As Sean turned his attention back to the stage and watched Alice, the March Hare, and the Queen of Hearts do what must be their tenth lap around the stage, he noticed Libby and Bernie peeking out at him from the curtain on the left. Libby waggled her fingers back and forth, and Sean reciprocated and forced a smile.

"Dad's not happy," Libby said to Bernie as she let the curtain drop.

"Told you that you shouldn't have foisted Ellen on him," her sister replied.

"Then what would you suggest?" Libby demanded.

"Waiting," Bernie said. "Michelle will screw up."

Libby shook her head. "I can't believe Dad is that dumb. What does he see in her?"

Bernie wiped a bead of sweat off her forehead. God, it was hot in there. "What do you think he sees in her? She laughs at his jokes, and she's twenty years younger than he is."

"Eighteen."

"Whatever."

"She's using him!"

"I don't think Dad sees it that way, and even if he did, I don't think he cares. In fact, let me go further. In this particular instance, I think he's happy being used." Bernie looked at her watch and cursed under her breath. They had to get going. In fifteen minutes, Erin (aka Alice) and Hsaio (aka The Dormouse) were going to pick up platters of pierogies from the prop table, re-enter stage right, walk down the steps into the audience, and offer the pierogies to the people sitting in the front rows.

While that was happening, the stage would go dark, and Zalinsky would take his teapot to the kitchen, fill it and a thermos up with hot water from the electric kettle, return to the stage, and start brewing the tea for the tea party. That was the plan.

Originally there had been no eating and drinking onstage, but Zalinsky had insisted that the tea party be "realistic." He wanted to both brew tea in his teapot and drink it, which of course created a whole slew of logistical problems for poor Casper. Bernie just hoped that Zalinsky didn't trip getting to and from the kitchen because it was going to be pitch-black backstage, and there were wires and cables snaking all over the floor.

"Can you imagine if Zalinsky dropped the teapot?" Bernie asked Libby, making sure to keep her voice low so it wouldn't carry out to the audience.

"Poof." Libby made a disappearing gesture with her hands. "Two million dollars gone, just like that."

"I don't think I'd drink out of it."

"I don't think I'd buy it."

"This is true. But you're not a collector."

"Even if I was . . ." Bernie's voice trailed off as she looked at her watch again. "We have to get going." They had two more scenes before it was time for the tea party. In scene number one, Alice bopped the Queen of Hearts with a croquet ball, and in scene number two, Tweedledee and Tweedledum recited their poem.

"I know," Libby said as she fanned herself with a playbill. She figured it was over ninety inside the theater. It was dark enough backstage as it was. When the lights went out they wouldn't be able to see anything. "I just hope we don't drop those damned platters."

"You and me both, sister," Bernie said as she turned and headed toward the galley kitchen.

Not only did she and her sister have to deal with the pierogies, they had to finish setting up for the high tea they were serving after the play. By Bernie's reckoning, they just had enough time to heat up the pierogies, arrange them on the platters, pour the milk into the silver creamer, which was also going on the tea table, and make sure the electric kettle had been plugged in before the stage went dark.

Five minutes later, Libby and Bernie were out the kitchen door. They were halfway to the prop table when the stage lights went out. Libby cursed under her breath. *Please don't let me drop the pierogies,* she silently prayed. She bit her tongue in concentration as she walked. She'd taken about twenty steps when she saw something in front of her that looked even darker than the surroundings. An object? Maybe a table? She wasn't sure. *It doesn't matter what it is,* she told herself. *Just go around it.* Which she did. She was just congratulating herself on not banging into it when she tripped on something on the floor.

"Damn," she cried as the platter tipped.

"Sssh," Bernie said.

"I'm trying," Libby replied as she righted the

platter. She didn't think any of the pierogies had fallen on the floor. At least she hoped not. It was hard to tell because she couldn't see them. She'd just taken another step when someone brushed by her, jostling her arm. "Watch it," she hissed.

"Then get out of the way," a person Libby decided must be a techie hissed back.

Libby bit back her retort and concentrated on getting to where she was supposed to go. She was almost at the prop table. By the time she got there, Bernie had already arrived and Erin and Hsaio were waiting for her.

"The lights are about to go on," Erin whispered as Libby put the platter on the table.

"I know," Libby whispered back.

A moment later they did.

Erin looked at the stage. Her eyes widened. "Where's Zalinsky?"

Bernie shook her head. She had no idea.

"He's supposed to be onstage by now," Hsaio noted, a hint of panic in her voice.

"Maybe he's still in the kitchen," Bernie suggested.

"Why the hell should he be in the kitchen?" Erin demanded. She was pissed. She hadn't wanted to do this play in the first place. "He should be sitting at the damned table brewing tea in that stupid teapot of his."

"I'll go look," Hsaio volunteered. Her tone was placating.

"Why don't you ask Casper what he wants to do in the meantime?" Bernie said to Erin. She could hear the audience getting restless.

Erin put her hands on her hips. "Do you see him around here?" she asked, jutting out her chin.

"No," Bernie allowed, which she thought was odd. She could have sworn she'd seen him near the prop table fiddling around with the Caterpillar's hookah ten minutes ago.

"Good, because neither do I," Erin replied. She turned to Hsaio. "Hurry up so we can start giving out the pierogies."

"I'm going, I'm going. No need to be unpleasant," Hsaio told her.

"I wasn't being unpleasant," Erin countered. "But we need to get this show on the road."

"Like I'm not aware of that," Hsaio huffed as she turned and headed toward the kitchen.

Great, Bernie thought as she watched Hsaio retreating into the backstage gloom. Now the picrogies will be cold on top of everything else. She peeked out around the curtain. The audience was definitely restless. They were leaning over and talking to one another while they fanned themselves with their playbills. She could hear phrases like "a waste of my time" and "when will this be over?" floating in the air.

Libby bit at her nail, realized what she was doing, and stopped. "I hope Zalinsky hurries up," she said.

19

"Me too," Erin agreed, shifting the platter of pierogies from one hand to another so she could pull down her skirt. Every time she moved, the dratted thing rode up. It was extremely annoying.

"I'll go see what's happening," Bernie offered.

"Hsaio already went," Erin pointed out.

"Maybe she needs help," Bernie replied. She couldn't stay still any longer. She had to do something.

She was halfway to the kitchen when someone screamed.

Chapter 2

Bernie's first thought as she hurried toward the sound was *Oh my God. What now?* Her second thought was *It's Hsaio screaming.* Her third thought was *Fantastic. More drama. Just what we don't need.* She didn't know why Hsaio was screaming, but she did know it wasn't because she'd seen a mouse.

Absolutely nothing had gone smoothly since she and Libby had taken this job. Nothing. And this was going to have been such an easy gig too. Simple as pie, Casper had said. A piece of cake. A chance for you to shine. Get some new business. Get in on the ground floor. You could become the go-to caterer for all the events at The Blue House. Etc. Etc. Etc. Yeah, right.

But how was she to have known things would turn out this way? Seriously, how hard could catering a community theater post-production party of *Alice in Wonderland* be? At least that's what she and Libby had thought. Some fancy scones with clotted cream and strawberries, a variety of crustless sandwiches of the cucumber and cream cheese variety, a summer pudding, different kinds of tea, both hot and iced, a little May wine, some sort of punch—in other words, a riff on a classic English high tea—and they were done. What they hadn't counted on was Zalinsky.

He'd turned out to be the proverbial client from hell. Of course, she and Libby hadn't known that when they'd taken the job. Neither had Casper, for that matter. If he had, he never would have signed on to direct this fiasco. When she and her sister had spoken to Zalinsky and presented their menu, he'd been positively enthusiastic. He'd thought an English high tea was a great idea. *Brilliant* was the word he'd used. But then as the weeks passed, he'd changed his mind about as often as Imelda Marcos changed her shoes. By the time they were done, the menu was a complete mishmash.

There was sushi (in deference to Zalinsky's precious Yixing teapot—never mind that the teapot was Chinese and sushi was Japanese), cucumber sandwiches, and a sprinkling of Polish dishes with unpronounceable names that Zalinsky had insisted on adding to the menu. To honor his mother's memory, he'd said—never mind that his mother was Irish. At least, that's what Casper Cumberbatch had told her. Individually the dishes were all fine, except for the headcheese, of course. But together? Together, they induced acute indigestion.

At that point, she and Libby would have backed out of the whole thing, except for the fact that they'd already signed a contract and Zalinsky had threatened to sue them for breach of it if they opted out. Libby had said he was bluffing, but Bernie was pretty sure he would have followed through on his threat. Evidently he had a history of drowning people in legal actions, which was one of the reasons Casper hadn't up and left.

At least that's what Casper had told her. Bernie sighed. Too bad she hadn't researched Zalinsky before they'd taken the job. In her defense, though, she'd never had to deal with this kind of situation before. But if she had it bad, Casper had had it worse. He had to deal with Zalinsky twenty-four/seven. If Zalinsky wasn't at the theater, he was calling Casper to discuss one of his ideas—all of which were terrible. It seemed as if nothing was immune from Zalinsky's meddling. Zalinsky had cast the play, pretty much rewritten it, and designed the set. It was the ultimate vanity piece.

To Bernie's mind, a perfect example of Zalinsky's meddling was Zalinsky insisting that the table where the tea party was going to take place be placed front and center on the stage. This was despite the fact that the tea party scene didn't happen until act one, scene five. But when Casper had pointed that out to Zalinsky, Zalinsky had called him a cretin and told him to get over himself. Everyone, he'd said, was coming to see the teapot. And maybe they were. Maybe Zalinsky was correct. Still, there was such a thing as being civil, a concept Zalinksy didn't adhere to. He just wanted what he wanted and used any means at his disposal to get it.

When she and Libby had argued with him about serving pierogies at the tea party, Zalinsky had gotten red in the face and told them they were morons and their food sucked. But when Libby had told him he had no sense of taste, he'd clutched his chest and told them they were giving him a heart attack. Libby actually thought he was having one, so she had apologized, at which point Zalinsky had told her he'd do whatever he wanted and he could do without her suggestions, thank you very much.

So when Zalinsky had decided that not *only* were pierogies going to be served for the tea but that Erin (aka Alice) was going to serve them to the audience as well, neither she nor Libby had uttered a peep. Pierogies! At an English tea! The thought still made Bernie shudder. As Casper had said, "It's enough to make one blush with shame." Which was only a slight exaggeration, in Bernie's mind.

Bernie sighed as she recalled the events of the past weeks. But wasn't that always the way? The things you thought were going to be hard were easy, and the things you thought were going to be easy turned out to be hard. At least her biggest nightmare hadn't happened. The food critic for the *New York Times* hadn't come. He'd sent his regrets instead. Evidently, he'd been invited to something more exciting in the Hamptons. Thank God for small favors. Their shop, A Little Taste of Heaven, would never have lived down the embarrassment.

Bernie pursed her lips as she recalled Zalinsky's temper tantrums, his clutching his chest and telling everyone they were giving him a heart attack when he didn't get his way. There had been no detail too small to escape Zalinsky's notice. The man didn't micromanage, he nanomanaged, which had built up a tremendous amount of resentment on the part of the cast and the crew.

Witness the scene in the lounge before the production had started. Bernie could smell the tension in the air when she and her sister had walked in. Everyone in the cast looked angry, while Casper looked as if he wanted to do a Cheshire Cat and fade into the sofa.

Erin Kenwood had been sitting next to him on the sofa, facing the door. She was wearing her *Alice in Wonderland* getup, a light-blue, knee-length dress, a frilly white apron, white knee-length socks, and black patent-leather shoes. A black velvet hair band was holding back her long blond hair. When she looked up, Bernie could see that her mascara and eyeliner were smudged. *Erin's been crying,* she remembered thinking.

Jason Pancetta, the March Hare, was sitting on the second sofa, alternately glowering at Zalinsky and swinging his pocket watch back and forth, while Hsaio Rosenthal was curled up on the sofa in her Dormouse costume, looking terrified. The next two members of the cast, Stan and George Holloway (aka Tweedledee and Tweedledum), were both leaning against the far wall.

Bernie remembered thinking that the costumes Zalinsky had chosen for them, tight T-shirts and vests and stripped knickers, must have been an act of revenge for some imagined slight—like maybe killing Zalinsky's best friend. The last member of the company, Magda Webster, who was Zalinsky's administrative assistant and the putative Queen of Hearts, looked as if she wanted to rake her long, red fingernails across Zalinsky's chest.

And then there had been *the scene*. Zalinsky had wanted to make yet another change, and she and everyone else had jumped in and told Zalinsky it wasn't possible, and he'd gotten really, really angry. Angry to the point where he'd stalked over to the coffee table and swept the vase filled with Erin's red roses onto the floor. Then he'd snarled at Erin to clean the mess up. If looks could kill, Zalinsky would have been dead.

But Zalinsky hadn't cared. Instead he'd railed at everyone. Bernie remembered his rant. "So this is what I get for trying to be nice," he'd screamed. "This is what I get for building you this lounge and furnishing it with top-of-the-line furniture." Then he'd ended with, "You people are going to be the death of me yet," and stomped off.

"From your mouth to God's ear," Bernie couldn't help remembering Casper whispering to Erin after Zalinsky had left.

It looks as if Casper has had his way, Bernie thought when she reached the kitchen and saw Zalinsky crumpled up on the floor, his arms outstretched, his hat covering his face. Zalinsky's favorite mug lay on the floor near his left foot, which was resting in a small puddle of liquid. Probably his tea, Bernie thought because that was all Zalinsky ever drank. He must have dropped it when he collapsed.

Bernie wrinkled her nose. The smell of something burnt lingered in the air. She watched Hsaio standing over Zalinsky, shrieking loud enough to wake the dead. Only in this case, Bernie didn't think there was going to be a resurrection. She'd just had time to register the fact that Zalinsky wasn't mostly dead, he was completely dead, when the two security guards who had been on the stage brushed her aside, slamming her into a wall as they rushed into the room.

It wasn't until an hour later, when the confusion had died down, that she and Libby realized that the two-million-dollar teapot was gone as well. So much for hiring security guards, Bernie had thought when she saw the empty spot on the table where the teapot had been.

Chapter 3

I didn't say that," Casper protested to Sean, Libby, and Bernie.

A week had gone by since Zalinsky's death. It was three in the afternoon, and the four of them were sitting in the Simmonses' flat above A Little Taste of Heaven. Casper was stirring another lump of sugar into his iced green mint tea, while Sean was finishing off a piece of blueberry pie.

"Yeah, you did Casper," Libby said as she flicked a crumb of crust off her lap.

"Okay," Casper admitted, backtracking, "maybe I did say *from your mouth to God's ear,* but that doesn't mean I killed him . . ."

". . . and stole the teapot," Libby added.

Casper gave her the evil eye. "Don't be absurd."

"I'm just repeating what the police are saying," Libby told him.

Casper put his cup down. "What the police are alleging. Alleging. I didn't steal the damned thing. Why would I do something like that?"

Libby supplied the obvious answer. "Because the teapot is worth two million dollars."

"Only to the right people," Casper retorted, "and they're above my pay grade. It's not the sort of thing you can pawn. They should talk to Hsaio. She's the one who knows about that world."

"She's getting a PhD in art education," Bernie objected. "That's quite a bit different."

Casper blotted the sweat off his face with a napkin. "But she still knows more about that world than I do. The police should look at her."

Bernie ate a raspberry. "They looked at everyone," she told Casper.

"They should look harder," Casper cried.

"They've pretty much settled on you," Sean informed him. "At least that's what Clyde tells me." Clyde was Sean's friend and a member of the Longely police force.

"Lovely," Casper muttered. "Wonderful. First that hell of a play, and now this." He looked up at the ceiling and put his hands together. "Will my trials never end, oh Lord?"

Bernie rolled her eyes. "Oh please!"

"But this is so unfair," Casper protested. "Everyone in the cast hated Zalinsky. You know they did."

"Yes, but not everyone had to spend as much time with him as you did," Libby pointed out. "Not everyone was about to have their professional career destroyed because of him."

"That's a slight exaggeration," Casper protested.

"Is it?" Libby asked. "I heard he was going to get rid of you . . ."

Casper interrupted. "Well, you heard wrong. *I* was the one who was leaving."

"Remember, you told me you couldn't get out of your contract," Bernie said.

"I said no such thing," Casper countered.

Libby continued with what she'd been saying. "Be that as it may, you were about to be reviewed by the drama critic of the *New York Times*. If the food critic had been at the play, I would have slit my wrists. Zalinsky's death stopped the play."

"He never came," Casper said.

"But you didn't know that," Sean pointed out.

"Do you really think I'd kill someone so I wouldn't get a bad review?" Casper demanded.

"People have killed for less," Sean told him. "And then there's the other stuff."

Casper put his glass down, sloshing the tea over the side onto the table. He wiped it up with a napkin Bernie handed him. "I've explained that. I mean if the police want to go after anyone they should go after Erin. If she had had a gun, she would have shot Zalinsky when he threw her roses on the floor. I'm surprised she didn't punch him. She sure looked like she wanted to."

Bernie and Libby remained silent.

Casper leaned forward. "She did," he insisted. He appealed to Bernie. "For that matter, you and your sister hated him just as much as I did."

"I'm not saying we didn't," Bernie replied. "But none of us threatened him. None of us left a note on his kitchen table that said, 'You'll get yours.'"

"I did not write that note," Casper cried.

"Then who did?" Libby asked. "It was on your letterhead."

"The person who wrote it is the person who is setting me up," Casper said. "Anyone could have gotten my stationery and printed it out on the computer. In fact," he leaned forward, warming to his subject, "I wouldn't be surprised if it was Zalinsky himself. It would be just like him to do this to me."

Bernie raised her eyebrows. "Seriously?" she asked.

Casper balled up his fists. "Would I have written that note if I intended to kill him?" he said. "Would I be that stupid? Give me some credit."

"Obviously someone thinks you are that stupid," Sean said. "Otherwise they wouldn't have sent an anonymous note to the chief of police the day after Zalinsky died."

Casper seized on the word *anonymous*. "If there was any credence to that note, whoever wrote it would have signed their name."

"The police aren't seeing it that way," Bernie said, thinking of what her dad had said about what Lucy, their chief of police, had said.

Casper crossed his arms over his chest. "This is nothing more than a scurrilous attack on me by a person of low moral character," he protested.

"Unfortunately, the police don't go by a gentleman's code of honor these days," Sean said dryly. "I think the days of dueling are gone."

"I come here for support, and I get the opposite," Casper said dolefully. He started to get up. "I thought you were my friend," he told Bernie, his voice brimming with indignation. "I thought you were going to help me."

"We are," Bernie told him. "Now, sit back down."

"Well, it sure doesn't sound that way to me," Casper said sulkily, but he sat down anyway.

Bernie leaned forward. "You need to calm down. My dad and I are just repeating what the police are saying. We're laying out their case so we can counter it."

Casper scowled. "The police are morons," he retorted. "Heaven preserve me from fools and vipers."

Bernie noticed that he'd started jiggling his right leg up and down. "That may be," Bernie said. "But here's the thing. You weren't where you were supposed to be right before Zalinsky died, and when you add that in to everything else . . ." Bernie put her hands out, spread her fingers, and shrugged. "Well . . ."

"I already explained that," Casper cried. "I was in the bathroom."

Libby added a dollop of cream to the top of her pie. "Unfortunately, no one saw you."

Casper looked indignant. "So now I have to tell everyone when I have to go off to the potty to poop? I need a witness?"

"In this case, it might have been a good idea," Libby said.

"No one could have seen me anyway," Casper retorted. "It was dark backstage. It's always dark backstage when a performance is going on. You know that."

Libby nodded her head. It was true.

Casper smacked the arm of the chair he was sitting in with the flat of his hand. "I can't believe this is happening to me," he moaned. "And my astrologer said this was going to be a good month. I'm going to fire him, the nincompoop." Casper waved his hands in the air. "I feel as if I'm in the middle of a bad movie written by a Hitchcock wannabe."

Sean put his fork down on his plate. "The thing is," he told Casper, "you could have gone in and substituted the hot-wired teakettle during the time you said you were in the john."

Casper gave a mirthless laugh. "Please. So could anyone else. It was so dark in there any-one could have gone into the kitchen and back again."

"Well, it was okay when I plugged it in," Libby said. "So that narrows the time frame down considerably."

"Maybe it wasn't the kettle," Casper suggested. "Maybe the plug was defective."

"No, it was the kettle," Bernie said. "They found the one we plugged in, in the kitchen cabinet. So someone changed up one for the other."

Sean leaned back in his armchair. "And here's

where we come to our problem. You have no one to vouch for your whereabouts, and you have the knowledge to have rewired the kettle."

"What you said goes for the crew as well," Casper protested.

Sean shook his head. "Their movements have all been accounted for."

"The guards," Casper suggested.

"I saw them," Sean said. "They were standing on either side of the stage, blocking the way."

"Fine." Casper took another sip of his tea. His leg jiggled faster. "Then one of the cast."

"Possibly," Sean said equitably. "But no one except you has any experience with wiring."

"I don't have any experience either," Casper protested.

"You worked in a lighting store," Sean said.

"So what?" Casper cried. "I worked on the floor. I sold things. I didn't work in the back of the shop."

"You told me you'd rewired a lamp in your living room," Bernie reminded him.

Casper rolled his eyes. "Jeez. Give me a break."

"I'm just sayin' . . . ," Bernie told him.

"I know what you're sayin'," Casper replied. "Okay. You're right. I did it." He extended his arms. "Here. Put the cuffs on me."

"Stop it," Bernie chided.

"Anyone can rewire a teakettle," Casper

continued, lowering his arms. "All you have to do is look on the Internet and follow the instructions. Anyway, it was probably an accident."

"I think not," Libby said.

"Electric teakettles can short out on their own," Casper protested. "It can happen. It probably happens a lot more than people think."

"Evidently not like this," Bernie said.

Thanks to her dad's friend Clyde, she'd seen the police report, and the report had been very clear. Someone had hot-wired the electric teakettle, and when Zalinsky had touched it, he'd received a fatal shock to his heart. Unfortunately, whoever had done it had wiped the handle and the teakettle itself clean. So, no fingerprints.

"Well, I didn't touch that teakettle," Casper said. "I didn't," he repeated when nobody in the room said anything. He raised his hand. "I swear."

Sean speared a crumb of crust on his fork and ate it. "It's not me you have to convince," he told him.

"I don't understand why they're so sure it's one of us," Casper said.

"Not us—*you*," Sean told him, speaking slowly to emphasize the gravity of the situation. "At the present time, *you* are the primary suspect."

"This is beyond the pale," Casper replied in a voice brimming with outrage.

Sean held up his hand. "May I continue?"

"Sorry," Casper muttered.

"In the mind of the police, *you* had the motive, the means, and the opportunity to commit this crime. Plus—and this is a big plus—there's the note accusing you, plus the note threatening . . ."

Casper broke in. "I already explained that."

"Do you want to hear what the police are thinking, or don't you?" Sean snapped. He was running out of patience.

"I want to hear," Casper said.

"Then let me finish," Sean commanded. He glared at Casper, who shrank back into the sofa. "As I was saying," Sean continued. "The police have two theories. In one, you killed Zalinsky because he was making your life a living hell and threatening to make sure you never got another directing job anywhere . . ."

This time it was Bernie who broke in. "Is that true?" she asked Casper.

Casper nodded. "But he didn't mean it. He was always saying that kind of stuff."

Sean went on as if no one had spoken. ". . . and then you stole the Chinese teapot because you figured he owed it to you. In their other theory, you intended to steal the teapot all along, so you hot-wired the electric kettle to provide a distraction, and Zalinsky's death was an unfortunate by-product of the heist."

Casper had gotten very still while Sean was

talking. "Do you believe that?" he asked anxiously when Sean was done.

"As a matter of fact, I don't," Sean assured him. "But what I think doesn't matter. If I were you, I'd get a lawyer."

Casper bit his lip. "I can't afford a lawyer. I don't have any money," he cried.

Bernie got up and put her hand on his shoulder. "Don't worry. I told you we'd help you and we will."

"How?" Casper asked.

"By talking to people," Bernie answered.

"Great," Casper grumbled. "Some people get Sam Spade, and I get the conversationalists."

Bernie glared at him. "Hey, we're doing you a favor here."

Casper looked down at the floor. "I know," he mumbled. "I'm sorry."

He looked so miserable that Bernie stopped being angry.

"You'd be surprised at what we can find out," Libby told him. "And you can help us by going home and writing down anything that Zalinsky said, anything that he did that made anyone in the cast mad at him."

"That list would be one hundred miles long," Casper protested. "I wouldn't even know where to start."

"Begin at the beginning," Libby suggested, echoing a phrase from *Alice in Wonderland*.

Casper ignored the reference. "But everyone hated Zalinsky," he pointed out. "Everyone."

"Yes, but there's someone out there who hated him extra specially," Libby said.

"Extra specially?" Bernie repeated. "What kind of phrase is that?"

Libby gave her sister the evil eye, then continued on with what she'd been saying. "Someone," she clarified, "who hated Zalinsky enough to kill him, and that's the person we have to find."

Chapter 4

Y ou think writing that list is going to help?"
Bernie asked Libby once Casper was gone.

"Even if it doesn't," Libby replied, "it'll give Casper something to do."

Sean took a swallow of his iced coffee and put the glass down on the side table next to his chair. "I can see why Lucy likes Casper for this," he remarked. Lucy, aka Lucas Broadbent, was the Longely chief of police.

"Casper wouldn't hurt a fly," Bernie protested.

"You'd be surprised what people will do when pushed hard enough," Sean told her.

"Not Casper," Bernie repeated.

"So you keep saying," Libby said.

"All the evidence is circumstantial," Bernie told her. "All of it!"

"Agreed," Sean said.

"Then why settle on Casper?" Bernie asked.

"The two notes," Sean answered. "They sealed the deal." He tapped his fingers on the arm of his chair while he thought about how he would conduct the investigation if he were still Longely's chief of police. "If I were you, I'd start with the teapot," he suggested after a minute had gone by. "I'd try to get a handle on where you'd unload something like that. And the security guys. I'd

39

talk to them and see what they have to say." Sean was about to say something else, but his attention was captured by the sound of the downstairs door opening and closing and someone running up the stairs.

Bernie was just thinking that they should really keep the downstairs door locked when the door to the flat opened and Sean's newfound friend Michelle came barreling through. Even though she was in her early fifties, to Bernie's mind she dressed as if she was in college. Today she was wearing a thigh-high denim skirt, which showed a lot of tanned leg, leg that Bernie had to admit looked pretty good, a tight black T-shirt, and flip-flops. Her blond hair was piled on top of her head in a loose bun—the hairstyle of the moment.

"Oh my God," she cried, advancing on Sean. "You poor dear. I just got home from Cabo and heard about what happened at The Blue House. That must have been terrible for you. Seeing that."

"And even worse for Zalinsky," Libby couldn't help noting.

Michelle threw back her head and laughed, displaying a set of perfect teeth. "That goes without saying." When she reached Sean, she bent down, gave Sean a hug, and kissed the top of his head. "I'm so sorry I wasn't there for you."

"That's okay," Bernie said sweetly. "Somehow we all managed to get along anyway."

Michelle laughed again. "Of course, you did." She grabbed Sean's hands and pulled him up. "If it's alright with you," she said to Bernie and Libby, "I'm going to steal your dad away. It's such a lovely day that I thought he and I could go down to the Hudson and sit in one of the cafés along the water and soak in the summer. It's so brief in this part of the world, I feel it's a crime not to enjoy it. Oh dear." Michelle looked around, taking in Bernie and Libby's expression. "I hope I'm not interrupting anything."

"Not to be rude or anything, but as a matter of fact, you are," Libby told her.

Michelle put her hand to her mouth. "I'm so sorry. I didn't mean to intrude. I just . . . got carried away. I should leave," she said, turning to go.

Sean patted her thigh, a gesture that did not go unnoticed by his daughters. "Don't be ridiculous, Michelle," he told her. "What we were talking about can wait."

"But Dad," Libby objected.

Michelle bit her lip. "I really don't want to cause trouble."

"Believe me, you're not," Sean said to her.

"Because you all looked terribly serious."

"Which is why a break would be perfect right around now," Sean told her. Then he turned to his daughter. "Libby," he said. "We'll talk about this when I get back."

Then before Libby could say anything else, he and Michelle were walking out the door.

"I just can't bear to be inside on a day like this," Bernie and Libby heard Michelle trill, her voice floating upward, as she and their dad walked down the steps.

"That's exactly how I feel," Sean replied.

Then Libby and Bernie heard the downstairs door close. A moment later, they saw Sean getting into Michelle's BMW.

"Where did she get that car?" Libby asked.

"No doubt from her last husband," Bernie replied.

"I can't figure out what she wants from Dad," Libby said. "It's not like he has any money."

"Maybe she just likes his company," Bernie replied.

Libby raised an eyebrow.

"Some women like older men," Bernie pointed out.

Libby shook her head. "I remain unconvinced." She brushed a strand of hair out of her eye. Her face was grim. "I think I may have an idea about what Michelle wants."

Bernie stopped watching Mrs. Johnson walking into their shop and turned toward her sister. "What?"

"Although it's pretty far-fetched," Libby admitted.

"I'm waiting," Bernie said when a minute had gone by and Libby hadn't said anything,

"Really far-fetched," Libby repeated. She was suddenly having doubts about confiding in Bernie.

"Tell me anyway."

Libby took a deep breath and let it out. "Okay, Debby . . ."

"The Debby from the Grist Mill?" Bernie clarified.

Libby nodded. "Last time I was there, she told me she'd heard that Michelle got her stretch bread recipe by cozying up to one of the bakers at Totonio's. Maybe she's after our cookie recipes."

Bernie made a disgusted sound and went back to watching the street. "That's ridiculous," she scoffed. "I know we don't like her, but let's get real here."

"It's possible," Libby countered.

"So is snow in July." Bernie turned away from the window and started picking up the dirty dishes and putting them on the tray to take downstairs. "Or how's this? Maybe she just likes Dad. Maybe that's all there is. Maybe we *are* jealous."

"Maybe you're right," Libby conceded. But in her heart of hearts she wasn't convinced, not one single bit.

Chapter 5

As Igor Petrovich scowled and flexed his biceps, Bernie decided he looked even larger standing in the doorway of his Brooklyn apartment on Ocean Parkway than he did standing on The Blue House stage as a security guard.

"Why you want to talk to us?" he asked her. He was wearing a wife beater and a pair of khaki shorts. "Why are you here from Longely?"

So Bernie explained why they'd made the trek into the city.

Obviously she didn't do a good job because the next words out of Igor's mouth were, "This what happened is not our fault."

It was the next day, and Bernie and Libby had taken the first part of their father's advice and gone to speak to the security guards Zalinsky had hired to keep an eye on the teapot. The two brothers shared an apartment on the sixth floor of a high-rise three miles from Coney Island in a building Bernie guessed had been erected in the 1930s.

"I'm not saying that at all," Bernie replied.

Igor's scowl grew. "So you saying what then?"

Ivan, who was wearing the same thing as his brother, joined Igor. He was slightly shorter and wider, and his hair was wet, but that was where the differences ended. "We hired to look good, that's all Zalinsky wanted us to do." He jabbed a stubby finger in the air to make his point. "He wanted us to look mean. That's what he said."

Igor nodded. "My brother Ivan is right. We do exactly what Zalinsky wants."

"Which was?" Libby asked.

"To make a show," Ivan said. "To stir up interest. We didn't know anyone was going to be hurt. We don't do things like that."

Libby clarified. "Hurt people?"

"Nyet. Be where people get hurt." Ivan stroked his jaw. "My brother and I, we do not like this. Also we have to be careful of our faces."

"I see," Bernie said, even though she didn't. Now that Bernie was looking at the two men, she was surprised she hadn't seen the strong resemblance between them before, but at the time she hadn't been paying much attention to them.

"You must have thought there was a chance someone would get hurt," Libby persisted. "You were wearing bulletproof vests."

"Fakes," Ivan said. "Not the real thing."

"Fakes?" Libby repeated, nonplussed.

Both Igor and Ivan nodded their heads.

"How about the guns?" asked Bernie.

"Also fakes," Ivan said.

"Really?" Bernie asked.

Ivan nodded. "They look real, no?"

"They look real, yes," Libby said. "Why would you do that?"

"You ask this question for real?" Igor said.

Libby and Bernie both nodded.

"We are actors," Ivan explained. "We hire ourselves for when people want to make themselves look important at nightclubs and other events. We become their bodyguards for the evening. We create . . . how you say . . . a buzz."

"And there's a market for that?" Bernie asked genuinely curious.

Ivan and Igor nodded their heads again.

"Da," Ivan said. "A big market. Everyone wants to be someone important. Sometimes we do some modeling too. Catalogs. That is why we have to be careful of our faces."

"Out of curiosity, how much do you get paid to be a bodyguard?" Bernie asked.

Bernie whistled when Igor told her.

Igor's face darkened. "But we did not get that from Zalinsky," Igor said. "He told us he didn't have the cash on him and he would go to the ATM afterward. But there was no afterward. How you find us anyway?" Igor asked, changing the subject.

"Casper . . ."

"The crazy little man in black shirt and black pants who is sweating like a mule all the time?" Ivan asked.

"Yeah, that's him," Bernie replied.

Libby continued. "He said that Zalinsky hired you and that his assistant . . ."

"Magda?" Igor asked.

"Yes, Magda might have your address, so we talked to her, and here we are," Libby said.

Bernie took a step forward. "May we come in?" she asked. "We'd really like to ask you about what happened that evening. Maybe you saw something that will turn out to be helpful, something that you don't even know is important."

"We tell the police everything we see. They already have talked to us," Ivan objected.

"I'm sure they have," Bernie told Ivan. "But we were hoping you could run through everything again for us." As she was speaking, Bernie thought she saw a flash of something inside the apartment—maybe a woman—moving across the hallway.

Igor rubbed the tattooed star on his bicep. "You are the caterers at the play, yes?" he asked.

"Yes," Bernie told him as she looked again. There was nothing there.

"So why you want to know about this?" Ivan asked.

"Sometimes we help people out," Libby told him.

"Help them out how?" Ivan asked, looking puzzled. "You bring food to their houses when they are sick?"

Bernie laughed. "No. We help them out when

they're in trouble with the law," she explained.

"So you are police too?" Igor asked. "You cook, and you do policing?"

"No," Bernie said.

Igor cocked his head. "Then you are like the private detectives I see on TV?"

"Kinda," said Libby, stretching the truth.

Igor scratched his arm. "So who is this person in trouble?"

"Casper," Bernie said.

"How he is in trouble?" Ivan asked.

"The police think he might have had something to do with Zalinsky's death, and we don't think that's the case," Bernie explained.

"So can we come in and talk to you?" Libby asked again.

The brothers exchanged a look, the kind of look she and Libby exchanged when they were about to make up an excuse for not doing something.

"Our apartment is a mess," Igor said.

"We would be ashamed to invite you in," Ivan agreed.

"Forgive us. But we will talk to you," Igor said, "if you want to meet us at the Kebob Shack in a half hour." Then, before Libby and Bernie had time to say anything else, Igor gave them the address and closed the door in their faces.

Chapter 6

What do you think that was about?" Libby asked, staring at the closed door. She wanted to ring the doorbell again, but decided there probably wasn't any point in it.

"I think there was someone else in there," Bernie said to her sister as she turned and walked toward the elevator. She trailed her fingers against the plaster wall as she went, enjoying the sensation of the coolness seeping into them. "Someone they didn't want us to see."

"I didn't see anyone," Libby objected.

"I think I did," Bernie replied.

"Who was it?" Libby asked.

Bernie shook her head. "Not a clue. Maybe a girlfriend. I didn't get a good look."

"So you don't think they're just giving us the brush-off?"

"No, I don't, but I guess we'll find out if they don't show up at the Kebob Shack," Bernie told her, although that was the last place she wanted to be. An ice cream parlor, yes; a kebob shop where there was a griddle going, no. On the other hand, she didn't want to have to drive back to Brooklyn again either. The Belt Parkway had been a nightmare.

The shop Igor had mentioned was located five

blocks away on Coney Island Avenue. By the time Bernie and Libby found another parking space near the restaurant, twenty-five minutes had elapsed. At that point, Bernie would have been happy to pay to park in a garage, but there were no garages in the area, so Bernie had endlessly circled the neighborhood until she found a parking space. It was tough to find one large enough for Mathilda.

"It would have been faster to walk," Bernie groused as they entered the restaurant.

"Yeah, but at least the van sort of has air-conditioning," Libby observed, referring to the fact that the Kebob Shack didn't. "This place feels like an oven."

It was in the eighties outside, but to Libby's mind with the heat radiating off the sidewalks it felt as if it were in the nineties. The Kebob Shack was empty, and as Bernie and Libby entered, the smell of old grease from the griddle rose to meet them. The word *shack* perfectly suited the place. It was a hole-in-the-wall with a grill, a Formica counter, a scuffed black-and-white tile floor, and five small round tables with two chairs apiece pushed under them. The menu tacked above the counter was in Hindi, and the walls were decorated with pictures of Pakistan. A fan whirred up above, and the door was open to let in any breeze that happened by.

Bernie and Libby had just ordered coffee, and

Bernie was fanning herself with a takeout menu when the two brothers arrived. They'd both shaved, slicked back their hair, and changed into khaki pants and tight-fitting, black T-shirts.

"We don't have much time to talk," Igor said.

"Then why did you tell us to meet you?" objected Libby, who was aggravated at having to be down here at all.

"Because we just got another job," Ivan said. "Last minute. At the Tatania. It's a big club in Brighton Beach. We have to get ready. At the time when we told you to meet us, we did not know this would be the case."

"I've heard of the Tatania," Bernie said as she took a sip of her coffee. It was surprisingly good. She sat down at the table in front of the window. "So how did Zalinsky get your name?"

"We are well known in the community," Igor replied.

"Which community is that?" Bernie asked.

Igor snorted as if the question was too obvious to answer. "The Russian community. We are asked for at many big parties. That is how Zalinsky hear about us. We think we make big money when he ask us to work for him. He is a big deal, very rich, and he would be having many parties, and many famous people would be at this play and see us, so we would get lots of business and that he would be paying us very well. But that's not what happened."

51

Bernie leaned forward. "So what did happen?"

Ivan took up the narrative. "We did not get paid. We should have listened to Magda."

Libby leaned forward. "You know Magda?"

"She is our cousin," Ivan said. "She tell us not to take the job. She tell us a lot of times he doesn't pay people."

"But we don't believe her," Igor explained.

"Anyway," Ivan said, "we think that even if he doesn't pay us it would be, how you say, good . . ."

"Exposure?" asked Bernie.

"Da," Ivan continued. "Good exposure, because there be many people there, and they would see us and like us. So when we get there and Magda comes running over and says she is sorry but Zalinsky does not have money in his account to pay us, we are not upset. But then a few minutes later, he comes over and swears our cousin is wrong and he will pay us the next day. This we believe."

Igor slicked back his hair with the palm of his hand and admired his profile in the window. "Magda, she was mad at us for coming. She tell us to go home."

"How come?" Libby asked.

"Because she no believe what Zalinsky tell us, and if we no get paid, she no get paid," Ivan said.

"She's your agent?" Bernie guessed.

Ivan nodded. "I tell her sometime you must give the cow away to get the milk."

52

"But she no agree," Igor said. "She say we no have any business sense, but we have good business sense. We talk to many people after the play and give out many cards."

"She still mad at us," Ivan confided. "But she always mad at everyone."

Bernie sat back and resumed fanning herself. "Why?"

Ivan and Igor both shrugged.

"It is the way she is," Ivan said. "She difficult person." He shook his head. "She not sunny-side-up kind of person. She brood."

"Aren't you Russians famed for that?" Bernie couldn't help asking.

Ivan burst out laughing. "Da." He pointed to his brother and back to himself. "We, no. We happy people."

"Can you tell us anything about Zalinsky?" Libby asked.

Igor thought for a moment. "I think he hard man to work for. I think maybe that is why my cousin is so unhappy."

Bernie sighed and took another sip of her coffee. "Anything else you can tell us?"

Igor shook his head. "We just speak to him on the phone. He call us up and tell us what he want and when he want us, and I tell him yes, and then at that date Ivan and I go there."

"Did you talk to Zalinsky before the performance?" Libby asked.

Ivan shook his head. "When we arrive, we come into the theater, but he was screaming at someone, so we left."

Bernie pushed her coffee away. "Did you see who he was yelling at?"

"A little Chinese woman," Igor said.

Bernie and Libby exchanged looks.

"Hsaio?" Libby asked.

"I do not know her name," Ivan replied. "But she very upset. Almost crying. We did not want to embarrass, so we shut the door and left. Then we go find Magda to tell her we are there."

"And what did Magda say?" Bernie enquired.

"She said we are idiots," Igor said. "But I still think not. I think we get business out of this."

Ivan nodded. "All publicity is good publicity."

"I'm not so sure of that," Bernie said. She looked down at the two addresses she had for Magda. "She lives around here, doesn't she?"

"She live with her babushka here," Ivan said, "and rent small house in Longely."

"Do you know if Magda's here now?" Bernie asked because Magda hadn't been at her place in Longely when she and Libby had stopped by.

"She still angry at us. She not talking to us now, so we do not know this," Ivan said.

"I don't think she talk to you either," Igor added.

"I guess we'll find out," Bernie observed, starting to get up.

"One thing," Igor said. "An important thing."

Bernie sat back down and waited. "The pierogies that you make."

"What about them?" Libby asked, even though she had a pretty good idea what Igor was going to say.

"You should not be making them again," Ivan told her. "They are not good for your reputation."

"This I know," Libby agreed. "There's one thing that doesn't make sense to me."

Now Igor and Ivan waited.

"How come he hired you to guard a two-million-dollar teapot?" Libby asked. "Wasn't he afraid it was going to be stolen?"

Ivan shook his head. "He tell us he taking care of everything. We just have to look good."

"Do you know what he meant?" Bernie asked.

Igor shrugged. "I think he mean he's guarding it himself. Magda tell us he always take care of everything himself. He always think he know better than everyone else."

"I'll go with that," Bernie agreed.

Chapter 7

Magda's grandmother lived in Little Russia at 3 Brighton Court, a house in a narrow alleyway between two major avenues. The address wasn't on Bernie's GPS, and after circling around the area for several minutes, she'd given up, stopped, and asked for directions. The first woman she asked had shrugged and shaken her head, but the second one had given her the information she needed.

It took another five minutes after that before Bernie found Brighton Court, and five more minutes until she found a parking space. The spot was a few feet away from an open fire hydrant, and when Bernie exited the van, she stepped into a stream of water running down the street, but she did manage to sidestep the horde of shrieking kids dressed in bathing suits and flip-flops running in and out of the water's spray.

As Bernie turned into the alleyway, a light breeze carried in the salty smell of the Atlantic. Bernie smelled it and smiled. To her mind, that smell was tanning lotion and grilled hamburgers and night-blooming flowers, all the smells of summer wrapped into one. She took another deep breath and thought about how nice it would be to be at the beach before getting back to the business at hand.

The address she and her sister were looking for turned out to be in the middle of the alleyway. It was one of five white clapboard bungalows with gray trim, all lined up with military precision. Each had a small backyard with a chain-link fence around it, and as Bernie walked toward Magda's grandmother's house, she wondered how this row of houses had escaped the developers' wrecking ball, or whether the residents were living in its shadow.

A short, white, wrought-iron handrail ran up either side of the three steps that led up to the front door. Two elderly, heavyset women—both with scarfs tied around their hair, both wearing floral print dresses and orthopedic shoes with Cuban heels—were sitting on the steps talking to one another. They stopped chatting when Bernie and Libby walked around the garbage cans on the curb and came toward them, waiting to see what the sisters wanted.

"We're looking for Magda, Magda Webster," Bernie said when she and Libby got close enough to talk.

The woman on the far right looked at Bernie and Libby and shook her head. Then she said something to her friend in Russian.

"She's not here," the friend translated.

"We were told she was," Bernie countered.

The English speaker translated the sentence for the other woman, who Libby and Bernie assume did not speak English. She shook her head again and began talking in rapid-fire Russian. Bernie and Libby waited. After a minute or so of animated conversation, the second woman asked Bernie and Libby who told them Magda was here.

"Igor and Ivan," Libby replied promptly.

Bernie decided that the first woman must have understood what she was saying because she leaned over and carefully spit on the ground.

"I guess she doesn't like them too much," Bernie said to the second woman.

"They are worthless," the second woman replied. She reached up to her shoulder and tugged her bra strap up. "They should be going to school and making something of themselves instead of running around like idiots with those stupid vests on."

"You could be right," Bernie said.

"I *am* right," the woman exclaimed.

"Okay. You are right. Can we speak to Magda?"

"What you want to talk to her for?" the second woman demanded, not bothering to translate Bernie's request for the first woman. "Are you police? Is she in trouble?"

"Definitely not," Libby answered. "We're here because we want to speak to her about her boss, Ludvoc Zalinsky."

"Also scum," the second woman answered.

"More than scum," the first woman said, for the first time using heavily accented English. She spit on the ground again. "It is good he is dead."

"Why are you saying that?" Libby asked.

"Why? Why?" The voice of the first woman, who it now seemed clear was Magda's grandmother, rose in indignation. "He make promises to my Magda, that's why she stay and work for him all this time and then he say 'no. I never say this'—and poof, just like this, it is gone. Gone. What she supposed to do now with the children? How she supposed to pay for their education?" she demanded of Libby. She looked her up and down. "You can help with this?" she finally said.

"Probably not," Libby admitted.

"Then why she should talk to you?" the second woman demanded.

"Because we're trying to help a friend," Bernie told her.

The grandmother leaned forward and let go a torrent of Russian.

"Does that mean you're not going to help?" Libby asked her when the torrent subsided.

"She did not say that," the second woman replied.

"So what did she say?" Libby wanted to know.

The second woman retucked the hem of her dress around her thighs before answering. "She say Magda, she is at the beach."

"Maybe we could go talk to her there," Libby suggested, although she was positive Magda's grandmother had said a great deal more than that.

"It is a big beach," the second woman told them. "You will not find them. And she is with her children and her cousins. Even if you do, it will not matter because she will not want to talk to you."

"Do you know when she's coming back?" Bernie asked.

The second woman shrugged. "When everyone is ready to come home."

"Could you call her?" Libby asked. "Tell her we're here?"

The second woman shook her head. "She no take her phone."

"Okay then. Can you have her call us when she does get back?" Bernie asked as she dug a pen and a scrap of paper out of her bag and wrote hers and Libby's phone numbers on it and handed it to the second woman, who said something in Russian to Magda's grandmother before handing the scrap of paper to her. Bernie watched the lady fold up the piece of paper she'd given her and slip it into her dress pocket.

"You go now," she said to Libby and Bernie, dismissing them with a wave of her hand. Then she went back to talking to her friend in Russian. After waiting for a minute, Libby and Bernie did as they were told.

As they walked back to the van, Libby ran her fingers along the wooden fence that demarcated the alley's boundaries. It was dirty, and after a moment, Libby had acquired a fine layer of soot on her fingertips. She wiped her fingers off on a ginkgo leaf and turned to Bernie.

"If Magda's grandmother is telling the truth about Zalinsky reneging on his promise to send Magda's kids to college," Libby said, "that would be quite a bit of money Magda would have to get her hands on."

"Hundreds of thousands," Bernie said.

"The teapot would certainly solve that problem," Libby noted.

"She'd certainly feel justified," Bernie observed.

"But if that were the case," Libby objected, "Magda would want to hire her cousins, not dissuade them."

"True. And anyway," Bernie mused. "If Magda were going to steal the teapot, why pick then to do it?"

"Maybe it was locked up in a safe before the performance."

"Okay. But then how did Magda plan to sell it? Who did she plan to sell it to?"

"Maybe Magda had a partner," Libby suggested. "A partner with contacts."

Bernie retied her DKNY wrap dress. "Which brings us back to Hsaio. I think we need to have a chat with her."

"Definitely," Libby agreed as Bernie reached into her tote and got out her cell phone.

Chapter 8

As it turned out, Bernie and Libby were in luck. Hsaio Rosenthal was at Zalinsky's office dealing with paperwork when Bernie and Libby called. She would, she told them, be there for another hour and a half before she had to go down to Columbia University for a meeting with her adviser about her thesis, which dealt with the beneficial effects of exposing six-month-olds to soothing colors.

"No problem. We should be there in forty minutes if the traffic isn't too bad," Bernie had told her before hanging up.

Bernie and Libby had been to Zalinsky's office before. They'd signed their contract there. His office was in his house, accessible by a separate entrance in the back. The house had originally been a farmhouse built in the mid-1800s. Supposedly, it had been part of the Underground Railroad.

Then it had been purchased and rebuilt by a man named Endicott back in the early 1900s. His wife, who had come from Alabama, had wanted to live in a southern plantation manor, and Endicott had obliged to the best of his ability. The house had gone from a farmhouse to a large, white, columned, two-story affair, with a wraparound veranda filled with wicker furniture that no one ever sat on. The irony was not lost on Endicott. He'd written about it in a letter to a cousin that was now sitting in the Longely Historical Society.

After Endicott and his wife died, the house had fallen on hard times, and by the time Zalinsky had acquired it, there was a leak in the roof and dry rot in the wood. He had spent a considerable amount of money restoring the place. Bernie had heard that the house was full of gold-plated faucets, spa-style showers, Japanese-style toilets, Swarovski crystal chandeliers, a media room, and a ball-room, as well as a separate exhibition space for Zalinsky's burgeoning art collection.

However, Bernie and Libby wouldn't know, because they hadn't seen any of the house. They'd walked around the back and gone directly into Zalinsky's office, signed the contract, and left. Zalinsky hadn't offered to walk them through the house, though they could see an adjoining room through the opened door, and they hadn't asked. The office had been small and spare, consisting of four rooms, probably the maids' quarters in a former iteration, Bernie had speculated.

There had been the entrance room where Magda Webster had sat, a slightly larger room furnished with antique Chinese furniture and blue-and-white pottery, which was where Zalinsky had his desk, a third room that seemed to be for storing files, and a galley kitchen. The walls of all four rooms had been painted cream white and were hung with Chinese scrolls.

Bernie checked her watch as she parked the van around the rear of Zalinsky's office. They'd made it back from Brighton Beach in an hour, which gave them a half hour with Hsaio. Bernie didn't think that would be enough time, but at least it would be a start.

Hsaio had five files spread out over Zalinsky's desk when the sisters entered the office. She turned and smiled at them.

"I'm just trying to get some paperwork in order," she explained, running a hand through her short, black hair.

Looking at Hsaio, the word coming to Libby's mind was wispy. Hsaio probably wore a double zero, Libby decided. If that. Libby was sure there was a downside to being that tiny, but for the life of her she couldn't figure out what it could be. Today Hsaio was dressed in a white T-shirt, a mid-thigh pleated chambray skirt, and white three-inch platform espadrilles, an outfit that emphasized her smallness.

"So how can I help you guys?" she asked, giving them a quizzical look.

Bernie leaned against Zalinsky's desk and redid her ponytail. "Tell us about the teapot," she said when she was done with her hair.

"The Yixing teapot?"

Bernie nodded. "How old is it?"

Hsaio laughed, showing a perfect set of white teeth. "Actually, it's modern. It was made by an artist from a province in China out of a special purple clay that can only be mined in a certain village, and the experts say that his craftsmanship compares favorably with the Ming court artisans of the fourteenth century. In addition, the clay from which it is made is supposed to have health benefits. Why are you asking?"

"Just becoming informed," Libby told her. "Can I ask why the teapot costs so much?"

Hsaio shrugged. "A matter of supply and demand. Lots of Chinese collect them, and these days they have a lot of money. Personally, I think Zalinsky paid way too much—he got caught up in a bidding war, and his ego got the better of him—but I was not consulted. I just did as I was told."

"Meaning?" Libby asked.

Hsaio pointed to herself. "I was the one who placed the bids for Zalinsky. He didn't want it known that he was the one who had bought it."

"And then he did want people to know," Bernie said.

Hsaio concurred. "Yes, and then he did."

"What made him change his mind?" Libby enquired.

"Personally, I think it was a matter of ego. He didn't want anyone to know if he lost the sale. But that's just me. I really have no idea,"

Hsaio told her. "As I said, I just followed orders."

Bernie picked up a ceramic statue of a horse and rider sitting on Zalinsky's desk. "Nice," she commented.

"Excellent copy of a Tang dynasty horse," Hsaio informed her.

Bernie put the statue down. "How come he picked you to place the bids?" Bernie asked her.

"Frankly," Hsaio said, "I think he confused art ed with art history. And then when he heard I used to work for an antiques dealer—kinda—he assumed I knew about the field, and I didn't correct him." Hsaio looked sheepish. "I needed the job."

"So then you would know where to sell the teapot," Libby observed.

Hsaio laughed. "That's what the police said to me too, and I'll tell you what I told them. I worked for Zalinsky, and I did what he told me, and as for knowing any serious collectors who would buy it, you probably know as many of them as I do."

"You didn't make any contacts when you worked for your antiques dealer?" Bernie said.

"Antiques is an elastic term. This is the place I worked," Hsaio said, and she took her cell phone out and went to Safari. "I'll let you be the judge. Here," Hsaio said, handing Bernie the phone.

"Everything Baseball?" Bernie asked. "Antiques seems like a bit of a misnomer."

"Hey, there are serious collectors of this stuff out there," Hsaio told her. "If you'd like, I'll get the owner on the phone for you."

Bernie put her hands up in the air. "That's not necessary," she protested.

"No, I insist," Hsaio said, dialing the number.

Bernie spent the next five minutes listening to the shop owner sing Hsaio's praises.

"Now," Hsaio said, taking the phone from Bernie when she was done, "if you ask me about baseball cards, that would be a different story. But selling the teapot to someone—that I can't help you with."

"Not even the Chinese?" Libby asked. "You said it's a hot item for them."

"It is," Hsaio told her. "The police asked me that too, but in case you're wondering, I'm adopted. I grew up in Scarsdale. Rosenthal. I'm Jewish. I have no contacts in the Chinese community. None. This whole thing makes no sense to me," she added.

"Do you mean Zalinsky's death?" Libby asked.

"No. The teapot," Hsaio told her. "That is what we were talking about, isn't it? The death I understand."

Bernie raised an eyebrow. "How so?"

"You worked with him," Hsaio said. "You know what he was like."

"Oh yes," Bernie said. "Indeed I do."

Hsaio laughed for the third time. "Well, there

you go. So did everyone else. He was an awful man. I had a terrible argument with him right before the show."

"So we heard," Libby said.

"The guards, right?" Hsaio asked.

Libby nodded.

"I saw them." Hsaio hesitated for a moment, then plunged into her story. "Zalinsky and I had this arrangement, you know. At least I thought I did." Hsaio shook her head. "I thought I was so smart. My mother told me not to do it, but I didn't listen."

"I remember a few of those," Bernie said.

Hsaio shot her a grateful glance. "I should have listened to her," Hsaio said. "What happened was that Zalinsky and I worked out a deal. Instead of paying me a salary for basically being his gofer, he was supposed to be paying my rent on an apartment he owned on the Upper West Side. I thought it was a fantastic deal." Hsaio made a face. "Then I found out about a month ago from a neighbor that the apartment building was going into foreclosure."

"That sucks!" Bernie exclaimed.

Hsaio snorted. "That's certainly an understatement."

"Did you talk to Zalinsky about it?" Bernie asked.

"What do you think?" Hsaio cried. "Of course, I did. He said there'd been a misunderstanding, and it was being taken care of, and I had nothing to worry about."

"And you believed him?"

"Definitely. I had no reason not to. I shouldn't have, but I did." Hsaio's voice trailed off. "That's what our fight was about. I found out he hadn't done anything at all. He swore it was all a misunderstanding and he'd done everything he was supposed to." She sighed. "Well, it's too late now. I guess I'm going to have to find another place to live. Not an easy thing these days. I'm probably going to have to move back home, God help me."

Libby gently ran a finger down the tail of the ceramic horse. For a moment, the only sound she, Bernie, and Libby heard was the quacking of the ducks in the pond in the backyard and the whoosh of the overhead fan. "So what's going to happen to Zalinsky's collection?" she asked.

"That's a good question," Hsaio responded. She bent down and picked up a scrap of paper that had landed on the floor and deposited it in the mesh wastepaper basket next to the desk. "I can tell you what Zalinsky wanted to have happen. He wanted this house to become a museum like the Isabella Stewart Gardner Museum in Boston." Seeing the blank look on the sisters' faces, she explained. "The Gardner museum was originally someone's home, and when the lady died, she stipulated in her will that

69

her house and art collection be opened to the public. Of course, she left a big endowment fund."

"Which I take Zalinsky did not?" Libby asked.

"Nope. Not even a little one," Hsaio replied. "Or if he did, I don't know about it. But then, as it turns out, I don't know lots of things," Hsaio concluded ruefully.

"Like the money situation?" Bernie guessed.

Hsaio nodded. "Like the money situation."

"I thought he was worth billions," Bernie said.

"So did I. So did everyone. But now I don't think that's the case," Hsaio replied. "I think maybe he was pulling one of those financial things . . . schemes. Of some kind." She gave an apologetic shrug. "I don't understand them, but that seems the only explanation. I mean, how do you go from billions to nothing?"

"So he was really broke?" Libby asked. "I find that hard to believe."

"I think everyone shares your opinion." Hsaio frowned. "Don't get me wrong, I don't know for certain, but what I *do* know is that there have been a lot of unpleasant calls coming in from people wanting to get paid."

"So we heard," Bernie said. According to Clyde, the police had checked out the calls and come up empty-handed.

As Bernie was talking, Hsaio rummaged around in her backpack, took out her cell phone, and checked the time. "Drats. Gotta go."

Bernie put her hand on Hsaio's shoulder. "One last question. How did you meet Zalinsky?"

Hsaio looked up from zipping up her backpack. "Erin introduced us."

"I didn't know you knew Erin before the play," Bernie remarked, slightly confused about the timeline.

"I know Magda from when she worked at Starbucks, and Erin is Magda's cousin. I think she's her third . . . or is it fourth cousin. I can't get the genealogy straight. Now if you want to talk about someone getting screwed over by Zalinsky." Hsaio gave a mournful shake of her head. "I feel so bad for her. She gave up so much for him . . ."

"Zalinsky?" Libby clarified.

Hsaio nodded. "He treated her so badly."

"What did he do?" Bernie asked, thinking of the scene she'd witnessed right before the play between Erin and Zalinsky.

"Ask her," Hsaio replied as she turned off the office lights. "She'll be more than happy to tell you, I'm sure. I'm sorry, but I'm late already."

She hurried out the door with Bernie and Libby trailing behind her. On the way out, Bernie noticed that Hsaio hadn't bothered to activate the house alarm. *Probably in her rush to leave she's forgotten,* Bernie thought. *Should I tell her?* she wondered. *Or not?*

Bernie wavered for a moment, but in the end the opportunity to get inside Zalinsky's house

71

won out over the shred of guilt she was feeling, so she didn't say anything. Instead, while Hsaio was futzing around, looking for her car keys, Bernie palmed a roll of Scotch Tape.

Once outside, Hsaio and the two sisters parted. Libby and Bernie walked over to Mathilda, while Hsaio trotted over to her old banged-up Civic. Libby got into Mathilda and Hsaio got into her vehicle, while Bernie lingered outside, pretending to take a pebble out of her shoe.

"You know," Libby said to her, "it occurs to me that we don't know anything about anyone in the cast."

"Why should we?" Bernie replied, glancing up. "We weren't there much."

"True," Libby agreed. "Coming?" she asked Bernie when Hsaio had gotten into her car and driven off.

Bernie straightened up. "After we take a quick look through Zalinsky's house."

Libby snorted. "I'm not breaking in."

"You don't have to."

"Neither are you."

"I didn't say I was."

"So how are we going to get in there?" Libby asked. "Levitation?"

"The way one usually does—through the door, smartass," Bernie told her sister as she turned and retraced her steps to Zalinsky's office.

"What about the alarm?" Libby called after her.

"Hsaio forgot to set it. Stay in the van if you want."

Libby sighed. She watched her sister for a moment. *Great,* she thought. *Just what I didn't want to do.* But then she turned Mathilda off, took the keys out of the ignition, got out of the van, and followed her sister. Just like she always did.

Chapter 9

By the time Libby got to the door, Bernie had her hand on the doorknob. She turned it, and the door swung open. "Tada. Magic," she cried.

"I thought Hsaio locked it," Libby said.

Bernie smiled contently. "She did, but it's amazing what a piece of tape over the lock plate can do."

"I don't know where you learned this stuff," Libby muttered, but Bernie didn't answer. She hadn't heard her because she was on the other side of the door already.

The sisters spent the next half hour going through Ludvoc Zalinsky's house. They started with his office. After listening to the voice mails on Zalinsky's answering machine, Bernie and Libby had to agree with Hsaio. There were a lot of calls about unpaid bills, but all of them were from agencies threatening legal action.

There wasn't anything else of interest in the office, or if there was, Bernie and Libby couldn't see it. It took less than twenty minutes to go through the rest of the office. The computer was password-protected, so that was a no go, and the few files that were there had to do with rental agreements and warranties. Evidently Zalinsky was renting his Mercedes, and it was about to be repossessed.

Then Bernie opened the door, and the sisters began exploring the rest of the house. It was not what they had been led to believe. In fact, it was the opposite. The kitchen was a big fancy affair with the requisite imported cabinets, double ovens, and granite counter tops, but it gave little evidence of being used.

"Zalinsky didn't cook much," Libby observed as she opencd and closed the cabinet doors. The pots and pans were pristine, and as for food, there were two boxes of pasta and a can of tomato sauce in one of the cabinets, and that was it. "It amazes me that the people who have the nicest kitchens never use them."

"Truc," Bernie said as she studied the pantry. The place was full of kitchen gadgets, including the same brand of clcctric teakettle that they had used in the theater. "I guess Zalinsky must have liked that brand," Bernie commented.

"Too bad it didn't like him," Libby said as her sister closed the pantry door, and they both walked into the den.

The walls were paneled, the books on the bookshelves seemed to have been chosen for their size and color, and the sofa was covered in a bad chintz. The room looked like a stage set, Libby reflected as she began going through the desk drawers. There was nothing in them, except a small toolbox in the bottom drawer. She opened it. The only things in it were a couple of instruction manuals and a basic tool set.

"It's like no one lived here," Libby observed as she put the toolbox back where she'd found it.

Bernie nodded. She was looking at a piece of paper from a yellow legal pad she'd found peeping out of a coffee-table book on American art. There was nothing on it except a number that had been circled.

"What do you have?" Libby asked, coming up behind her.

Bernie showed her as she took out her phone and dialed the number. Her call went directly to an answering machine that said, "Art Unlimited. Please leave your number, and we will get back to you." Bernie did as instructed and hung up. "Interesting," she said, tapping the phone against her chin.

She lowered it, opened Safari, and typed in "Art Unlimited." A moment later, the site came up. It was tasteful, and the copy on the opening page read, "Discreet rentals for the discerning."

"I wonder what they rent?" Libby said.

"Art."

"Ha. Ha."

Bernie tried clicking on the listed links, but none of them worked. "I'll tell you one thing," she said to Libby. "They have a lousy website."

"Maybe that's on purpose to keep the hoi polloi out," Libby said.

"Then why have a website at all," Bernie countered as she walked into the living room. "I feel as if I'm in a fancy corporate office," she said, looking around.

"I wonder if this stuff comes from Art Unlimited," Libby said, pointing to the pictures hanging on the walls. They were mostly modern art. She indicated a large canvas with a white background and a white square in the middle. "I just don't get it," she said.

"Me either," Bernie agreed. "I wonder if he rented the furniture as well? This place has no personality at all. I think I would have preferred what people said this place was like to what it really is like."

"Ditto," Libby observed as she started toward the stairway that led to the second floor. "It's as if he got everything out of a catalog."

It wasn't until Bernie and Libby got to Zalinsky's bedroom that they found anything that really caught their attention. The bedroom was huge, a fact emphasized by the lack of furniture. The only things in it were a king-sized bed, an antique red-lacquered dresser, a leather-covered armchair, and a sixty-inch TV mounted on the wall across from the bed. The walls were bare except for three small paintings: a Monet, a Cezanne, and a Picasso.

"Do you think they're real?" Libby asked Bernie.

"I don't know," Bernie said, studying them.

Libby pointed to the Monet. "I didn't know you could rent stuff like this."

"Me either," Bernie replied. "But you probably can. After all, you can rent a Prada bag."

"This is a little different."

"Just in scale."

"I wonder what it would be like to own a Monet?" Libby mused.

"Somehow, I don't think we're ever going to find out," Bernie said. Then she walked over and opened the closet door. "Jeez," she muttered as she took in the size. "I've slept in bedrooms in Chelsea that were smaller than this."

She stepped inside. Zalinsky's clothes were arranged according to season, color, and function. There was a shelving system for his shirts, sweaters, underwear, and socks.

"Well, this stuff isn't rented," Libby observed as she joined her sister in the closet. "I guess he really cared about his clothes."

Bernie looked at the suit labels. "And paid a lot for them. I'll tell you one thing, Ludvoc would have made Imelda proud," Bernie said as she studied the rows of custom-made shoes neatly lined up in racks.

She was thinking about how boring men's shoes were when she noticed a very thin line starting at the floor and going about a quarter of the way up the wall. It was probably a crack in the wallboard. Probably. But still. Bernie bent down to get a better look.

"What are you doing?" Libby asked.

Bernie tapped on the wall beside the crack. One side sounded different than the other.

"Do you hear that?" she asked Libby.

Libby nodded.

"I think there might be a door here or something," Bernie said as she moved the shoes away and lightly ran her fingers over the wall. She could feel some sort of seam. She stepped back and took another look. The seam seemed to be a square. "There's definitely something here," she noted, moving out of the way so Libby could see what she was talking about.

"You're right—there is," Libby acceded, after she'd knelt down and traced the crack like her sister had. She sat back on her heels. "Probably some sort of safe."

"A very large safe," Bernie said. She could fit her shoulders in there. Then she recalled something. "Or a passageway out. Remember, this house was on the Underground Railroad."

"But I thought Endicott gutted the farmhouse and rebuilt it," Libby objected.

"He did. But he could have rebuilt the tunnel as well."

"Why would he do that?"

Bernie shrugged. "I don't know. Because it pleased his fancy?"

"Maybe that's why Zalinsky bought the house in the first place," Libby suggested.

"Could be," Bernie said. "It's something that might appeal, especially if you thought you were going to have to make a quick getaway. Have you noticed there's no personal stuff in this house? No picture albums, no books, nothing."

"Yes, I noticed. And your point is?"

"Maybe what we're looking for is in the tunnel."

"What are we looking for?" Libby asked.

"I don't know," Bernie admitted. "Something."

Libby massaged her calf muscle. "Okay, let's suppose you're right," she told her sister. "How do we get into it? There's no opening for a key, so I'm guessing the door to the tunnel has to open with some sort of hidden spring or lever."

"That's what I'm thinking too," Bernie said.

She and Libby stood up and began looking around the closet. They moved the clothes and the shoes and studied the walls and the floor. Nothing. Then they ran their hands underneath the shelving. They didn't feel anything except wallboard.

"Maybe the lever is outside," Bernie suggested after she and her sister had explored every last inch of the closet.

"Maybe," Libby agreed as they trooped into the bedroom.

After ten minutes of fruitless searching over, under, and behind the bed, tapping on the headboard, looking behind the dresser, moving the chair, lifting up the rug, feeling behind the curtains, and peeking under the paintings on the wall, Bernie and Libby conceded defeat. They plopped themselves down at the foot of Zalinsky's bed.

"Maybe the story about the tunnel isn't true," Libby said. "Maybe those cracks are just signs of the house settling or a bad wallboard job."

"Maybe." Bernie sighed and looked out the window. She had been so sure too. From where she was sitting, she could see the tops of the oak trees as well as the neighbor's perennial garden, which was bordered by a small stream that meandered down the hill. For a moment, she watched two robins on the branch of a crab apple tree. Then her gaze shifted to the window. "It's a nice view," she commented. "But the window treatment really detracts from it."

"What would you do?" Libby asked.

"Well, for openers, I'd get rid of those curtain rods." Bernie sat up straighter, warming to her topic. "Those curtain rods are truly awful. Could they be any bigger? Your eye goes right to them. They're completely out of character with the room. And those supports! Dragons? Seriously, why would anyone do that?"

"Why indeed," Libby said. Suddenly she had an idea. "Unless . . ."

Bernie turned to look at her sister. "Unless what?"

"Look how big the dragons are."

Bernie's eyes opened wider. She put her hands up to her mouth. "Oh my God," she cried.

"Are you thinking what I'm thinking?" Libby asked.

Bernie gave a snort of a laugh. "All this time we were poking around, and the answer was right in front of us."

"Maybe," Libby said.

"Why else would the thingees . . ."

"Thingees?"

Bernie waved her hand impatiently. "The whatever you call the supports for the curtain rods . . . why else would they be so large?"

"Bad design?" Libby replied.

Bernie didn't answer. Instead she and Libby got up off the bed and rushed over to the window. Now that they were looking carefully, Libby and Bernie could see that the support on the left was slightly bigger than the support on the right. Bernie walked over to the left side. She stood on tiptoe and raised her hand. Nope. She was too short. She couldn't reach it.

"I need something to stand on," Bernie said, looking around the room. The armchair. She pushed it across the floor and hopped up on it. "Here goes nothing," she said as she reached up, grasped the dragon's tail with both hands, and yanked down on it.

Bernie and Libby heard a creak and felt motion. She pulled down harder. This time the dragon moved. Bernie instinctively held up her hand to catch the curtain rod in case it fell, but it stayed in place. "We have game," she said as she jumped off the chair.

She and Libby rushed back inside the closet. There was a small, visible space where the crack in the wall had been.

"It *is* a door," Bernie said as she bent down, grabbed hold of the edge, and pulled.

The door opened a little wider.

Libby looked at the opening. "I don't know," she said. "This opening would be a pretty tight fit for Zalinsky."

"He could still wiggle his way through," Bernie said as she peeked inside.

She couldn't see anything. It was all blackness. She took out her phone and opened the flashlight app. Suddenly the tunnel came into view. She moved her phone up and down. The ceiling was low. She wouldn't be able to stand upright, but she could get down on on her hands and knees, and she'd been right, it was wide enough to get her shoulders through with a couple of inches to spare on either side.

She crawled in a little way and played the light over the walls. A couple of feet down, she spotted a box sitting on the floor. Books were piled on top of it. She crawled in a couple more feet, removed the books, and dragged the box out. It was your standard brown cardboard carton, the kind one sent packages in, and it was sealed with packing tape.

"It's heavy," Bernie noted as she lifted the carton up and put it on Zalinsky's bed.

Then she got her keys out and slit the tape with the key to the van. Libby looked over her shoulder as Bernie opened the flaps. There was a dark green backpack smushed inside. Bernie lifted out the backpack and unzipped it.

She let out a low whistle. "Wow," she said as she shook out the contents.

"For sure," Libby agreed.

Chapter 10

Libby studied the backpack's contents lying on Zalinsky's bed. There was a small notebook with nothing inside, twenty thousand dollars in cash, a small envelope containing five one-carat diamonds, probably one hundred gold Krugerrands, a Glock .9mm, two boxes of ammo, and an American passport sporting Zalinsky's picture and the name Louis Zebb.

"Interesting that Zalinsky kept the same initials," Libby commented as she picked up the passport and thumbed through it. It gave no evidence of being used.

"I suppose it's easier to remember your new name that way," Bernie observed. She pointed to the issuing date. "He got this in April. Maybe he knew trouble was coming."

"Or maybe he was just covering all his bases," Libby said as she picked up a large, square| leather case that had been inside the backpack and opened it. It was full of jewelry, each piece wrapped in purple tissue paper.

"Could be," Bernie said. "I guess if you're someone like Zalinsky, you've got to have all your bases covered."

"Not bad," Libby commented, lifting out a tennis bracelet and a pair of two-carat diamond earrings. "Not bad at all." She went through the rest of the jewelry. There were two Cartier watches, several more diamond bracelets, four sets of diamond earrings, two diamond pins with stones set in a flower design, and a number of necklaces. Seven of the pieces had women's names attached to them, none of which, Libby noted, were Erin's. "He was quite the ladies' man," Libby observed.

Bernie picked up a pair of earrings and held them up to the light. "I wonder if they're real?"

"You think they're phony?" Libby asked.

"Yeah, I do," Bernie said after studying them for a minute. "Good phonies, but phonies nevertheless."

"What makes you say that?" Libby asked.

"The clarity of the stones in these earrings looks off. Either that or they're low-grade diamonds."

Libby took a pair of earrings and held them up to the light. "They look fine to me."

"That's because you never worked in a jewelry store," Bernie told her sister.

"Give me a break," Libby retorted. "You worked there for a week before you got fired."

Bernie put her hands on her hips. "First of all, I quit; and second of all, I learned a lot during that week."

"Like what? You were doing computer stuff in the office and running errands."

Bernie ignored her sister. "Well," she said,

tapping the fingers of her left hand on her chin, "there's only one way to tell."

"Get them appraised?"

"That would take time."

"What are you doing?" Libby cried as she watched Bernie place the earrings she was holding on the floor.

"Finding out," Bernie said, bringing her foot up and stamping down on the earrings as hard as she could. When she picked her foot up there was a mound of white powder on the floor. "Paste. If they had been real they would be intact," she went on to explain.

Libby gestured toward the jewelry case. "So all of these are fake?"

Bernie nodded. "That's probably a good bet."

"Even the watches?"

"I don't see why they should be real when everything else is fake, do you?"

"No." Libby started to chew on her cuticle, realized what she was doing, and stopped herself. "But the money and the unset diamonds and the gold coins are real?"

"They look real to me."

"And Zalinsky's passport? Real or fake?"

Bernie thought about that for a minute. Then she said, "Fake. I don't see why he would be using a false name in his day-to-day dealings. Too complicated."

"Then how come the jewelry . . ." Libby began.

"Is fake?" Bernie said, finishing her sister's sentence for her.

Libby nodded.

"Like you said, Zalinsky was quite the ladies' man. I'm guessing the jewelry was for his girl-friends," Bernie answered. "Of which, judging by the names on the pieces, he had a fair number besides Erin."

"Well, he was definitely economical," Libby said. "Why spend money on the real stuff when the fake stuff will get you what you want?"

That got Bernie thinking about the diamond earrings and bracelet she'd seen Erin wearing. They looked just like the ones in Zalinsky's leather case. Then Bernie remembered over-hearing Erin bragging to Magda about all the jewelry Zalinsky was giving her. "I wonder if the stuff Zalinsky was giving Erin was real, and if it wasn't, I wonder if Erin found that out?" Bernie mused.

"It's certainly the type of thing that would get a girl upset," Libby commented. "Really upset. Especially if one were going out with said guy for monetary reasons alone."

"What other kind of reasons would there be for going out with Zalinsky?" Bernie asked.

"None, as far as I can see," Libby responded promptly. "I mean you wouldn't be going out with him for his looks or personality. Maybe he's good in bed."

"Doubtful. He's too selfish and in too much of a hurry." Bernie put her hands above her head and stretched. "You know what they say about hell hath no fury like a woman scorned? In this case I'd say, hell hath no fury like a woman scammed."

"You think Erin rigged the teakettle?" Libby asked.

Bernie thought over her sister's question for a moment. "Why not?"

"It just doesn't seem like her."

"Totally disagree. Did you see the look on Erin's face when Zalinsky threw her roses on the floor? If she had had a gun, she would have shot him. No. I think she's capable of lots of things if she gets pissed enough, and finding out that her jewelry was fake would definitely be something that would piss her off."

"Yeah. But is she capable of rigging the tea-kettle? I see her more as someone who would slip antifreeze into someone's coffee."

"I don't know. She could have looked up how to do it on the Internet, and even if she didn't, she could have gotten someone to do it for her."

"Now that," Libby told her sister, "I could totally see her doing. Well, one thing is for sure," Libby continued, changing the subject, "Zalinsky was definitely prepared to get out of town."

"Evidently," Bernie agreed. "Maybe that's why he bought the teapot. Because it was small and portable, and he could sell it. If anyone would know an interested buyer, he would."

"Or," Libby said, another explanation having occurred to her, "maybe Zalinsky was a prepper. Maybe he was one of those guys who believed in being prepared for Armageddon."

"A prepper?" Bernie replied. "No. Preppers have supplies of food, water, batteries, and medical supplies." She pointed to the backpack. "This is a go bag. This is for when something bad happens and all you have time to do is grab the bag and get out of town."

"Well, he didn't get out fast enough," Libby observed. "Obviously, he didn't see whatever . . ."

"Whoever," Bernie corrected.

"Fine. He didn't see whoever coming. He thought he still had time." Libby was just about to ask Bernie how much the Krugerrands were worth when she heard a car pulling into the driveway.

Bernie cursed under her breath.

"Now what?" Libby asked.

Chapter 11

Bernie didn't answer her sister. She was too busy listening to the sounds below. A moment later, she and Libby heard footsteps crunching on gravel, then footsteps on the veranda, then the front door to the house opening, and the sound of the alarm beeping as someone punched in the code. Libby and Bernie looked at each other.

"Lucky we went in through the office," Libby whispered.

"I figured it was a two–tiered security system," Bernie whispered back.

"No, you didn't."

Bernie put her finger to her lips. Now Libby could hear it too. There were footsteps coming up the stairs.

"Damn," Bernie cursed as she shoved the money, jewelry, and gun lying on the bed back into the backpack, while Libby returned the chair under the curtain rod back to where it had been and grabbed the carton the backpack had come in. Then they both ran for the closet. They were trapped. There was nowhere else to go.

"Please, don't come in the bedroom," Libby prayed.

"I wouldn't count on that if I were you," Bernie

told her. Then she added, "It could be worse. At least our van is parked in the back."

Libby didn't reply. Her body was rigid as she contemplated the footsteps in the hallway. There were two sets. One tread was heavy, while the other was light. Then she heard voices. They sounded familiar, but she couldn't place them.

"I think it has to be in his majesty's bedroom," a woman said.

"Are you sure?" a man's voice asked.

"No, I'm not. But I've looked everywhere else."

"Glad you have the code," the man says. "It saves us the trouble of breaking in."

The woman laughed. "Not because he wanted me to have it."

"Now, that I can believe. He was a control freak," the man said.

"That's a nice way of putting it," the woman replied.

"Okay," the man replied. "He was an asshole."

"Exactly. He thought I was just a dumb blonde." The woman sniggered. "Boy, did he make a mistake." There was a pause, then she added, "I just want what's mine . . ."

"Ours," the man said.

The woman corrected herself. "Yes. Of course. Ours. He owes us. He owes us big-time."

"What about the others?" the man asked.

"That's their problem. They can take care of themselves," the woman replied.

It had taken Libby a while, but she recognized the voices. "It's Erin and George Holloway," she whispered to Bernie.

Actually, Bernie had made them the moment she'd heard their voices. She could see them now. Erin, model slim, her blond hair caught back in a bun, her perfect makeup—which never ran, no matter what the temperature was—and George, stocky, with his black hair in a samurai-style bun, and his tight, black T-shirt showing off the dragon tattooed down his arm.

"I wonder what Zalinsky owes them?" Bernie whispered.

"Money. He probably hasn't paid them either," Libby responded.

"Maybe it's more than that," Bernie replied, retelling the story her boyfriend, Brandon, had told her about Zalinsky putting the two brothers out of business, then forcing them to work for him.

"That wouldn't surprise me," Libby said when her sister was done.

Bernie sat back on her haunches. Based on the direction the sounds were coming from, Bernie could tell that Erin and George were standing in front of Zalinsky's bedroom. They'd be inside in another second, and then it was a short step to the closet door.

"The tunnel," she told Libby. "We should get into the tunnel."

"I like where we are now," Libby said. She hated small spaces.

"What if they open the closet door?" Bernie demanded.

"We can hide behind the hangers in the back."

"Get serious," Bernie said.

"They won't see us there," Libby said, defending herself.

"They will if they step inside."

"Then we'll say we were . . ." Libby's voice trailed off while she struggled to come up with a plausible explanation.

"Exactly," Bernie said.

Libby tried a different tack. "So they find us? So what? What's the worst that can happen?"

"They could kill us," Bernie said.

"Okay, that would be bad," Libby agreed. "But also highly unlikely."

"Really. After all, they might have killed Zalinsky. Who's to say they won't do the same to us."

"Who's to say they will?" Libby countered. "Anyway, there's the gun in the backpack."

"Do you want to use it?"

"Not if I don't have to."

"Fine. Neither do I. On a lighter note, they could call the police and have us arrested for breaking and entering."

"We didn't really break in," Libby replied.

"I'd like to hear you explain that to Dad after we're arrested," Bernie told her.

"True." That would be worse than getting shot. Libby rubbed her calf muscles. They were beginning to cramp. She had to remember to drink more water, especially in the summer.

Erin and George started talking again. Their voices were clear. *If voices were color,* Bernie found herself thinking, *Erin's would be coral and George's would be slate.*

"I think we're looking for a bag," Erin said.

"Like a paper bag?" George asked.

"No, like a suitcase or a backpack," Erin replied.

Bernie noted a certain peevishness in her tone. George must have noted it too because he said, "Hey, don't get your back up with me."

Erin apologized. "Sorry. I'm just . . . upset. This whole thing is such a mess. I can't believe he was going to do that to me."

"He was a moron," George said.

Bernie heard some shuffling. For some reason, she thought Erin and George were kissing.

"How do you know we're looking for a bag?" George finally said after a couple of minutes had gone by.

Erin sighed. "I told you."

"Tell me again," George commanded.

"Like I said," Erin recounted, "a couple of weeks ago I heard his majesty talking on the phone when he was at my place. He said to whomever he was talking to that he was good to go and that he had his nine mil and everything else he needed for Belize in his trusty bag."

"Belize?" Libby mouthed, turning to Bernie. "Can't you buy a citizenship there?"

Bernie nodded. "I guess he was planning to get out of the country as well as the town," she mouthed back.

"So it would seem." Libby blinked away a drop of sweat that had landed in her eye. God, it was hot in here. She didn't know how much longer she could stay put. "Maybe they'll leave soon."

Bernie shrugged. "Maybe. But I wouldn't count on it." She gestured to the tunnel and patted Libby's arm. "You'll see, it won't be as bad as you think it's going to be in there."

Yes, it will, Libby wanted to scream. *It'll be worse.* Just thinking about being in the tunnel gave her the heebie-jeebies. *God only knew what was inside there. Probably spiders. She hated spiders. Or those things with all those legs. Silverfish? Centipedes? Ugh. She could feel her stomach turning already. Or rats. What about rats?* Libby took a deep breath and let it out. She could hear Erin and George talking again and tried to concentrate on that.

"You want to take the bedroom or the closet?" Erin was asking.

"The closet," George said.

Bernie and Libby looked at each other. Bernie

96

raised an eyebrow. Libby put her palms up in a gesture of defeat.

"You can do this," she murmured to herself. "There's nothing in there. Nothing." Much as she hated to admit it, Bernie was right. They'd be better off in the tunnel.

"You first," Libby said to Bernie.

Bernie gave her a thumbs-up. Then she pushed Zalinsky's go bag into the tunnel and crawled in after it on her hands and knees. Libby followed her in. Then she wiggled around, grabbed the tunnel door by two indentations near its edge and pulled it shut.

The first thing that hit Libby when the door closed was the darkness. Except for the beam of light from Bernie's phone, it was so dark she couldn't see her hand in front of her face. And it was hot. Extremely hot. Suffocatingly hot. Libby felt as if she couldn't breathe. She'd hated tight spaces ever since she was a little kid and had gotten stuck in the laundry chute and the fire department had had to come and get her out. *Concentrate on your breathing,* she told herself as she could feel herself begin to panic. *Breathe in to the count of seven and out to the count of eleven. Or was it the opposite way? She never could remember.*

Libby was just about to inhale when she heard the scrape of the closet door opening. She froze. So did Bernie. Then they heard footsteps walking in and the tinny sound of hangers being moved along their metal rods.

"Why do you think there's a tunnel in this house anyway?" George said.

Bernie assumed he was speaking to Erin. It was harder to hear what he said, though, and Bernie thought that was because he was turning his head to talk to Erin, who was outside in the bedroom.

"You just don't listen, do you?" Erin replied. Her voice was slightly muffled. "I already told you. This house was part of the Underground Railroad."

"So why do you think the bag is in the tunnel?"

"Because I've looked everywhere else," Erin snapped.

Bernie could tell from the tone of her voice that Erin was losing her patience again. It seemed to be in short supply.

"And why do you think the tunnel is in the closet?" the sisters could hear George asking.

"Jeez," Erin answered. "Give it a rest."

"Hey, I don't like wasting my time."

"Do you think I do?" There was a pause. Then Erin explained. "It's just the way Zalinsky acted. He always acted weird when I went in the closet to hang something up. Nervous like. He'd yell at me for messing things up."

"Maybe you were," George suggested. "Maybe he just liked things neat."

"It was more than that. He'd never let me sta in this room when he wasn't here. He always made me leave. I figure there has to be a reason for that."

"Maybe he didn't want you snooping around, looking in his things."

"But he didn't know I was doing that," Erin protested.

"I think maybe he did."

"Do you want to look, or do you want to talk?"

George chuckled. "I've got a third possibility in mind."

Bernie and Libby could hear Erin giggle.

"Is that all you ever think about?" she asked.

"Like you don't," George crooned.

Erin giggled again. "I got a new tattoo—just for you."

"In my special place?" George's voice was hoarse.

"You're a bad, bad boy."

"Let me see."

"Later, baby," Erin cooed. "Work first, play second."

George laughed. "Then let's make this fast. You want me to move the shoes and stuff?"

"Absolutely," Erin told him.

That, Bernie decided, was their cue to go. She began crawling forward on her knees, traveling farther into the tunnel. She'd gone about a foot when she realized that Libby wasn't following

99

her. She crawled back and tugged on the hem of Libby's T-shirt. When her sister turned around, Bernie motioned for her to go forward.

Even though she wanted to stay where she was, Libby started moving. She went slowly, pausing every minute or so to check out the path in front of her in the small amount of light that Bernie's cell phone provided. The tunnel wound to the left, sloping slightly downward, and Libby tried to picture where in the house they were, but she couldn't. She'd lost her sense of direction.

As the sisters advanced, Erin and George's voices fell away till all Bernie and Libby could hear was the sound of their own breathing and the swoosh of the backpack on the tunnel floor as Bernie pushed it in front of her. She continued on, shining the light generated by her cell ahead of her. *Thank God, she'd gotten the app,* she thought, as she slowly advanced forward. She didn't think she'd be able to do this in total darkness. As she moved, she noticed that the floor was starting to slope downward at a more pronounced angle. She'd gone two more yards when she got a shock. Her light revealed nothing except blackness up ahead.

Chapter 12

B ernie stopped. Oh my God. Her heart started hammering in her chest.

"What's the matter?" Libby asked.

"Just a minute," Bernie replied.

"Is there a problem? Why are we stopped?"

Bernie could hear the rising note of hysteria in her sister's voice. "No problem. It's fine," she lied. "There's nothing wrong. I've just got a cramp in my leg," Bernie said as she slowly inched forward.

This was not good. Please, God, don't let the tunnel end here, she prayed, because now that she thought about it, that was a definite possibility. She'd just assumed everything would be fine. Why? If it weren't, she and Libby would be stuck. Nothing to do but wait out George and Erin. Think positive, she told herself. At least they had the light. Without it, she might have fallen down the hole.

But that brought up another issue. How long was the battery in her phone going to last? Would using the flashlight drain the battery? How charged was her battery anyway? She should have paid more attention because she didn't know. Bernie shivered in spite of herself as she inched forward, going as far as she could go.

She came to the edge of the abyss and aimed

the light from her cell phone down into the blackness. When she saw what was down there, she started to giggle.

"What's so funny?" Libby asked.

"It's stairs. Really steep stairs." Bernie started to laugh harder. From relief. She couldn't help herself.

"What's so funny about that?" Libby demanded.

"Nothing. Nothing at all," Bernie said as she wiped the tears from her eyes. She'd explain after they got out of here.

"Then why are you laughing?" Libby demanded. "Are you okay?"

"I'm fine. Excellent, in fact. I'm just glad we're getting to the end of this thing," Bernie told her, pushing aside another alarming thought. What if the door they were heading to was stuck? *Put that thought right out of your head,* she told herself as she explained about the stairs to her sister. "Just turn around and go down on your ass and you'll be fine."

"I knew there was a reason I haven't lost my last ten pounds yet," Libby wisecracked. "At least I'll have some padding."

Bernie was smart enough not to say anything about the size of Libby's behind. Instead she turned around, clasped Zalinsky's backpack to her chest, and inched forward until her butt was on the top step and her feet were on the one below. Then she carefully lowered herself down to the next step. "Give me a couple of seconds before you come down," she instructed Libby as she cleared the next step. The last thing she wanted was Libby bumping into her and both of them tumbling down the stairs.

Libby silently counted to fifteen. "Are you ready?" she called.

"Ready whenever you are," Bernie answered as she slid down a third step.

Libby inched forward. She had her butt on the top stair, her feet firmly planted on the one below, and she was busy telling herself this was no big deal when she heard the sound of something opening above her and felt a rush of air. Then she heard George say, "Erin, you were right about the curtain rod." Thirty seconds later Libby heard another set of footsteps going into the closet. Erin's, she presumed.

"Wonderful," Bernie said through clenched teeth. "Just what we don't need." Then things got worse.

She heard George say, "You stay here while I go in." There was a pause. Then he said, "Somebody has to stay up here in case something goes wrong. You think I'm going to steal the bag or some-thing?"

Bernie and Libby's hearts began to beat faster.

"Maybe he won't come down all the way," Libby whispered.

"Maybe," Bernie whispered back. But she knew

he would. He would because he'd be looking for the backpack, the backpack that she was clutching to her chest.

A few seconds later, she could hear cursing, then the sound of George sliding into the tunnel. Well, one thing was for sure. It would be a tighter fit for him than it had been for her and Libby. So that would slow him down slightly.

Bernie turned her head to Libby. "Come on," she said. "We gotta hustle." And with that she began to slide down the stairs as fast as possible.

Every time she hit the edge of one of the steps, she could feel it digging into her butt. *I'm never going to sit down again,* she thought as she slithered down. Libby was right behind her. When Bernie got to the last step, Libby plowed into her, knocking her onto the floor.

"Sorry," Libby hissed as Bernie rubbed the side where Libby's shoe had hit her.

Bernie didn't bother to answer. Instead she got on her hands and knees and started crawling again.

"How much longer till we get out of here?" Libby whispered. She could hear George above her. She'd thought he'd be slow, but he wasn't. He was making good time—better time than they had made.

"I'm not sure, but we'd better get to that door soon," Bernie replied. She was going as fast as she could go, but judging from the sounds coming from above, it wasn't fast enough.

Focus, Bernie told herself. Focus on what you're doing. So Bernie stopped thinking about George. She stopped thinking about Libby. She stopped thinking about anything except the tunnel, her breathing, and putting one hand and knee in front of the other. Finally, after she wasn't sure how much time had elapsed because she'd lost track in the blackness, she came to the end.

Her light showed a door. A small one. Made of wood. With a latch on it. Bernie uttered a silent prayer and let out the breath she didn't know she'd been holding. She lifted her hand and pulled on the latch. It was stuck. Maybe rusted out. She tried again. It wasn't budging.

"What?" Libby asked.

"I can't get the latch to move," Bernie hissed, fighting to keep her voice calm.

"Your lip gloss."

"My what?"

"Use your lip gloss," Libby repeated. "The expensive one with shea butter. Maybe it'll act as a lubricant."

"I hope so," Bernie said. She handed Zalinsky's backpack off to Libby, opened her bag, and began rummaging around inside it.

"Hurry," Libby whispered. "He's getting closer."

"You think I don't know that," Bernie snapped. A second later, her hand closed on her lip gloss. "Got it." She took the top off and began

105

applying the gloss to the lock. Then she pulled. The latch moved a little. She pulled harder. The latch moved some more. Then nothing. She applied more gloss. The latch was well and truly stuck.

"Give me the backpack," she told Libby.

Libby handed it over. She watched while her sister opened it up and took out the Glock.

"Are you shooting the door open?" Libby asked.

"Not yet. But I will if this doesn't work." And with that Bernie used the butt of the gun to hammer the latch open.

"Piece of cake," Bernie said as she handed the backpack and the Glock back to Libby. "Say a prayer," she told her as she grasped the door handle and yanked. The door jumped back. Light flooded the tunnel. Bernie crawled outside. Libby followed.

"Good call about the lip gloss," Bernie told Libby as she turned and closed the door, never mind that she was out the thirty bucks the gloss had cost her.

Libby just nodded. She didn't say anything because she was too busy giving thanks for being out of the tunnel. No matter what happened now, it had to be better than being in there. For a moment, she and her sister stood blinking in the daylight. Little specks of color exploded across their eyes. It took them a couple of minutes to be able to see again after spending all that time in the dark. The trees had never seemed so green or the sky so blue.

Libby was admiring the leaves of a maple in front of her when Bernie said, "George."

"What about him?" Libby asked.

"He's going to come barreling through that door any second. It would be nice if we could block it and slow him down."

"With what? Superglue?" Libby said.

"I was thinking that rock," Bernie said, pointing to a large one five feet away. It wouldn't stop George from opening the door, but it would slow him down.

Bernie and Libby ran over to it. The rock proved harder to move than Bernie had anticipated because the bottom half was buried in the dirt, but after several tries they finally succeeded in getting it out and rolling it toward the door.

"I think I pulled a muscle in my shoulder," Libby complained when they were done. She looked around. "Do you know where we are?"

Bernie brushed the dirt off her hands, then pointed to the left. "I think we're in the woods in back of the office. If we go straight, we should come out next to the van."

"I hope you're right," Libby said.

"Me too," Bernie replied as she picked up Zalinsky's backpack and started moving off in that direction. She wanted to get out of there before George came out of the tunnel. "I guess we'll find out."

Bernie walked quickly, keeping her eyes on the ground so she didn't trip over any roots or rocks. It took her and Libby five minutes to get to the van, longer than she had anticipated.

"Oh my God," she cried when she saw a reflection of herself in the van's side-view mirror. "I look horrible." And she took a tissue out of her bag and began wiping off the eyeliner and mascara that had migrated to her cheeks.

"Yeah, you do look pretty bad," Libby concurred.

"Well, you don't look so good yourself," Bernie retorted.

"At least my makeup is where it's supposed to be."

"That's because you don't wear any," Bernie shot back.

"Exactly my point. That way nothing can go wrong. Okay, we both look like hell," Libby conceded, looking down at her knees. They were scraped and bleeding from crawling through the tunnel, plus she had a tear in her T-shirt and black stuff across the leg of her Bermuda shorts, while Bernie had a circle of muck on the bodice of her DKNY wrap dress and a tear on the skirt. Bernie sighed. Hopefully the tailor would be able to fix it.

"Come on," she told Libby, opening Mathilda's

door. "Let's get in the truck before George gets here." She was thinking she was hearing a twig popping kind of noise, but she wasn't sure.

Libby jumped in, while Bernie started Mathilda's engine. Mathilda coughed and spluttered.

"You can always count on Mathilda not to start when you need her," Bernie groused. Finally Mathilda's engine caught. "About time," Bernie said.

Then, just as Bernie was going to switch into drive, she saw George through the trees.

Chapter 13

Step on it," Libby cried, having seen George as well.

Bernie shook her head. She'd changed her mind. "No. We're staying put."

"Why?"

"Because I have a better idea." Then Bernie turned off the van, leaned over, and opened the door.

"What do you think you're doing?" Libby asked, aghast.

"Playing a hunch," Bernie replied.

"First we practically kill ourselves to avoid meeting George, and now we're sitting here waiting for him?" Libby asked as she saw her chance for a cool shower followed by a watermelon and feta salad with a slice of French bread disappearing.

"*Autre temps, autre mores,*" Bernie chirped airily.

Libby fought off a desire to strangle her sister. "What the hell is that supposed to mean?"

"It means, loosely translated, different time, different situation," Bernie replied, stepping onto the ground. She could see George coming out of the woods. He was putting his phone away as he came toward her. *He's probably telling Erin where we are,* Bernie thought as she crossed her arms over her chest and waited for him.

"Fancy seeing you here," Bernie said to George when he was a couple of feet away from her. She looked him up and down. "Wow. Where were you? You look like you were digging in a mine or something."

"You don't look too good yourself," George replied while he wiped a smear of blood off a small cut on his arm. "Maybe we were digging in the same place."

"I don't do well in the heat," Bernie told him. Out of the corner of her eye, she could see Erin running up to meet them. *Good,* Bernie thought. *The more the merrier.*

"What are you doing here?" George demanded as Libby got out of the van and joined her sister.

"Yes," Erin seconded, coming up behind George. "I'd like to know that too."

As Erin stopped to catch her breath, Bernie was heartened to note that her eye makeup had migrated down her cheeks as well. Then she noticed there was something different about Erin's appearance, but Bernie just couldn't put her finger on what it was.

"Funny you should ask, Erin," Bernie said. "Hsaio and I must have gotten our times mixed up. She asked Libby and me to meet her at the office, but when we got there the door was locked. I guess she must have gone to class. Too bad, because she said she had some important information to tell us concerning your benefactor's death, but since that wasn't happening, we decided to take a little jaunt through the woods. It's really quite lovely this time of year."

Erin smiled sweetly. "Yes, Ludvoc could be incredibly generous. The world will miss him." She put her hands up to her eyes to wipe away a tear.

"That's what Hsaio said," Bernie lied. "We'll all miss him."

"Yes, we certainly will," Erin agreed.

George coughed, while Libby tried to keep a straight face.

"We just came to collect a few things that Ludvoc wanted me to have," Erin explained.

"Keepsakes can be such a comfort," Libby chimed in.

Erin nodded. "That is so true."

"I didn't know you were Magda's cousin," Libby said.

"Third cousin," Erin said.

"Are you Russian?" Libby asked.

"On my mother's side," Erin said.

"Because Erin isn't a Russian name," Libby said.

"It was Irina. I changed it," Erin said.

"So, as I was saying," Bernie said, jumping back into the conversation, "since Hsaio wasn't here, my sister and I decided to look around, and the most amazing thing happened. You'll never guess what we found."

"A unicorn?" George said. He swatted at a bee and then plucked a thorn out of the palm of his hand with his teeth.

Bernie smiled at him. "No. A backpack. Just lying out in the woods."

"Really?" Erin said. "Probably something some kid dropped."

"One would think, but one would be wrong," Bernie replied. "At least in my experience, most kids don't carry gold coins, cash, a gun, diamonds, and a fake passport in their backpacks. Although there are always going to be exceptions to that rule."

Bernie looked at Erin as she spoke. She reminded Bernie of a setter spotting a bird. Erin was vibrating with excitement; she was trying very hard to be Miss Cool—and not succeeding.

"So whose backpack was it?" Erin asked.

"Zalinsky's. Imagine that," Bernie said.

"Imagine," Erin echoed weakly.

"I guess he was planning on leaving," Bernie said. "Did you know about that?"

Erin rallied. "No," she asserted, unconvincingly in Bernie's mind. "I didn't."

"Do you have any idea why he would do something like that?"

"Leave?" Erin asked.

"Yes," Bernie said.

George took a step forward. "He told my brother he was afraid someone was out to get him."

Erin put her hand to her mouth. "You never told me that," she cried.

"I thought I did," George said.

"I would have remembered if you had," Erin replied.

"Did he say who?" Bernie asked, interrupting.

"Not to my brother," George answered.

"How about to you?" Bernie inquired, swallowing. Her mouth felt dry, probably from all the dust she'd swallowed in the tunnel. She needed water. There was a bottle in the van, but she didn't want to interrupt the conversational flow to get it. "Did he say anything to you?" she asked for the sake of thoroughness, because she didn't believe that Zalinsky had said anything to George's brother, Stan, let alone to George.

"Nope." George scratched a mosquito bite. "So what are you going to do with the backpack?"

"We're turning it over to the police, naturally," Bernie said.

Erin smiled and smoothed down her hair with the palm of her hand. "Of course you are. You know, George and I are going that way." She turned to George. "Aren't we?"

George nodded. "Definitely."

"We'll be happy to drop it off."

"Thanks for the offer, but I think we'd better do it," Bernie told her. And then what was bothering her about Erin hit her. She wasn't wearing her earrings, her necklace, or her bracelet. "What happened to your jewelry?" she asked. "I hope it wasn't stolen or anything."

"Oh no," Erin replied. "I just don't like to wear anything in the summer when it's this hot. I get rashes."

"I do too," Bernie said. "It's such a drag. That's why I can only wear the real stuff."

"Me too," Erin said.

George snorted.

"What's that supposed to mean?" Erin demanded, turning to him.

George threw up his hands. "Nothing. Nothing at all. A fly just flew up my nose. Damned insects. They're all over the woods this time of year."

Right, Bernie thought, her ears perking up. *She wondered what George was alluding to.* She decided to throw out some more lines and see what she reeled in. If that didn't work, she and Libby could always talk to him alone later. "Which reminds me," she went on. "Did I tell you we found some jewelry in Zalinsky's backpack?"

Erin's eyes widened slightly. "No, you didn't."

"There was a whole bunch of it in a leather case. A lot of it looked like the stuff you wear, except of course yours is real and this was paste." Bernie shook her head in mock dismay.

George snorted again.

"Really?" Erin said.

"Really," Bernie replied, pausing to retie the sash on her dress as she assessed the expression on Erin's face. She couldn't tell what Erin was thinking. Was the jewelry Zalinsky had given Erin real, or wasn't it? Obviously, George's snort had meant something. But what? Bernie admitted to herself that she didn't know.

"Frankly, I'm surprised," Erin said.

"Me too," Bernie agreed. "I would be so pissed if that happened to me—thinking I'd been given something real and it turns out its fake! I'd feel . . ." Bernie flung her hands out, "I don't know . . . furious."

Erin cleared her throat. "Well, mine was"—she corrected herself—"is real."

"I remember," Bernie reminisced, wondering what Erin's change of tense meant, "this guy I was going out with in San Fran giving me this emerald ring, and I was showing it off, and someone I knew took me aside and told me it was a fake. I wanted to kill Ollie. I think doing someone like that shows such a lack of respect.

"But then I don't think Zalinsky had any respect for most people. Look what he did to Libby and me. Making us serve that terrible menu. I mean, we would have been the laughingstock of the food world. But did he care? He did not. On top of everything else, he didn't even pay us for all our time and effort. No, Zalinsky really screwed us over. Lucky he didn't do that to you," she told Erin.

"Yes, isn't it," Erin replied evenly.

"Even if he did throw your flowers on the floor and tell you to clean up the mess. I have to say you handled that very well, better than I would have. I would have wanted to brain him."

"He did have a temper," Erin allowed.

"That's for sure," Libby agreed.

"He was always nice to me, though," Erin said, her voice getting stronger.

George snorted for the fourth time. Erin pointedly ignored him.

"But he did have his dark side," she continued. "He could be ruthless." She turned to George. "Look what he did to you and your brother."

George gave Erin a warning look. "What are you talking about?"

"Just the way he made you and your brother come work for him after he ruined your business," Erin said.

"We wanted to work for him," George protested. "We did," he told Bernie and Libby. "He said he'd help expand B & G Biometrics."

"Instead of which he closed it down," Erin said. She tsk-tsked. "And after all that money you borrowed from your family. What did Stan say? That your parents took out a second mortgage on their house, and now the bank might take it?"

George glared at her. "We're paying everything

back," he said through gritted teeth. "It's going to be fine."

This time it was Erin's turn to snort. "What are you paying it back with?" Erin asked pleasantly. "I mean, I'm sure Zalinsky stiffed you just like he stiffed everyone else."

"Maybe that's true," George said, advancing on Erin. Bernie noted that his face had grown red. "But at least I still have a place to live. At least he wasn't ditching me for a younger, prettier model and throwing me out of my apartment."

"That's a lie," Erin cried. She balled her hands into fists. "An absolute lie. How can you say something like that?"

"Really, is that why you were asking Magda if you could live with her?"

"She totally misunderstood what I was saying," Erin snapped. "Totally."

George licked his lips. Bernie decided he looked as if he wanted to strangle Erin. "She's not the only one who is misinformed."

"That man brought out the worst in everyone," Bernie commented.

Erin and George turned to look at Bernie. It was as if they'd forgotten she and her sister were there, Libby reflected.

"He certainly did," Libby said, echoing Bernie's sentiments.

For a moment, neither George nor Erin spoke. Then George started in again.

"He certainly was a piece of work," George said, laughing. "Look at what he did to Erin."

"He didn't do anything to me," Erin told Bernie.

"She had this promising career," George explained to Bernie and Libby. "And now . . . it's pretty much over."

Erin punched George in the arm.

"Ouch," he said, moving away from her. "That hurt."

"Sorry," Erin said, although Bernie didn't think she looked contrite. At all. "He doesn't know what he's talking about."

"Yeah?" George put his hands on his hips. "Well, that's what Igor said, and he should know," he told Erin. "He's in the business."

"He's a wannabe," Erin scoffed. "Now, are you sure we can't take the backpack for you?" she asked Bernie, changing the subject. "I'd hate to see you go out of the way. I mean, you're so busy with the shop and all."

"I'm positive," Bernie said, and she turned and climbed back in the van. "But thanks for the offer."

Erin and George looked at them for a moment, and then they moved off. Even though they couldn't hear anything, Bernie and Libby could tell from the way Erin's and George's arms were moving that they were arguing.

"Talk about throwing someone under the bus," Bernie commented when Erin and George had disappeared into the woods. She reached for her bottle of water and took a big gulp. "Erin was pretty quick to do that to George."

"And George was pretty quick to reciprocate," Libby noted.

Bernie leaned over, turned the air conditioner on high, and fanned the tepid breeze toward her face. "So much for young love," she said. "Did you hear that Zalinsky was throwing Erin out?"

Libby shook her head. "No. Did you?"

"You think George was telling the truth?"

"Yup," Libby said. "Or let me just say Zalinsky doing that wouldn't surprise me. At all."

Bernie took another gulp of water and passed the bottle to Libby. She'd heard something about Erin . . . now what was it? Then suddenly she remembered.

"You know," she began, "I think I remember hearing that Erin was engaged to this investment banker and that Zalinsky took her away from him."

"That's funny," Libby said, "because I heard she was going out with Jason and Zalinsky took her away from him."

Bernie did a rat-tat-tat with her fingernails on the steering wheel. "We should find out."

"Without a doubt," Libby told her as Bernie shifted into drive and started toward the Longely police station.

Chapter 14

"That's the last time I ever do the police a favor," Libby grumbled as Bernie pulled the van in front of their shop, A Little Taste of Heaven. "We should have kept the money."

"It would be nice," Bernie agreed, thinking of everything they could have done with it.

The transfer of the backpack to the police had not gone as smoothly as Bernie had anticipated it would. She'd figured she'd hand Zalinsky's backpack off to her Dad's friend Clyde, explain that she'd found it in the woods, and leave. Unfortunately, Clyde wasn't there. Lucy, aka Lucas Broadbent, Longely's chief of police and her dad's nemesis, was.

"Damn," Bernie muttered when she saw him come out of his office. The Simmons family didn't like him, and he sure didn't like them. She knew he wasn't going to buy her story on general principles, but it was too late to leave now. "Looking good," she told him. Actually, Lucy had gained even more weight since she'd seen him last. Between that and his bald head, he looked like an egg.

"Ah, the Simmons sisters." He rubbed his hands together. "Seeing you just makes my day. Why are you here?"

So Bernie told him.

"How do I know this isn't a setup to divert suspicion from your friend Casper?" he'd demanded.

"Brilliant deduction. Yeah, I always have twenty thousand dollars in cash, gold coins, and diamonds hanging around the flat," Bernie had replied.

"Maybe you do," Lucy had said, at which point Bernie had rolled her eyes, which had just pissed Lucy off even more. He'd then spent the next half hour asking Bernie and Libby where they'd found the backpack.

Bernie kept repeating the same story. She said they'd gone for a hike in the woods, and Lucy kept saying that he didn't buy it.

Finally, he'd pointed at her clothes and said, "Where were you hiking anyway? A mud pit?"

"We fell," Bernie had told him.

"Both of you?" he'd asked. "At the same time?"

"No," Libby had said. "Bernie fell first, and I tripped over her. Is there a law against that?"

"No, but there's a law against lying to the police," Lucy had replied.

"We're not lying," Libby had asserted.

"You know what I think," Lucy had begun.

Bernie yawned. "No, but I'm sure you're going to tell us."

Lucy had ignored her and continued on. "I think

you found the backpack somewhere else. I think you're trying to muddle up the crime scene."

"The crime scene is at The Blue House," Libby said. "How did we get muddied up if we found the backpack there?"

"I know where the crime scene is, thank you very much," Lucy had snapped.

At which point, Libby decided she'd had enough. She was tired and dirty and hungry, and she wanted to go home, clean up, and have something to eat. "This is ridiculous," she said, standing up. "We're leaving."

Lucy had glared at her and told her to sit back down, but Libby had glared right back and said that as far as she knew she was free to go. There was nothing Lucy could say because it was true.

"This isn't going to help your friend," Lucy had told Libby as she and Bernie had walked toward the door. "There's still the threatening note Cumberbatch left on Zalinsky's table . . ."

"He didn't write that," Bernie objected.

Lucy went on as if Bernie hadn't spoken ". . . the anonymous letter we got, not to mention the suspect's whereabouts at the time of Zalinsky's death."

"He's Bernie's friend, not mine," Libby had retorted for want of something better to say.

That had silenced Lucy long enough for her and Bernie to walk out the door. On the way home, they stopped at the supermarket to get food for their cat and bought two five-pound bags of lemons because they were on sale.

"I'm thinking lemon chicken," Libby said once they were back in the van.

Bernie nodded. It was always a good seller for them. They spent the rest of the ride back discussing tomorrow's lunchtime specials. They'd settled on five dishes in addition to the lemon chicken: a cold poached salmon; a BLT made with farm-cured bacon, avocado, local beefsteak tomatoes, and butter crunch lettuce served on a store-baked baguette slathered with homemade mayonnaise; a corn, tomato, and feta cheese salad; a watercress, arugula, walnut, and goat cheese salad; and fresh peach ice cream. They were almost in front of the shop when Bernie cursed and slammed on the brakes.

"What's the matter?" Libby asked.

Bernie pointed. Their cat, Cindy, was sitting in the street right by the curb. Another minute and Bernie would have run over her.

"Oh, my God," Libby cried as she unbuckled her seat belt and dashed outside.

Bernie was right behind her.

"You could have been run over," Libby told Cindy as she scooped her up in her arms and pressed her against her chest. Their main street was full of fast-moving cars and was distinctly not a cat-friendly place.

Cindy meowed a response.

"How'd you get out?" Bernie asked her.

Cindy looked up at Libby and meowed again. Then she began to purr.

"That was close," Bernie said as she reached over and rubbed the tips of Cindy's ears. Cindy purred louder.

Bernie shuddered as she thought about what could have happened to the cat if she hadn't been paying attention. Loath as she was to admit it, she'd become quite fond of Cindy since she'd been foisted on them last year. The fact that she was a good mouser didn't hurt either. Bernie was about to suggest to Libby that she take Cindy upstairs, while she went into the shop and talked to Amber and Googie when Amber came running out of the store.

"Thank God you're here," she cried.

Chapter 15

"A mber, what's the matter?" Libby asked as their counter girl headed toward them with all the fervor of a homing pigeon heading for its coop, not that Libby was too alarmed since Amber tended to be dramatic.

As Libby watched Amber approaching them, she remembered the first three months she'd worked in the shop. One day Amber would show up as Marilyn Monroe, the next day she'd be Goth Girl, and the day after that she'd be imitating a beatnik. Not knowing what Amber would look like when she came to work had driven Libby crazy, but the customers had loved Amber's chameleon act, and after a while Libby had too. Now she looked forward to seeing what Amber was going to look like when she walked through the door.

Today she was impersonating a twelve-year-old with her purple braids, Frozen T-shirt, pink wraparound skirt, and numerous multicolored bangles on her arms.

"I like the hair," Libby said as she watched Amber bearing down on her and her sister. "So what's up?" she asked, as she scratched Cindy under her chin.

"I am so sorry," Amber told her as she clasped

Bernie's hands to her bosom. "I tried to call you, but it went straight to voice mail."

"That's odd," Bernie told her as she gently worked her hands free. That's when she remembered. She'd turned off her phone's ringer when she and Libby were hiding in the closet, and she'd never put it back on.

Amber turned to Libby. "I tried yours too," she said reproachfully. "But I couldn't even leave a message. Your voice mail is full."

"Sorry," Libby said. Her phone was in the van's glove compartment. She hadn't glanced at it since last night. She really had to get back in the habit of checking her messages.

Amber looked close to tears. "I didn't know what to do."

"Tell us what's wrong," Libby said. For the life of her, she couldn't imagine what was so bad. There was no fire truck, no ambulance, no police car parked outside the shop. Maybe the credit card machine was down or the cooler was failing again, but neither of those warranted tears.

"It's Michelle," Amber said.

"What about her?" Libby asked.

"She's in the back."

"You mean the back of our shop?"

"Yes."

Cindy hissed, and Libby realized she'd tightened her grip on her. "Where?" she asked again, hoping she hadn't heard right.

"In the back," Amber repeated.

"That's what I thought you said," Libby replied. To say this made her unhappy was a massive understatement.

Amber bit her lip. "I tried telling her you didn't like anyone who doesn't work in the shop back there, but she said that you said it would be fine."

"Really?" Libby said. "Is that what she said?"

Amber shrank back at the ice in Libby's voice. Bernie patted her arm.

"It's okay," she reassured Amber. "It's not your fault. It wasn't your place to stop her."

"I tried," Amber said. "But she went right by me."

Bernie patted her arm again. "Don't worry. It's not your responsibility. I'll go talk to Michelle," she said, turning to Libby. "You take Cindy upstairs."

"No. We'll both go talk to Michelle," Libby replied. She wanted to hear what Michelle had to say for herself. This was not a conversation she was going to miss.

Bernie looked at her sister. If she didn't like Michelle, Libby absolutely loathed her. "I'd like to keep the conversation civil, if you don't mind."

"Why would I mind?" Libby asked, for the moment the personification of reason.

"It was a figure of speech," Bernie told her.

"I know that. Anyway, I'm always polite."

Bernie rolled her eyes.

"I am," Libby insisted. "You're the one with the big mouth."

"Not in this case," Bernie told her. "Just don't say anything. I want you to leave the talking to me."

"I won't say a word," Libby replied.

"Promise?"

"I promise," Libby said. "Anyway, I really want to hear what she has to say about the cat."

"How do you know that she had anything to do with the cat?" Bernie asked.

"I don't know. I'm just connecting the dots."

"Meaning?"

"Well, how else did Cindy get outside? It's not as if she opened the door by herself."

"Maybe it was the FedEx guy."

"We're not expecting a delivery."

"Maybe Dad ordered something."

Both Libby and Bernie turned to Amber.

"I didn't see the truck," she told them. "Not that that means anything. I could have been waiting on a customer."

"How was lunch, by the way?" Bernie asked.

"Good," Amber answered. "Lunch was good. We had a run on the gravlax, and we're out of pumpernickel and the three-bean salad. Oh, and we're going to need some more French roast soon."

Bernie nodded. She made a note to speak to

Mike over at Joe's Brew and see if he'd give them a discount if they bought in larger quantity. "I'll pick some more up later today," she assured Amber. Then she turned, and the three of them headed into A Little Taste of Heaven.

Bernie reflexively inhaled as she walked into the shop, drinking in the scents of fresh coffee, butter, vanilla, basil, and toast. Then her eyes took in the sparkling counters, the display cases filled with freshly made salads, local cheeses, and store-made baked goods, and the small tiled tables and wire chairs where the local moms came to sip coffee and chat after they'd dropped their kids off at school.

Three years ago, she and Libby had repainted the walls a pale blue and the ceiling a mint green, and the combination worked. Then she and Libby had hung large photographs of Longely that they'd reproduced from snapshots they'd found in the Longely Historical Center on the walls. Her mom had created a warm, inviting place, and Bernie was proud of the fact that she and her sister had continued the tradition. No matter what the problems were, she was always glad to walk into the shop. It was home.

Bernie looked over at Libby. She could tell from Libby's expression she was feeling the same way—maybe even more so. That's what made Michelle's being in the back so galling. It was an invasion, and if there was one thing she knew about Libby it was that she didn't do well when someone barged into her home without an invitation. And then there was the matter of the cat. If Michelle did have something to do with Cindy getting out, that was worse than being in the back without permission.

"Do you want me to take Cindy upstairs?" Amber asked.

Libby shook her head. Cindy didn't like Amber very much and would probably scratch her, then Amber would drop her, Cindy would run away, and they'd be back where they started. "Thanks," she told Amber, "but we'll manage."

Bernie bit her lip. "Are you sure you won't let me handle this?" she asked Libby.

"I'm absolutely positive," Libby replied. "How long has Michelle been in the back?" Libby asked Amber.

"I'm not sure," Amber replied. "Maybe a half hour. I'm really, really sorry," she said for the third time.

Bernie patted Amber's arm again. "You did good," she told her, looking around.

At least A Little Taste of Heaven was empty. The last thing they needed if there was going to be drama was a shop full of customers. That kind of thing was most definitely not good for business. Right now they were in a lull, and they'd be in a lull until four, when people would start coming in to pick up dinner. Then, at seven, business would drop off to zero. You could set your clock by it. They had three rushes a day, and the rest of the time the shop was empty. At first, the pattern had bothered Bernie, but she'd come to realize that that was why they were able to run their shop with the crew they had.

On their way to the back, Bernie and Libby stopped for a moment to exchange a few words with Googie, their second employee. Unlike Amber, he had no interest in Michelle, no interest in any of the gossip that swirled through the shop. He was totally focused on his job, and that was it, which was one of the things Bernie liked about him.

Plus, he was good with machinery and never panicked, no matter what the circumstances. He was the cool to Amber's hot. At night, he performed with his group, The Wolfmen, and Bernie had to say she thought they were pretty good. One of these days, Bernie knew that both he and Amber would leave, a thought that filled her with sadness, but today wasn't the day.

Bernie was thinking about what she'd do when that happened while she walked into the kitchen. Michelle was standing in the middle of the room, with her arms folded over her chest and a triumphant expression on her face. Clearly she'd heard them coming and had prepared herself.

Not even a shred of guilt on her face, Libby thought as she followed Bernie in. *Amazing.* Then she noticed that the door to their office was slightly open. She was positive she'd closed it before she and Bernie had left.

"Hello," Bernie said to Michelle.

Michelle smiled. "Nice day."

Not even a hint of a fluster, Bernie thought. *She thinks she has this all sewn up.* "Can I help you with anything?" she asked.

Michelle laughed. "No. I'm fine." She gestured to a tray on the nearest prep table. "I was just fixing your father a little snack."

"Really?" Libby said. She was going to say more, but Bernie gave her a warning look, and remembering her promise, she shut up.

"Amber is perfectly capable of doing that," Bernie said, taking over the conversation. "And anyway, Dad doesn't like Camembert on pumpernickel. He likes Brie on a baguette, and he prefers nectarines to peaches."

Michelle laughed. "That's not what he told me. I just thought it would be nice if I got something for Sean, especially with you two running around and playing detective."

"Playing?" Bernie echoed. She could feel her hackles rising.

Michelle tittered. "Sorry if I offended you, but you're not licensed, are you?" She leaned toward them. "Confidentially, I think your dad is feeling a little neglected." She went on before Bernie could reply. "I love your setup here. My prep| room is much smaller. I don't even have an office."

"Do tell." Bernie folded her arms over her chest.

"Yes," Michelle continued. "I hope you don't mind that I peeked inside yours."

Bernie shot Libby a sideways glance. Her sister was getting ready to lose it. Not that she blamed her. All their recipes, the list of vendors they used, their financial info, were in there. She was furious too.

"Actually, I do mind. I mind a lot," Bernie told her, which was a massive understatement.

"I'm sorry," Michelle said, though she didn't sound sorry at all. Then Michelle looked down at the cat in Libby's arms and made a pronouncement. "You know, cats really belong outside," she said.

"Not this one," Bernie replied as Libby clasped Cindy a little more tightly to her chest.

"I think she likes being outside," Michelle said. "All cats do."

"And you know this how?" Bernie inquired in the quiet voice she used when she was really, really mad.

"They should be hunting mice in the barn," Michelle blithely continued on.

"Well, we're not living on a farm, we're living

in Longely, and Front Street is dangerous," Bernie said. She could hear the edge in her voice as she spoke to Michelle.

"Wow. That's exactly what your dad said." Michelle laughed. "Like father like daughter, I guess."

"So you're the one who let Cindy out?" Libby asked, breaking her vow of silence. Actually, Bernie was surprised she'd been quiet for as long as she had.

Michelle straightened her shoulders. "She was mewing at the door. I could tell she wanted to go out."

"So now you're gifted with cat ESP?" Bernie demanded.

"If that's what you want to call it," Michelle replied sweetly.

Bernie took a deep breath and exhaled. "The cat stays in, understand?" she said through clenched teeth.

"Fine," Michelle said. "If that's the way you want it."

"That's definitely the way Libby and I want it," Bernie told her, "because we don't want a dead cat. And next time, if we're not here, ask Amber to get Dad whatever he wants, although, truth be told, he's perfectly capable of coming down here by himself."

Michelle sniffed. "I'm just trying to take care of Sean. I'd think you'd be happy to have

135

someone who cares for your dad and wants to make him comfortable."

"I guess that depends on who that someone is," Libby told her, regretting the words the moment they flew out of her mouth. *Bernie was right,* Libby thought. *I shouldn't have come in.*

"What are you saying?" Michelle demanded.

"What do you think I'm saying?" Libby challenged.

"You think you're so smart. We'll see just how smart you are," Michelle rapped out. Then she picked up the tray with the food she'd prepared for Sean and flounced out of the room.

Libby turned to Bernie. "What did she mean by that?"

"I have no idea, but I don't think it's going to be good," Bernie declared, hazarding a guess.

"I think you may be right," Libby agreed. "I should have kept my mouth shut."

"Yes, you should have," Bernie told her.

Five minutes later, Libby and Bernie found out how not good it was going to be when their father came storming into the kitchen and demanded they go upstairs and apologize to a weeping Michelle, who looked at Bernie and Libby and said, between sobs, words to the effect that she only wanted to do the right thing and was sorry if she'd caused them any problems.

Of course, Bernie and Libby apologized. They had to. At which point Michelle had wiped away her tears with the back of her hands, hugged both of them, and trilled that they were all going to be best friends, and wasn't that going to be wonderful?

If Libby had a knife, she would have stabbed her. Instead she'd smiled and said she was looking forward to it.

Chapter 16

I don't think your daughters like me," Michelle declared as she massaged Sean's shoulders.

Sean was sitting on a bench facing the Hudson, while Michelle was standing behind him.

"Of course they like you," Sean declared, reaching up and patting her hand. "What's there not to like?"

"I don't think they do," Michelle said, contradicting him. "All I wanted to do was help," she added, her voice taking on the plaintive quality she excelled at.

Sean gave her hand a squeeze. "Maybe you just need to give them a little more time. After all, we've just been seeing each other for a month."

"Two months," Michelle corrected. "But I don't think it would matter if we'd been seeing each other for a year," Michelle said as she came around and sat down next to him. "I think your daughters would still feel the same way. Do you know, they think I'm stealing their recipes," she said indignantly.

"No, they don't."

"Yes, they do!"

"They didn't say that, did they?" Sean demanded.

Michelle's eyes misted over. "They didn't have to."

Sean stiffened, and Michelle swallowed and made a show of being brave. She patted his shoulder.

"Promise me you won't say anything to them. It'll just make things worse. Please," Michelle implored when Sean didn't answer her.

"Fine," Sean said gruffly. "If that's what you want."

"It is," Michelle said. "It is. I so want all of us to be friends."

Sean sighed. He felt as if he was swimming in the ocean and couldn't see the currents that were tossing him this way and that. He knew there was something going on between the three women, but he was damned if he knew what— which was depressing since he prided himself on his ability to read social situations.

For a moment, he and Michelle watched a man fishing from his outboard anchored near the shore. Sean followed the arc of the line with his eye, remembering when he used to go fishing for trout with Rose at a little river in the Catskills before the girls were born. Things seemed so much simpler then. Or maybe that was just the way he remembered it. He wasn't sure.

"So you like it?" Michelle asked after a couple of minutes had gone by.

"Like what?" Sean asked, turning to her. He'd been so immersed in his thoughts that he hadn't heard what she was saying.

"The shop's name," Michelle repeated, Sean noticing a definite edge to her voice. They'd just been to see the place. According to the contractor, it would be ready to open in another three weeks, which in Sean's experience meant at least four or five weeks, if you were lucky.

"Oh, definitely," Sean lied. "Love it." Actually, he hadn't heard what Michelle had said. He'd been thinking about deep-sea fishing and wondering if he could convince his buddy Clyde to go on another trip with him.

"You don't think they'll mind?" Michelle asked.

"Who?"

"Your daughters, of course."

"No. Why should they?" Sean replied, a comment he would come to deeply regret. In retrospect, he realized he should have taken Michelle's comment as a hint of stormy waters ahead.

Michelle reached up and stretched, leading Sean to focus his gaze on her breasts. "I don't know," she said, dropping her arms back down once she'd attracted his attention. "But I'm pretty positive your daughters don't like the idea that I'm opening up a shop so close to theirs."

"I'm sure its fine with them," Sean told her, even though he had a vague suspicion that Michelle was correct, that it wasn't alright with his daughters. He just thought that if he kept ignoring the situation it would eventually go away.

"I've been thinking," Michelle said, rubbing a thumbnail up and down his arm.

Sean waited.

"Maybe we can join forces."

Sean turned to look at her. He didn't understand.

Michelle explained. "I can sell some of Bernie and Libby's stuff in my shop, and they could sell some of my stuff in theirs."

"What would be the point of doing that?" Sean asked, genuinely bewildered.

"That way we could expand our brands," Michelle said.

"Brands?" *What was that?* Sean wondered.

"It's our product names. Like Nike. Nike is a brand."

"I know what Nike is," Sean replied, shifting his weight. He still got stiff if he sat too long. "I just don't understand how that pertains to what you were talking about."

Michelle took in a deep breath and let it out. "What I meant is your daughters and I could cooperate instead of compete. That way it would be a win–win situation all around."

Sean shook his head. He was pretty sure—no, he was positive—that Libby and Bernie wouldn't agree to that. "I don't think they'll see it that way."

Michelle ruffled his hair and walked her fingers down the back of his neck. "Will you talk to them about it? Please," Michelle cajoled.

"Maybe we could even combine our shops if this works out—my lease is just for a year. Then you and I could see each other all the time."

"Sure," Sean said, thinking how nice that would be.

The truth was that he enjoyed being around Michelle. She was warm and soft, and she held his hand and rubbed his back, and he liked that. Plus, she made him laugh. She made him feel attractive and wanted, things he didn't know he could feel anymore. But the girls didn't get it, and he was too embarrassed to tell them he was ready to go out in the world again, not just be their dad.

Chapter 17

I wanted to puke when he told me," Libby said, recalling hers and Bernie's conversation with their dad about Michelle's proposal. "She didn't even have the guts to tell us herself."

"Michelle?" Brandon asked, clarifying. It was ten o'clock in the evening, and he, Bernie, Libby's boyfriend, Marvin, and Libby were at the bar at RJ's, drinking beer and eating pretzels.

"Whom else have I been talking about," Libby demanded, her face flushing as she remembered the conversation she and Bernie had had with their father. Talk about nerve! And the thing that got her the most upset was that their father hadn't seen anything wrong with Michelle's plan.

"Can we use the words manipulative and conniving to describe her?" Bernie asked.

"You can use whatever words you want," Marvin replied as he took a sip of his Brooklyn Lager.

"Sounds as if you guys had a really bad day," Brandon noted as he put another bowl of pretzels in front of them.

The four of them were the only ones in RJ's at the moment. There'd been a rush at six, a slight trickle at seven, then everyone had cleared out, and things had been dead ever since, dead to the

143

point where Brandon had been able to finish restocking the cooler, clean the counters, and sweep up, but then August was always a slow month, Brandon reminded himself. August was when three-quarters of his regulars took their vacations. Hopefully, it would stay quiet until two, when he could close the place up and go back to his flat with Bernie—if the gods were kind.

Libby took another sip of her IPA and carefully put her glass back on its coaster. "Between the tunnel and Michelle, we had a no-good, absolutely terrible day," she declared, paraphrasing the title of one of her favorite childhood books, but as she looked around, she realized that no one had gotten the allusion, which depressed her.

Marvin started to say something, changed his mind, took a sip of his beer, and ate a couple more pretzels instead.

Libby turned toward him. "What?" she asked.

"I didn't say anything," Marvin protested.

"But you were going to," Libby pointed out.

Marvin took another sip of his beer. "But I didn't. I changed my mind."

"Tell me," Libby ordered.

"Yeah, Marvin," Brandon said in a mocking tone as he planted his elbows on the bar. "Tell us."

"Brandon, just drop it," Marvin replied, his voice rising.

Brandon grinned. He loved needling Marvin. You could always count on a response. "Ah, come on," he wheedled, doing an excellent imitation of a high school girl.

"It's nothing," Marvin said. He rubbed his hands together. "Let's play some darts."

But Libby wasn't going to be put off that easily, especially since Marvin was now writhing in discomfort. "Why won't you tell me?"

Marvin made one last attempt to avoid the conversation he was about to have. "Because you won't like it."

"Try me," Libby told him.

"You're going to be really pissed."

"Marvin . . ."

"Fine. If that's what you want." And Marvin shrugged. Maybe it was better that Libby hear what he had to say. After all, it wasn't that terrible. "Have you ever considered that Michelle isn't as bad as you think she is? That she's actually seeing your dad because she likes him, not because she wants to steal your recipes? That maybe your dad likes having someone in his life? That maybe you're being paranoid?" There. He'd said it.

Libby glared at him. The phrase "if looks could kill" came to Marvin's mind.

"See," Marvin said, "I knew I should have kept my mouth shut."

Brandon leaned forward and cleared his throat.

Now that he'd gotten this started, he figured he needed to say something. Number one, he owed Marvin, and number two, he thought Marvin might be correct. "You have to admit Marvin may have something there," he said. "Maybe you girls are overreacting . . . Or not," he said looking at the expression on Bernie's face and thinking about tonight. "But even if you're right . . ."

"We are," Bernie declared firmly.

"There's nothing you can do about it," said Brandon, finishing his sentence, grateful that he hadn't mentioned the phrase *geriatric sex.*

"That's true," Marvin said. "If you go on this way, you'll just get your dad even madder, and he'll be less likely to listen to you."

"So what would you, with your great font of relationship advice, suggest?" Libby asked.

Marvin decided to overlook the sarcasm and take Libby's question at face value. "That's easy," he answered. "If it were me, I'd kill Michelle with kindness."

"Easy for you to say, but hard for me to do," Libby retorted. "She makes me so angry."

"No kidding," Brandon threw in. "I'd never have known."

"She had no right," Libby pounded on the bar, "to be snooping around in the back of our place the way she was. No right at all. I mean our recipe for our chocolate chip blondies was right out on the desk!"

"Oh no!" Brandon cried, putting his hand to his heart. "Is that as bad as stealing the secret of eternal life?" he asked, forgetting himself again.

"Ha, ha," Bernie said. "Lest you forget, our recipes are our livelihood."

"Sorry," a contrite Brandon said. "Maybe she really was curious about your setup," he suggested. "It is possible."

"Then why didn't she ask to see the back of the shop when we were around? Or make an appointment?" Libby challenged. "We would have shown it to her."

"Would you have?" Brandon asked.

"Of course, we would have," Bernie countered.

Brandon thought for a moment. "Okay, her place is going to open soon, right?"

Libby and Bernie nodded.

"Three weeks. A month. Something like that," Bernie said.

"So why don't you guys see what she's serving at her place when it opens," Brandon suggested. "If the menus are the same, you'll know."

"And meanwhile just say nice things about her to your dad," Marvin suggested.

"Like what?" Libby demanded.

"I don't know," Marvin replied. "Come up with something."

"I can't," Libby responded. "There's something off about her. When I look at her, I get a bad feeling."

"I like her shoes," Bernie interjected. "I can compliment her on those."

Everyone ignored her.

"Then don't say anything to your dad about her, Libby," Marvin said. "Don't say anything at all. Just smile."

"Fine," said Libby pantomiming a smile.

"I'm serious," Marvin told her.

"I'll try," Libby agreed, relenting.

"Do not try. Do, little grasshopper," Bernie said.

"Shut up," Libby told her.

Brandon intervened. "A toast," he said, lifting up his glass of IPA, even though he generally made it a rule not to drink while on duty. "A toast to trying."

Libby, Bernie, and Marvin raised their glasses, clinked them, and drank.

"Are you coming to the funeral?" Marvin asked after he'd put his glass down.

"Whose funeral?" Bernie asked.

"Zalinsky's, of course. Who else?"

"He's being buried here?" asked Bernie. She couldn't keep the surprise out of her voice.

"Yup. He is. Zalinsky bought and paid for everything himself."

"Paid, paid?" Bernie asked, thinking of Zalinsky's empty bank account.

"In cash," Marvin informed them. "Evidently, he came into the funeral home last month and arranged the whole thing with my dad. He even wrote his own obit. It's going in the paper as soon as the police release the body."

"We should go," Libby declared.

"I would expect no less," Marvin told her.

"Interesting," Bernie murmured, thinking about Zalinsky's get-out-of-town bag that she and Libby had found in the tunnel.

"That's fairly unusual, isn't it?" Brandon asked Marvin.

"Not really," Marvin said. "You'd be surprised by the number of people who prepay."

Bernie swiveled on her bar stool until she was facing Marvin. "Did Zalinsky tell your dad why he was doing it?"

"Yeah. As a matter of fact, he did." Marvin popped a couple more pretzels into his mouth and crunched them up. "He said that he liked living here, and he wanted to be buried here, and since his experiences in life had taught him how fickle fate was, he believed in buying what he wanted while he had the money. Then he added that he'd learned that if you wanted something done right, you had to do it yourself."

"Well, he certainly took that to heart with the play," Libby observed.

Bernie reached over, took a pretzel, broke it into three pieces, and ate them. "I wonder what happened to make him change his mind?" she mused after she'd chewed and swallowed.

"Change his mind about what?" Marvin asked.

"Staying," she answered.

Marvin drained his glass, considered having another beer, and decided not to. "He was leaving?"

"Remember Zalinsky's go bag? The one we found in the tunnel?" Libby reminded him.

"What about it? That doesn't prove anything. He could have packed that bag a long time ago," Marvin pointed out. "That could have been his equivalent of my grandmother sewing diamonds into the seams of her coat for, as she used to say, 'just in case.' "

Bernie took a sip of her beer. "One thing is fairly clear," she said. "He obviously didn't see it coming."

"Obviously," Brandon agreed. "If he had, he would have taken the guy out first."

"Definitely," Bernie replied, thinking back to her dealings with Zalinsky.

"I wonder who is going to be at the funeral," Libby said, changing the subject.

"He doesn't have any family," Marvin said.

"None?" Bernie asked.

"None that he listed," Marvin replied.

Brandon ate a couple of pretzels out of the bowl and refilled it for the third time. "Here's what I'm wondering. I'm wondering whether Zalinsky was killed because someone wanted the teapot or they took the teapot as an after-thought?"

"You and everyone else," Bernie said. She was about to add something to her comment when her cell began to ring. She dug it out of her tote and answered. It was Casper.

"You have to come," he cried when Bernie picked up. "You have to come now."

"Where are you?" Bernie asked.

"At my house. Please."

"Are you okay?" Bernie asked.

"Physically or mentally?"

"Either."

"I'm not sure," Casper replied before he hung up.

"Great," Libby groused when Bernie filled her in on the call. Talking to Casper was the last thing she wanted to do at the moment. "Do we have to?"

Bernie thought about Casper's tone. Even though Casper was inclined to the dramatic, there had been a genuine note of panic in his voice. "Yeah. I think we do."

"It's probably nothing," Libby said.

"No. I think it's something," Bernie said as she slid off her bar stool. She turned to Brandon. "I'll be back as soon as I can."

Brandon grinned. "I'm counting on it."

Chapter 18

The house Casper Cumberbatch had rented for his stay in Longely was a ten-minute drive from RJ's, as was most everything else inside the town, for that matter, Bernie reflected. It was a smallish, fourteen-hundred–square-foot split ranch off of Greenwood Place, and Casper had told Bernie he'd fallen in love with it the moment he'd seen it. One of the things he adored about it was the amount of space it afforded him as contrasted with his studio apartment down in Dumbo.

The house had been built in the fifties and boasted a two-car garage, a paneled basement, a living room with sliding doors that led out onto a patio, three bedrooms up a short flight of steps, two bathrooms, both tiled in pink, and a kitchen featuring harvest-gold appliances, an appliance color Casper rather fancied since it reminded him of the house he'd been raised in.

Casper was sitting on the steps, smoking a cigarette, and fiddling with the ivy growing over the stair railing when Libby, Bernie, and Marvin pulled up.

"I thought you quit," Bernie called out to Casper as she killed the van's engine and hopped out.

"I did," Casper replied. "This is an e-cigarette."

"Is it like smoking the real thing?" Libby asked as she exited the van.

Casper frowned. "Unfortunately, no. Alas, it is but a poor, pale substitute for the real thing. It is nothing but a fake, a fraud."

"So why smoke it?" Marvin inquired once he'd exited Mathilda and finished stretching. He'd forgotten how tight the front seat was when three people were sitting in it. Fortunately, they hadn't had to go far.

"That's a question I frequently ask myself," Casper replied.

Bernie twisted her skirt around so the front was in the front and the back was in the back. She kept forgetting that she had to have the waistband taken in an inch so it would stop moving around as she wore it. "And your answer is?" she prompted Casper.

"Ah, a good question," Casper replied. "My answer is simple. I am a weak-willed individual who needs to have something in my mouth at all times or I blimp up. The last time I gave up smoking completely I gained eighty pounds. I've lost forty of that, but I have forty more to go. So it's either this thing," Casper raised his e-cigarette, "or eating, and I've just donated all of my fat-fat clothes to Goodwill. Now, I'm wearing my medium-fat clothes."

"Maybe I should start smoking too," Libby

said, thinking of the weight she kept trying . . . and failing . . . to lose.

"Don't even think about it," Marvin retorted, giving her the evil eye. Anyway, he liked Libby just the way she was. He didn't want someone who was all skin and bones.

Libby was going to tell Marvin she was just kidding, but before she could, Casper got up and brushed the dirt off the bottom of his chinos.

"Shall we proceed?" he said, starting for his front door.

"What are we looking at?" Bernie asked.

"You'll see," Casper told them. Then he opened and held the door until everyone was inside. "Now I won't be able to sleep tonight. Every time I hear a noise I'm going to think that someone's coming into the house."

"Take a sleeping pill," Marvin suggested.

"Just what I want," Casper snapped. "To be unconscious when someone comes in to slit my throat."

"Sorry," Marvin said as his thoughts jumped to how neat Casper's place was as opposed to his— but then he reminded himself that Casper didn't have Petunia the Pig living with him.

It wasn't that Petunia wasn't clean; she was. She was cleaner than any dog he'd had. It's just that she had a tendency to root, which meant that Marvin always found all the sofa pillows, books, and magazines on the floor when he came home at night from the funeral home. Also she could open the cabinet doors with her snout, so there was that to contend with. He really had to get around to pig-proofing his house.

As Marvin thought about what Petunia might possibly be doing and the fact that he should probably get back to his flat fairly soon, Casper was walking his visitors through the living room, with its beige carpeting and beige furniture and white walls, into the dining room, which was also a sea of beige.

"There," he said, pointing to a package of tea and a piece of computer paper sitting in the middle of the dining room table. "That's what I found."

"What about it?" Bernie asked. The whole thing looked innocent enough to her.

"Read the note," Casper instructed.

Bernie went over and picked up the piece of paper. " 'Don't think I don't know what you did,' " Bernie read out loud. " 'Be careful or you're next.' "

"Well, that doesn't sound good," Libby said. "Maybe you should call the police."

Bernie put the sheet of computer paper back on the table. "So what did you do?" she asked.

"See," Casper said to Libby as he pointed to Bernie, "this is why I didn't call the cops." He turned to Bernie. "And for your information, I didn't do anything, except, of course, make the mistake of agreeing to direct *Alice in Wonderland* for the lunatic."

Bernie studied him for a moment. "So someone broke into your house and left a random note and a tin of tea for laughs?"

"I don't know. Maybe whoever did this wants me to go to the police and give them this note so they can use it as another piece of evidence against me," Casper said. "That's right, blame the victim," Casper added when Bernie didn't say anything.

"I'm not blaming you," Bernie told him as she turned her attention to the square, light-green tin. It had both English and Chinese lettering on all four sides, proclaiming that its content consisted of first-quality Chinese gunpowder green tea. "I'm trying to understand." She pointed to the tin. "Have you opened this yet?"

Casper shook his head. "No, Bernie. I was waiting for you."

"Why?" she asked.

Casper gave an embarrassed little shrug. "Who knows what's inside of it? It could be anything."

"Like tea," Bernie said.

"Or scorpions or black widow spiders," Libby said.

Casper visibly shuddered. "I hate bugs."

"Or anthrax," Libby added. "What if it's anthrax?"

"You're not funny," Bernie told her sister.

"I'm just seeing how you like it when the shoe is on the other foot," Libby answered.

"Oh my God." Casper put his hand to his mouth. "I didn't think of that," he said.

"I was just kidding." Libby told him, feeling sorry she'd opened her mouth.

Casper waved a finger at her. "No. You could be right. Maybe we should call the police. Or the FBI. Or the CDC."

Bernie stifled an exasperated sigh and snuck a look at her watch. At first she'd thought, if that's what Casper wanted to do, it was fine with her. The sooner she got out of here and back with Brandon the better, as far as she was concerned. But then she realized that waiting for the police and having to talk to them would eat up the rest of the evening.

"Hey, it's your decision," Bernie told him. "But for what it's worth, I think Libby's suggestion is way off the mark."

"It was a dumb thing to say," Libby said. "It really was. If Zalinsky's killer wanted to kill you, you'd be dead already." She pointed to the piece of computer paper on the table. "If you ask me, this looks like a bad joke from someone who doesn't like you."

"Me?" Casper pointed to himself, his face a mask of outraged innocence. "That's absurd. Everyone likes me."

"Right," Bernie said.

157

"They do," Casper insisted.

"Fine. They do," Bernie replied. "So do you want me to open the tea tin or not?"

Casper shook his head. "I just . . ." He waved his hands. "It's just . . . I guess I don't know what to think anymore." He paused for another minute, then said, "I can't . . . You decide."

"Fine. I will," Bernie said. "Let's see what's in here, shall we?"

Chapter 19

Libby, Marvin, and Casper all took a step back as Bernie picked up the tin and began to try to twist its top off. It didn't budge. Very anticlimactic. She handed it to Marvin.

"You try," she told him.

He did, even though he didn't want to. The results were the same. "I think I need a screwdriver," he said.

"Or a knife." And Bernie went into the kitchen, got a butter knife, came back, inserted the blade end between the top and the body of the tin, and pried the top up, keeping the tin as far away from herself as she could. Then she carefully lifted the top off and peeked inside. Whatever this was, it wasn't gunpowder green tea. Gunpowder green tea had leaves that were rolled into little pellets, hence the name gunpowder—or at least the kind she'd seen did.

"So?" Casper asked as he watched Bernie click her tongue against her teeth.

"I'm not sure what this is," Bernie admitted. "I've never seen tea this color. It's yellow."

"What are you doing?" Libby cried as Bernie took a cautious sniff.

"Smelling it," Bernie said. Whatever it was smelled like what? She identified a grassy note and something else. Maybe a slight residue of bleach? She wasn't sure.

"Yellow?" Casper repeated.

"Yup," Bernie said. "Why?" Bernie asked, noting the look on her friend's face.

But Casper didn't answer. Instead he said, "Here, let me take a look," elbowing Bernie aside. "That's yellow tea," he told them after he'd peeked in.

"That's what I just said," Bernie told him.

"No," Casper replied. "You said whatever it was, was yellow, and I'm saying it's yellow tea. That's what it's called."

"Yellow tea?" Libby said. "I've never heard of that."

Casper nodded. "Me either until Zalinsky showed it to me one day. He was bragging about it being pretty rare stuff. I guess it's pretty expensive. I take that back. It's really expensive. Big surprise there. Then Zalinsky told me the tea was called yellow not because of its color but because yellow was the color that the Chinese emperors wore for centuries, so if you want to call something special, you name it yellow." Casper scratched his head. Bernie watched a dandruff flake land on Casper's black T-shirt. "I don't get it," he proclaimed, indicating the note and the tea. "I don't get it at all. Any of it. What's this supposed to mean?"

"I dunna know," Bernie replied, doing a bad imitation of a Scottish accent.

Libby and Marvin didn't say anything because they didn't know either.

"I mean what's the point?" Casper asked,

"That *is* the question, isn't it?" Bernie said. "But there has to be one because someone went to a certain amount of trouble to leave this for you, not to mention getting a tin of gunpowder green tea, emptying it out, and refilling it with this other stuff."

"Maybe whoever did this just wanted to spook you," Marvin suggested.

"Well, they've succeeded," Casper replied.

Bernie turned to Casper. "So whose enmity have you incurred? Who would want to do a number on your head?"

"No one," Casper answered promptly, repeating what he had before. "Everyone loves me."

Bernie raised an eyebrow. "Seriously?"

Casper sniffed. "Of course, seriously."

"In the cast?" Bernie had been at the rehearsals.

Casper stood up straighter. "I don't know what you're talking about," he declared. A distinctly defensive note had crept into his voice.

"Well," Libby replied, having been at the rehearsals as well. "Let me think. There was the time you called Erin a sow, and the time you told the twins they were too stupid to live, and the time you asked Magda if she got her hair cut by someone who used a bowl, and then there was the time you told Hsaio she was beyond talentless, not to mention the time you told the twins there was nothing redeeming about them, and you could see why their business had gone belly-up."

Casper held up his hand, staunching Libby's torrent of words. "Okay," he allowed. "I get it. So maybe I did get carried away. So maybe I was a little . . . harsh . . . once in a while."

"Harsh?" Bernie asked. "Harsh? How about downright mean?"

"I wasn't being mean, I was motivating," Casper protested.

Bernie crossed her arms over her chest and fixed him with an accusing glance. "Really? Surely you could have motivated some other way. You had Erin in tears one of the days I was there," she said.

"Hey, I'm a director, and sometimes as such I have to yell to get what I want," Casper told her. "I admit I get carried away once in a while. But so what? Professionals know that's what happens, especially the closer you get to an opening. In fact, they appreciate it. No one wants to look bad in front of an audience."

"That may be true," Bernie said. "But we're not talking about card-carrying SAG members here. These people aren't even community theater people. They didn't want to be there. They were all forced to sign up by Zalinsky."

"I know. I know." Casper licked his upper lip.

"You're right. I shouldn't have treated everyone the way I did, but in my defense, Zalinsky was making me crazy. He was calling me at all hours of the day and night wanting to change this scene and that piece of staging, and wanting to put the spots upstage instead of downstage. And then he kept rewriting scenes. Every time I turned around, he had come up with a different line of dialogue. And that stupid teapot." Casper groaned. "Oh my God. First it was going to be onstage for the tea party scene; then he wanted it onstage all the time. It would have been easier to direct a full-bore production of *Le Miz* than what I was going through."

"I understand," Bernie said, remembering Zalinsky and the constant menu changes for the tea she and Bernie were supposed to be serving. "I do."

"And then there were those costumes," Casper continued, still focused on the injustices Zalinsky had dealt him. "They were horrible." Casper jabbed himself in the chest with his finger. "They were beyond horrible. They showed everyone in the worst possible light. Zalinsky designed them and paid someone to run them up, but everyone in the cast blamed me for them. Me." His voice shook with anger. "I tried, oh how I tried to get him to change them, but he wouldn't. I was a victim just like everyone else, and now I'm being persecuted by someone who wants to kill me."

"We don't know that," Bernie said.

"Whoever is doing this might as well have," Casper moaned. "My life as I know it is over." And with that he collapsed on the sofa and buried his head in his hands.

Bernie walked over and patted his shoulder. "There, there. It'll be okay."

Casper looked up. "Don't patronize me. It won't be okay. If the police don't get me," he gestured to the dining room table, "this maniac will."

"We'll find him before that happens," Bernie told him, trying to reassure.

Instead, Casper groaned louder. "I had a bad feeling about this play from the get-go," he said. "Why didn't I listen to myself? Why didn't I trust my instincts? And on top of everything else, I still haven't gotten paid, and now I never will."

"Neither have we," Libby said. "Has anyone?" she asked, even though she knew the answer.

"Not that I know of," Casper said.

"That's why whoever killed Zalinsky stole the teapot," Bernie said.

"Or maybe they just hated Zalinsky," Marvin suggested.

"It's like the chicken and the egg," Libby observed. "Which came first?"

"Who cares?" Casper cried. "What difference does it make?"

"Casper, you of all people should know that motive matters," Bernie remonstrated.

"Yeah," Casper mumbled. "I guess you're right."

"So who among the cast was having money problems?" Bernie asked.

Casper let out a moan. "Everyone. Everyone was counting on Zalinsky paying them for being in *Alice*."

"Isn't that a little unusual, this being an amateur production and all?" Libby inquired.

"Definitely," Casper replied. "But it wasn't just about the money. He promised people stuff—stuff that never materialized."

Libby thought about Magda, Erin, and Hsaio. "What did he promise you?"

"The creative directorship of The Blue House."

"What did he promise Jason?" Bernie asked.

"I have no idea," Casper replied. "He pitted everyone against one another. He made secret deals."

"Why am I not surprised?" Bernie muttered.

Conversation stopped. No one could think of anything more to say. Instead Libby, Bernie, Marvin, and Casper stared out the living room window and watched the moths fluttering around the house lights and listened to the sounds of laughter from a party someone was throwing a few doors over.

"So we're agreed, no cops?" Bernie asked, rousing herself.

"No cops," Casper repeated.

Bernie sighed. She wanted to go back to RJ's and Brandon, but she and Libby still had to establish a credible timeline for the intrusion into Casper's house.

"Okay," Bernie said, turning to face Casper. "When did you find the tea and the note?"

"I told you. They were on the table when I came in. Why?"

Bernie raised her hand. "Just bear with me for a second. When was that?" she asked.

Casper thought for a moment. "About an hour ago. More or less."

"Was it more or less?" Libby asked.

Casper turned toward her. "Don't be ridiculous," he said irritably. "How should I know? I don't time everything I do. I wasn't looking at my watch. Anyway, I called your sister right after I read it."

"Fair enough," Libby said. "So you came home and walked straight into the dining room?"

Casper shook his head. "No. I walked in the door, then I went into the kitchen and got a drink of water and ate some strawberries, then I visited the bathroom, after which I walked in here, read the note, and called you."

Bernie pointed to the sliding doors. "Were those locked?"

Casper shook his head. "Probably not. I usually don't bother."

"Is this house alarmed?" Libby asked, though she pretty much knew the answer already since there was no sign out front announcing that fact.

"No, it isn't," Casper told her.

"So anyone could have walked into your house, left the tea and the note, and walked back out," Libby said.

"I suppose they could have," Casper replied. "Not," he added, "that the locks on those doors would be difficult to get through if one wanted to."

"Who knows you don't lock your sliding glass doors?" Bernie asked.

"Everyone in the cast, I would imagine," Casper said promptly. "I've been holding some of our rehearsals here. I told Erin and Magda that if they arrived here before I did to just come in through the doors and wait for me."

"Were they the only people you told?" Libby asked.

"I think so. But they could have said something to someone else. Anyway, I remember Zalinsky making a comment when we were rehearsing at The Blue House about my not locking my sliding doors and telling me that I should be more careful, that you never know what's going to happen. Maybe he was right for a change." Casper shook his head. "It's just that it's hard for me to imagine something bad happening here in Longely. It seems so . . . so peaceful."

Bernie laughed. "*Seems* being the operative word."

"What did Zalinsky say exactly?" Libby asked.

"Nothing really. He just said that he wouldn't feel comfortable leaving doors unlocked like I was doing. That I was inviting trouble in."

"And everyone was at The Blue House when he said it?" Bernie asked.

"The cast was there, though the tech crew wasn't. We were still just doing readings."

"So essentially everyone in the cast knew they could get in and out of your house if they wanted to?" Libby said summarizing.

Casper worried a cuticle on his thumbnail. "When you put it that way, I suppose they did."

Libby nodded. "How do you get into your backyard?" she asked, changing the subject.

Casper pointed to the left. "There's a gate along one side of the chain-link fence. You just unlatch it and go in."

Bernie sighed, walked over to the sliding doors, and looked outside. It was a dark night. The moon and the stars were hidden under a dense cloud cover. Rain had been predicted for tomorrow, and judging by the sky, it was on its way. All Bernie could see was a perfectly ordinary fenced-in backyard with two oak trees growing toward the back, a swath of grass, and a patio with a glass table and chairs and a gas grill sitting on it.

Obviously, Bernie thought, whoever had done this had left the note inside Casper's house because he or she wanted to scare Casper by showing him that they could come and go as they pleased.

"Maybe you should lock the sliding doors from now on in," Bernie suggested, for lack of anything better to say.

"Oh, I definitely will," Casper replied. "That's for certain."

"The tea," Libby said suddenly.

Everyone turned to look at her.

"What about it?" Casper asked.

"You said it was rare, right?"

Casper nodded. "Right. That's what I was told."

"So where did it come from?" Libby asked.

"Zalinsky's house?" Bernie said, going for the most obvious answer.

Casper shook his head. "No. He kept it under lock and key at The Blue House. He liked the idea of drinking the tea out of that stupid teapot. 'An emperor's tea for an emperor,' he used to say. He also told me he needed to get some more. That he was running low on the stuff."

"That's not what I meant," Libby said, interrupting.

Bernie and Casper stopped talking and looked at her.

Libby explained. "I meant where did he buy the tea?"

Casper shrugged. "I think he told me some store over in the next town. Maybe Wycliff?"

"It's Tea Time," Bernie and Libby exclaimed in unison.

"I don't want any tea, thank you very much," Casper said crossly. "I will never take a sip of that beverage again," he declared.

Libby laughed. "It's Tea Time is the name of the shop," she informed him.

"I think we should pay the store a visit," Bernie said to Libby. "Like tomorrow. Maybe when they open."

Libby nodded. "Works for me." Then she watched as her sister walked over to the table, took the tin of tea, and dropped it into her tote bag.

"So we can show them what we're talking about," Bernie explained. She'd explained because she'd expected Libby to object, which, to her surprise, she hadn't.

"Good idea," her sister had said instead.

Chapter 20

U nfortunately, the next day didn't go exactly as planned. First, the shop's credit card machine went down, which meant that Libby had to spend an hour and a half on the phone while she futzed around with it before getting it back online. Then they got a rush order from a good customer for three trays of mint brownies, two trays of chocolate chip cookie bars, a red velvet birthday cake, and two dozen chocolate cupcakes with mocha frosting for an impromptu birthday party.

After that, Bernie had to run to the store for more paper goods, then despite the rain, the shop got swamped with an unexpectedly large noon rush, and to cap things off, Amber had an emergency at home, so it was a little after four by the time Bernie and Libby got out of the shop and headed over to Wycliff.

The drive took about twenty minutes. Bernie could have chosen the shorter, more direct route, but she decided to go through town instead because a small coffee house had opened up a couple of weeks ago on the outskirts of Longely and Bernie wanted to check out their window. Plus, it didn't hurt that Michelle's shop was down the block from the coffee place since Bernie wanted to see how that was coming along as well.

It had stopped raining, and the sun was out when Bernie passed Grind's and headed toward Michelle's new place. Bernie had been distinctly underwhelmed by Grind's window, and she was thinking about what she would have done with that display space had the shop been hers when she looked off to the left and spotted the new sign in Michelle's place. *It must have just gone up today,* Bernie thought as she hit the gas, hoping that she'd get by it before Libby saw the sign. But she wasn't fast enough.

"Oh my God," Libby screeched, pointing at the sign. "Did you see that?"

"It's not so bad," Bernie said, trying to calm her sister down.

"Are you kidding me," Libby cried. "It's called A Taste of New York."

"I know what it's called. I can read," Bernie replied.

"And our place is named A Little Taste of Heaven. Michelle even used the same type face we did."

"It's a pretty common one," Bernie pointed out, trying to pacify Libby.

Libby snorted. "Close, but no cigar."

"I don't smoke cigars," Bernie said.

Libby ignored Bernie's comment. "I told you Michelle was copying us. I told you. I bet she's going to serve our brownies there too."

Bernie made soothing noises. "Relax. We don't know she has the recipe, and even if she does, it's not worth getting upset about."

"Not worth it?" Libby shouted, her face now red. "Not worth it?"

"Okay," Bernie said, pausing for a stop sign. "Maybe it is worth it, but we can't do anything about it."

"Watch me," Libby said as she reached over and grabbed her cell out of her backpack.

"Who are you going to call?" Bernie asked.

"Michelle. Who else?"

"And tell her what?"

"For openers, that she has to stop copying us and get a new name for her place, or I could simply tell her that she's a lying, conniving bitch."

"Very laudable. And that will accomplish what, Libby?"

"Well, Bernie, it'll make me feel better, for one thing."

Bernie held out her hand. "Think for a minute. Do you really want to give Michelle the satisfaction of knowing how you feel?"

Libby scowled at her sister. "And I should care, why?"

"Remember what happened in the kitchen the other day?"

"Of course I do. So what?"

"Remember how Dad reacted then? Think what

will happen when Michelle tells him what you said."

Libby clicked her tongue against her teeth as she ran through the scenario Bernie had suggested. "You're right," she concluded. "I'm not going to give Michelle a chance to spin her version. This time I'll go straight to Dad."

"And say what?" Bernie challenged.

"Duh. Obviously, I'll tell him what Michelle's doing. I'll tell him our side of the story before she gets to him."

Bernie didn't say anything. She just kept driving.

"What's wrong with that?" Libby demanded in the face of Bernie's silence.

"Libby, don't you think he already knows?" Bernie asked quietly.

"No, I don't," Libby answered.

"Are you sure?"

"You think he'll take her side, don't you? Don't you?" Libby repeated.

Bernie sighed. "I just don't want to give her any more ammunition."

"So you *do* think he will take her side," Libby stated, correctly interpreting her sister's lack of an answer.

Bernie took her eyes off the road and looked at Libby. "Honestly?"

"Yes, honestly."

"I think it's a definite possibility."

"I don't get it," Libby exclaimed.

"What's to get?" Bernie retorted, bringing her eyes back to the road. "Dad likes her."

"So?" Libby said. "He's liked other women."

"Not this way. He really, really likes her. He and Michelle could even get married. Do you really want to start a feud with your possible stepmother?"

Libby's eyes flew open. She clutched her chest. "They're not going to get married. That's the most ridiculous thing I've ever heard."

"What if they do?" Bernie asked. She considered it a real possibility. "What then?"

Libby sucked in her breath. "So are you suggesting we do nothing?" she demanded. "That we just sit there and eat it?"

"No. I'm suggesting we do what Brandon suggested until we devise some sort of coherent strategy to counter the Michelle effect."

"And that strategy would be?"

"I don't know yet," Bernie confessed. "Believe me, though, I'm working on it."

"Well, work faster," Libby told her.

Bernie tapped her fingernails on the steering wheel as she mulled over her options. "I think the first thing we have to do is find out more about Michelle."

"It's true. We don't know a lot about her, do we?" Libby observed.

"No, we don't," Bernie said. Up until this point

she'd considered Michelle her dad's passing fancy, not someone worth firing up her intelligence network for. "I think I'm going to ask Brandon to ask around and see what he can find out, while we do some asking around as well."

Suddenly something Michelle had said when they'd first met popped into Libby's head. "Didn't she say something about having a shop in Syracuse a couple of years ago?"

"I think you're right," Bernie exclaimed. "Don't you know someone who runs a cookie shop up there?"

Libby nodded. "Yeah. Marsha. Her place is on Westcott Street."

"Excellent. Talk to her. Maybe she knows Michelle."

Libby started reaching for her phone.

"But in the meantime," Bernie warned, "please try not to say anything negative about Michelle to Dad."

"Nothing?" Libby asked.

"Nothing," Bernie said firmly. It felt good to be the voice of reason for a change. "We don't want to make Dad defensive about her."

"He already is," Libby pointed out.

"This I know," Bernie replied. She was just about to reiterate that they didn't want to make the situation any worse than it already was when her cell started ringing. "God, I hope it's not the shop," she said as she answered it. There'd been enough problems there for one day.

It wasn't. It was one of Casper's friends, calling to inform Bernie that Casper had been taken into custody. Bernie cursed under her breath. Not that she was surprised. She had just been hoping that this would come later rather than sooner.

"Forget Michelle and Dad for the moment," she told Libby after she hung up. "We need to put all our energy into finding out who killed Zalinsky." Then Bernie told Libby why.

Libby wasn't surprised either. Unlike Bernie, she wondered why it had taken Lucy as long as it had.

Chapter 21

Five minutes later, Bernie and Libby arrived at the strip mall that housed It's Tea Time. It had been built twenty years ago and was showing its age. There was a big box store on either end, and between them was a random selection of mid-level shops ranging from a jewelry store to a shop that specialized in lacrosse equipment to a baby boutique.

It's Tea Time sat between a cobbler and a consignment shop, and as the sisters entered the store, Bernie couldn't help wondering whether a shop like this wouldn't fare better on the main street of the town, where the wealthier people shopped.

The thought had occurred to her because at the moment she and Libby were the only people in the place. There were no customers, and whoever was manning the counter—Bernie guessed she or he was in the back attending to something or other—wasn't there either.

"Not good," Libby observed.

"Not good at all," Bernie agreed.

For several reasons. The obvious one was the risk of robbery, but the more cogent one was that a customer who walked into an empty store was likely to turn around and walk out. The word that came to Bernie's mind as she looked around the shop was *nice*—that was nice with capital N. Or the N could also stand for *neutral,* Bernie decided. As in gender-neutral, to be specific. The walls were painted a cream color, while the floor was done in an unobtrusive light-blue linoleum tile. The photos on the walls were the only things that stood out. Bernie took a moment to examine them. They showed a large, lush flower garden through the various stages of the year.

Most stores have a definite vibe to them. That's part of the reason people come in to shop, especially these days when you can get everything online. But from what Bernie could see, this place had no personality. It wasn't a ladies' tea parlor with frills and flourishes. It wasn't a hipster joint. It didn't have a Zen feel to it. It looked cold and uninviting. A minimum of time, money, and thought had been lavished on its decoration. Bernie decided she would be surprised if It's Tea Time was in business next year.

On the other hand, the store was well stocked. Bernie had to give it that. One side of the shop was devoted to a broad selection of tea paraphernalia, while the shelves on the other side of the place were packed with an impressively large array of loose and packaged tea. There were teas from England, Ireland, Russia, India, Japan, and China. There were herbal teas and green teas and black teas and oolongs, as well as teas to help you go to sleep, teas to wake you up, and teas to help you lose weight.

A blackboard tacked on the wall above the counter announced the tea menu for the day, with the day's specials highlighted in red chalk. Next to the cash register was a small display case offering a selection of foods, mostly cookies and muffins, all of which Bernie could tell had been bought at BJ's even though the sign proclaimed they were homemade.

Over to the left, toward the back, was a small alcove. Clearly even less thought had been given to its furnishings. The walls were bare. Three rickety-looking wooden tables with paint peeling off their tops and six chairs that looked as if they would collapse at any moment were the sum and substance of the furniture.

What a waste of space, Bernie thought. If the shop had been hers, she would, at the very least, have switched out the florescent light for a hanging lamp, gotten rid of the tables and chairs, and put in a love seat, a few easy chairs, some small tables, and a colorful area rug instead.

She was wondering why Alla Feldman had made the choices she had made and about whether she and Libby should expand and put more seating in their place, when a woman Bernie assumed was Alla Feldman came out of the back.

Alla was of medium height. Her dark hair was pulled back into a bun, which emphasized her aquiline nose. Her eyes were ringed with heavy black eyeliner and her lashes beaded with mascara. The rest of her makeup consisted of a pale foundation that was too light for her olive skin and scarlet lipstick. Bernie put Feldman in her early thirties, and as she walked toward them, the way she carried herself made Bernie wonder if she'd studied dance at some time in her life.

"Can I help you?" Feldman asked in lightly accented English.

"Nice photos," Bernie said, pointing to the pictures hanging on the wall.

Alla Feldman smiled. "Thank you. They are of my garden." She gestured to five large glass jars on the back counter. "I grow the chamomile and lavender and the comfrey that I sell here."

"Excellent," Libby said. She cleared her throat and smiled back. "We're looking to buy some yellow tea," she said, following the script she and Bernie had rehearsed in the van coming over.

The woman's penciled eyebrows lifted. "Yellow tea? Are you sure you don't mean green."

"I'm positive," Libby said emphatically.

The woman toyed with one of her gold bangles. "I'm sorry, but this is not something we sell here."

"Are you sure?" Bernie asked, wondering where Alla Feldman hailed from. She was having difficulty placing the accent. Israel perhaps? Somewhere in the Middle East?

181

The woman sniffed and drew herself up before turning to Bernie. "Of course, I am sure. I am the owner. I know what is in my place."

"I don't understand," Libby said, feigning puzzlement. "A friend of ours told us he bought it here."

Alla looked bored. "Then your friend gave you the incorrect information."

"Ludvoc, Ludvoc Zalinsky," Bernie said, mentioning the name. She thought that she saw Alla Feldman startle before she went back to her bored expression, but she wasn't positive. The shift in expression had happened too fast.

Alla corrected Bernie. "Ah. I know of him. I read about him in the papers."

"But you don't know him?" Bernie asked, repeating her question.

"That is what I said," Alla repeated firmly. "He is the dead one, correct?"

Bernie and Libby both nodded.

"He was murdered," Feldman added. "I read this in the newspaper."

"Yes, he was," Bernie agreed.

"It is too bad. Then you could have asked him where he got the tea."

"Too bad that's not a possibility now." Libby stifled a cough. "So you're saying he never came in here and bought yellow tea from you?"

"Why you keep asking me the same question?" Alla demanded. "I already tell you the answer. I don't sell it. This is my shop, and I know what is in it and who comes in and buys things. This Zalinsky," Alla sniffed, "he never . . . how you say . . . darken my door."

"Well, perhaps the person that told me made a mistake," Libby conceded, even though she didn't think that Casper had. "Is there any other place around here that sells it?"

Alla Feldman shook her head and made an impatient noise. She was turning to go when Bernie took the tin out of her tote, opened it, and placed it on the counter in front of her.

"What is this?" Alla asked.

"This is the yellow tea he supposedly got here," Bernie told her.

Alla knitted her brows together and tapped the writing on the tin with a blood-red fingernail. "This says green tea."

"That's not what's in there now," Bernie said.

"This," Alla said, nodding toward the tin, "is a brand we do not carry here at It's Tea Time. You buy this at the supermarkets," her tone indicating that that was the same as buying it at the Dollar Store. She looked from Bernie to Libby and back again. "I do not understand," she said.

"Neither do we," Libby replied. "That's why we're here."

Alla was silent for a moment while she thought. Then she reached out her hand. "May I look?" she asked.

"Please do," Bernie replied.

The sisters watched as Alla took the top off the tin and looked inside. Then she lifted the tin up and smelled it, after which she took a pinch of the tea and put it in the palm of her left hand.

"This tea has been bleached," she announced, pointing to it.

"Bleached?" Libby echoed.

"Yes, bleached, and then color has been added. Yellow dye."

"So it is not yellow tea?" Libby asked.

"That is what I have just said. Yellow tea is very expensive. It is very rare. I do not sell things like that in my shop. There is no market for something like that here."

"If I wanted yellow tea, where would I get it?" Libby asked.

"Maybe over the Internet," Alla replied. "Maybe down in the city. Flushing. Lots of Chinese there. Many places."

As Alla talked, Bernie noticed that her gaze was focused on the parking lot. Bernie turned to look at what Alla was looking at. It was Stan walking across the lot.

"You know him?" she asked Alla.

"Who?" Alla asked.

Bernie pointed. "Him. Stan Holloway."

Alla gave a casual shrug. "He comes in and buys a cup of tea once in a while. All he does is talk, talk, talk. He a very angry young man."

"Why do you say that?" Libby asked.

"I hear him on the phone. Sometimes he is yelling, saying he's going to kill his boss. He gets red in the face. He is so loud I have to go over and tell him to be quiet." She shook her head. "He is not good for business."

"Did you tell the police?" Bernie asked Alla.

Alla looked at her like she was crazy. "Why I do that?"

"Because Zalinsky was Stan's boss," Libby told her.

"Ah. This I did not know."

"Maybe you should," Bernie suggested.

"I think maybe this is not my business," Alla told Bernie. "I think you should talk to this person yourself." And with that she turned and marched into the back of the store, leaving Bernie and Libby standing there.

Chapter 22

B y the time Bernie and Libby stepped out of Alla's shop, Stan was halfway across the parking lot.

Bernie cupped her hands and yelled. "Stan, wait. I want to talk to you."

Stan kept going.

"Maybe he didn't hear you," Libby suggested.

"Maybe," Bernie agreed. The parking lot was noisy, what with cars pulling in and out. She picked up her pace to a trot. She was glad she was wearing her three-inch wedges instead of her stilettos. Less chance of tripping, and she could move faster.

"Or maybe he doesn't want to talk to us," Libby said. Already she could feel a trickle of sweat working its way down her back. It had to be at least ninety, maybe more.

"That too," Bernie replied as she dodged a car that was backing out of its parking spot.

The woman rolled down her window. "Watch where you're going," she snarled.

"Let's not kill ourselves," Libby said as she grabbed a handful of the back of Bernie's sundress and pulled her sister out of the way of another car backing out.

"I'm watching."

"You're obviously not."

Bernie grunted as she maneuvered between two parked cars in an effort to head Stan off. Libby slowed down. She could feel the pain in the back of her knee start. Damn. She'd done something to it last week, and she thought it was better, but evidently it wasn't. She was rubbing it when Bernie called out to Stan again. This time he turned, looked at Bernie, made a sharp right, and headed in the direction of the nail salon. Any doubt that Bernie or Libby had harbored about Stan not hearing Bernie vanished.

"I think we can safely say that Stan doesn't want to talk to us," Bernie said.

"Maybe because he's talked to his brother," Libby suggested, "and he doesn't want to make things worse."

"Or maybe he's in a rush because he's going to be late for his mani-pedi," Bernie proposed.

Libby laughed. "Or he could be working on his tan."

"Or he could be going out the back exit."

"That too," Libby agreed. Shops in strip malls were mandated to have a rear exit as part of firecode regulations.

"Unless he works there and he's late," Libby said.

"Can you see that, Libby?" Bernie asked as she headed to the salon.

"About as much as I can see you eating Little Debbies," Libby replied.

"But I like Little Debbies," Bernie protested.

"Yeah. Me too. It's a guilty . . ."

"Pleasure," said Bernie, finishing her sister's sentence for her. "Like frozen Reese's Peanut Butter Cups and Snickers Bars."

"And Popeyes fried chicken."

By this time they were at the salon door. Bernie opened it and went inside. Libby followed. *At least it's air-conditioned,* Libby thought as a blast of cold air hit her. The place was full, and the woman behind the cash register looked up and smiled as Bernie and Libby entered.

"What can I do for you? You want manicure? Pedicure? Waxing? Tan?" the woman asked as Bernie spotted Stan exiting the rear door and took off after him.

"We're just passing through," Libby explained to her.

The woman lost her smile. "Hey," she said. "What are you doing? This isn't a street. This is a place of business. You can't go running through here like this."

"Sorry," said Libby, pausing to apologize.

The woman glowered at her. "I'm calling the police," she declared reaching for the phone.

"Please don't," Libby said. "Everything's fine. Really."

"It is not fine with me," the woman announced as she dialed.

Libby took off. No use sticking around now, she reasoned. She kept on bobbing her head and saying "Sorry, so sorry" to the women who had put down their magazines and were staring at her as she went by them. She knew it wouldn't help anything, but being polite was a reflexive action.

By the time Libby caught up to her sister, Bernie had caught up with Stan Holloway.

"Why didn't you stop?" Libby could hear Bernie asking him, as she bent over and massaged her legs.

"I didn't know you were chasing me," Stan told her.

Bernie snorted. "At least if you're going to lie, put a little effort into it, for heaven's sake. Use some imagination."

"It's the truth," Stan protested, doing a really good job of looking outraged.

"Of course it is," Bernie replied. "Why else cut through the nail salon like that?"

"Because—if you must know, not that it's any of your business—I was taking a shortcut." Stan wiped the sweat off his face with the hem of his T-shirt. Despite herself, Libby couldn't help noticing his abs, which were textbook washboard. They took her mind off the stitch she'd developed in her side.

Bernie looked around. They were in the alley in back of the shop. It was lined with dumpsters brimming with garbage. Clouds of wasps and hornets buzzed around them, while crows hopped in and out, scavenging for food.

Pieces of fast-food wrapping paper peppered the asphalt. It was hotter here than it was in the front of the strip mall, the heat bouncing off the concrete walls and the black tar, and between it and the smell Bernie felt mildly nauseous. She heard someone talking and looked around. A couple of Best Buy employees were standing in front of the store's loading dock taking a smoking break. She brought her attention back to Stan.

"Really," she said, getting back to the matter at hand. "So where were you taking a shortcut to?" She pointed to the weed-strewn lot that began where the asphalt stopped. "Wait. I know. You were scouting out a camping space."

Stan scowled at her. "Maybe I was."

Bernie smiled and brushed a fly away. "Somehow I doubt that."

"Doubt away." Stan's lips curved into a mocking smile. "In fact, I don't have to answer you if I don't want to, so why don't you just get lost?"

Bernie clicked her tongue against her teeth. "So rude."

"Hey, you were the one chasing me."

Bernie let that one go. "I take it you don't have

an answer for my question," she said instead.

"Oh, I have one alright. I just don't want to tell you. You're not the cops," Stan said smugly.

"No kidding," Bernie replied. "And if you're really lucky I won't call them either."

"You won't have to," Libby said. She'd finally managed to straighten up. "The lady at the register in the nail salon is doing that for you."

"Great," Bernie muttered. She looked around. "We should get moving before they show up." She didn't want to have to explain what she was doing to the cops because she was about ninety-nine percent sure they wouldn't understand. Or approve.

"Works for me," Stan replied, being of the opinion that any meeting with the police was a bad meeting. "Why would you call them on me anyway?"

"Maybe because you killed Zalinsky. Or maybe because you broke into Casper's house and left a note and a tin of doctored tea on his dining room table," Bernie said.

"Which?" Stan asked.

"How about both?" Bernie said.

"Wow." Stan put his hands up in the air. "You got me. Hey, I've changed my mind. Let's wait for the police. That way I can charge you with harassment."

"Okay by me," Bernie said. She and Stan glared at each other.

Libby pointed toward Best Buy. "Have fun, you two. I'm leaving."

Stan thought about the weed he had in the glove compartment of his car and changed his mind again. "You're really crazy," he told Bernie as he fell into step with Libby.

"So I've been told," Bernie retorted.

"Where did you come up with this?" Stan demanded.

"Alla," Bernie said, following in her sister's footsteps.

"Who the hell is Alla?" Stan demanded, looking puzzled.

"The lady who owns the tea store," Libby replied.

"That's her name?" Stan shook his head. "That's one crazy lady."

"She said she overheard you say you wanted to kill your boss, and since your boss is Zalinsky . . ." Bernie let her voice trail off.

"I was pissed at the time," Stan said.

"So you don't deny you said that?" Bernie asked.

"Like you've never said anything like that when you're angry," Stan shot back.

"I have," Bernie said. "But the person didn't die."

"Jeez." Stan rolled his eyes. "See. This is why I didn't want to talk to you in the first place. Because you're looking to pin Zalinsky's murder on anyone but your friend, and you're grasping at straws."

"I'm looking for the person who killed Zalinsky, and it wasn't Casper," Bernie replied.

"So you say," Stan said.

"I most certainly do," Bernie replied, taking a quick step back from a wasp that was flying around her face.

"How do you know that? Because he told you he didn't?" Stan demanded.

"All the evidence against him is circumstantial," Bernie replied.

"There's more against him than against anyone else," Stan said.

"Not true," Bernie said.

Stan jutted his chin out. "Really?"

"Yes, really," Bernie replied.

Stan folded his arms across his chest and planted his feet firmly on the ground. "Since you know so much, why don't you tell me why I did it?" he demanded.

"Fine," Bernie said. "Here's what I think. I think you killed Zalinsky and then framed Casper."

Stan laughed. "Did I leave the note and the tea on Casper's table as well?"

"How do you know about that?" Bernie asked.

"Easy," Stan said. "Your friend has a big mouth. He called and asked me."

"And what did you tell him?" Libby asked.

"I told him yes, of course," Stan sneered.

"What do you think I told him? I hung up on him."

"Maybe you did do it," Libby posited. "Maybe you wanted to get back at Casper for the way he treated you and your brother during rehearsals and for the costumes you and your brother were wearing."

"They made us look like the laughingstocks of the town," Stan muttered. "I wouldn't even make my dog wear that."

"But Casper didn't have anything to do with those costumes," Bernie protested. "And I'm betting you knew that. No. What I think happened is that you killed Zalinsky and were trying— albeit clumsily—to frame Casper by writing that note to the police."

"You certainly had a motive," Libby added, stepping back into the conversation. "You killed Zalinsky because of what he did when he took over your business. He promised to grow it, but he didn't, did he?"

Stan shook his head. The mention of what Zalinsky had done infuriated Stan to the point that he had trouble talking about it.

Libby continued in a calm voice. "Instead he did just the opposite. He shut your business down and made you work for him, and now your family is in deep trouble, since they loaned you the start-up funds and you can't repay them."

"They're losing their house," Stan blurted.

"That would certainly get me really upset," Libby noted.

"And how," Bernie said, thinking of her dad.

Libby swatted at a hornet buzzing around her face. "So you killed Zalinsky and then you tried to frame Casper for it. I think it's as simple as that."

"Where'd you hear that stuff about Zalinsky and the business?" Stan asked. The words came out through gritted teeth.

Libby took a step back. "Erin," she replied. "We heard it from Erin."

"And when did you see her?" Now a vein was pulsing under Stan's left eye.

Libby told him. Judging from the expression on Stan's face, she guessed he hadn't known about his brother's escapade in Zalinsky's house.

"He went there?" Stan asked.

"Yup," Libby answered.

"With Erin?" Stan said.

"Yes, again," Libby replied.

Stan took a deep breath and let it out. Then he took another. Libby and Bernie could see his body begin to relax. "George is never going to learn," he said.

"He's never going to learn what?" Bernie asked.

"He's never going to learn about women. Ever." Stan rubbed beads of sweat off his forehead with the heel of his hand. "Talk about someone with a motive."

"Erin?" Libby clarified.

"No. Madam Curie." Stan bit his lip. "Hear that?" he asked a moment later.

Bernie and Libby stopped talking and listened. They heard sirens, and they were heading their way.

"Come on," Bernie motioned toward the back exit of Best Buy. "Let's get out of here."

Libby and Stan nodded. At least that's one thing everyone could agree on, Bernie reflected.

Chapter 23

H ot day," Libby said to the two smokers in front of the loading dock as they went by them.

The smokers grunted and continued smoking. Bernie pulled open the glass door and went inside. Libby and Stan followed. A moment later, they were engulfed in the store's air-conditioning. Libby rubbed her arms. Now she was freezing.

"You were talking about Erin's motive," Libby reminded Stan as they walked by the bank of TVs, all of which were tuned to news channels.

"Was I?" Stan said. He didn't turn his head. He was watching a clip of a baseball game.

"Yeah, you were," Libby replied.

Stan tore his eyes away from the TVs. "Hypothetically speaking?"

"If that's the way you want it," Bernie replied.

"It is," Stan said.

"Go on," Libby urged.

"I don't know," Stan said, having last-minute doubts.

"Hey, let's not forget that she-who-must-not-be-named was willing to throw you and your brother under the bus."

"True. Very true." Stan gave a nervous cough and shuffled his feet. "Well, in that case," he began, "if you were engaged to someone, someone wealthy, and you left him for another even wealthier person with the expectation that you would marry that person, and you found out he was going to throw you out of your apartment, which he was paying for, not to mention finding out that all the pieces of jewelry he'd given you were worthless fakes so that he was leaving you with nothing because he was hooking up with a younger, sexier model, you'd be pretty pissed, wouldn't you?"

"Yeah, I think I would," Libby said, remembering how she'd felt when Orion left her.

"Definitely," Bernie declared. "He'd be so dead."

Stan smiled. "Exactly. What is it they say about hell hath no fury like a woman scorned?"

"And does this person who she-who-must-not-be-named was originally engaged to have a name?" Libby asked.

"Ah," Stan said. "That would be telling."

"You've already told," Bernie pointed out.

"Not really. You can't expect me to do all your work for you, now can you?"

"Fine," Bernie said. "We'll figure that out for ourselves. But I still want to know why you put that tea on Casper's dining room table."

"Okay." Stan clutched his chest. "You got me." He held his hands in the air. "Bring on the cuffs."

Bernie whipped around and faced him. "So you do admit you left the tea there?"

"No, I don't," Stan answered. "I don't at all. I was kidding. Kidding."

"I'm not so sure," Libby told him.

"Good for you," Stan replied. "You shouldn't be so quick to jump to conclusions. And as for the name of she-who-is-an-incredible-pain-in-the-ass's former boyfriend, I suggest you ask her majesty." He sniggered at the idea. "I'm sure she'd love to tell you." Stan bowed. "It's been a pleasure, ladies, as always." Then he took off.

Bernie started to go after him, but Libby held out a restraining hand. "Don't bother," she said. "We've gotten everything we're going to get out of him."

"You're right," Bernie replied as she watched Stan head for the door. "At least for now."

"Good. Because I'm too tired to chase him."

"And too hungry," Bernie added.

"Yeah, that too. Yogurt doesn't do it for me."

"Me either," Bernie said. That was all she and her sister had had for lunch, and it wasn't enough. "I'm thinking something light. Maybe a couple of opened-face brie and cucumber sandwiches on toasted French bread and a perfectly ripe Pennsylvania peach for dessert."

"With an iced coffee," Libby added. She was imaging the explosion of flavor and the juice of the peach in her mouth.

"And a couple of madeleines," Bernie said.

"Definitely those," Libby agreed. They were her new favorites. She loved the subtle flavor of the little cakes and the slight resistance when she bit into one. "I wonder what Dad will say about what Stan said."

"We can ask him when we get home . . ."

"If he's home." It seemed as if she and her sister never saw him anymore.

"I just hope that Michelle isn't with him, if he is."

"Tell me about it." Libby sighed. Michelle always had something to say. Unfortunately, her comments weren't particularly helpful.

Bernie changed the subject. Michelle was simply too depressing to talk about. "Well, at least we do know that Stan's story confirms the one George was hinting at," she noted.

"Too bad Stan didn't give us a name," Libby said.

"An omission the Internet might be able to remedy," Bernie observed. She removed her smartphone from her bag with a flourish. Five minutes later, she'd found the information she was looking for.

"I wonder if it was Erin who broke off the engagement," Bernie mused as she passed her cell to Libby.

Libby squinted. "I can't read this. It's too small," she complained.

"Jeez. Maybe you should get your eyes checked," Bernie told her.

"Maybe you should get a bigger phone," Libby retorted.

Bernie grabbed her phone back and read the article to her sister. According to it, Adam Benson, a stockbroker for the firm of Smith and Miller, had announced his engagement to Erin at the Bridgeview Yacht Club in Hudson, New York, on the fifth of November in 2014.

She checked some more. "Evidently Mister Benson is still doing business at the same firm."

"Ah ha. Our next victim," Libby said.

Bernie nodded. "It'll be interesting," she said.

Chapter 24

Two days after making an appointment with Adam Benson, Libby and Bernie found themselves sitting across from him in his office on Fifty-Sixth Street and Seventh Avenue in Manhattan. It was a corner office on the thirty-ninth floor of a building that housed a variety of financial companies.

The building had been built with an eye to impress, and Libby and Bernie were admiring the view and complimenting Benson on the examples of early Chinese art he had dotted around the office. Bernie and her sister were ostensibly there to talk about an investment strategy for the three million dollars they were about to inherit from their mythic Aunt Pearl.

"She did well," Libby said, smoothing out her pale blue silk dress with the palm of her hand. It was one of two dresses that she owned. The second one was reserved for funerals.

"Evidently," Adam Benson said, smiling pleasantly.

Pleasant was one of the words that came to Bernie's mind when she looked at him. The second word that came to her mind was *expensive*. Benson's haircut was expensive, as were his suit, his shirt, and his tie. Although

Bernie didn't know that much about men's clothes, she was pretty sure that Benson's suit was bespoke, his shirt was Turnbull and Asser, and his tie was Italian silk. She decided that everything about Benson and his surroundings screamed money, the subliminal message being *Trust me with your dough and you too can have this lifestyle.*

Bernie was glad she was wearing her white cotton pique Dolce & Gabbana sheath with her cream-color Manolos. It was her grown-up outfit, the one she wore to business meetings when she wanted to be taken seriously. It was also the outfit that made her legs look really good, which didn't hurt. These days one had to use any advantage one had.

Bernie was also carrying her Prada bag, while Libby was carrying a small Valtrex Bernie had loaned her. She and Libby did look pretty good, if she had to say so herself, Bernie reflected. At the very least, they looked like the type of people who had enough money to invest to make this meeting worthwhile for Benson.

Adam Benson steepled his fingers together and smiled blandly as his secretary brought in a tray filled with a pot of coffee and a selection of cookies and put it down on top of the round, marble-topped table Bernie, Libby, and Benson were sitting at.

"So," he said after Libby and Bernie had served

themselves, "your Aunt Pearl must have been quite the lady."

"Oh, she was. She was very, very smart," Bernie assured him. "We knew she was good with money—she was a bookkeeper, you know—we just didn't know she was that good." She took a sip of coffee. It was excellent. "Sumatran?" she asked.

Benson nodded. "We get it roasted for us in Brooklyn."

Bernie nodded, lifted a Linzer torte to her lips, and took a bite and chewed. She decided she liked A Little Taste of Heaven's better. This one didn't have enough butter in the dough, and the raspberry jam the baker had used was a tad too sweet. "And the cookies?" she asked.

"From a little place on Thirty-Ninth and Ninth."

"I'm surprised they're not from Brooklyn," Libby observed. "Everything else seems to be from there these days."

"Quite so," Benson said, doing an imitation of an English banker on the BBC. He gave Libby another bland smile. "So," he said after a few more minutes of polite chitchat had gone by, "what were you thinking of in terms of investment strategies."

"Art," Libby said promptly. "We were thinking of investing in art."

Benson raised an eyebrow. "Really. That's an interesting choice."

"Asian art, to be specific," Bernie added, falling in line with her sister's lead. She made a gesture that encompassed the office. "It looks as if you know something about it."

Benson bowed his head modestly. "I admit I know a little."

"And you've done well?" Bernie asked.

"I've been lucky," Benson told her.

"I'm sure there's a certain amount of knowledge involved," Libby said.

"A bit," Benson allowed.

Libby turned to Bernie. "See," she said. "I told you we came to the right person." Libby turned back to Benson. "We know someone who made a lot of money collecting oriental art, and we were hoping to follow in his footsteps," she explained.

"And who would that be?" Benson asked, even though, Libby reflected, he didn't seem at all interested in the answer.

Now it was Libby's turn to smile. "Ludvoc. Ludvoc Zalinsky." If she'd hoped to get a strong reaction out of Benson, she was disappointed. His expression remained the same. This, Libby decided, might be harder than she thought it was going to be.

"Really," Benson said. He took another sip of coffee, carefully put his cup down on his saucer, reached for a small butter cookie, ate it, then brushed off a crumb that had landed on his suit jacket. "Of course, I'm familiar with the name.

He was in the papers recently." Benson looked up at the ceiling while he mimed thinking. After a moment he mimed remembering. "He's the one who met an unfortunate demise at the hands of a teakettle, isn't he?"

Bernie and Libby both nodded.

"So bizarre," Benson said.

"That it was," Bernie agreed.

"It happened at the opening benefit for The Blue House, didn't it?" Benson asked.

"Correct again," Bernie replied.

"On which," Benson put a hand up and stroked his chin, "if I rightly remember, the article said he had lavished a great deal of money."

It was Libby's turn to reply. "That he did," she said.

"I thought so." Benson flicked a speck of dirt off of his jacket lapel. "Of course, the article said he had a lot of money to spend," Benson reflected. "A lot of these Russians do."

"You sound as if you didn't know him," Libby said.

"I don't," Benson told her.

"Sorry for our mistake," Bernie said. "I guess we were misinformed."

"I guess you were," Benson said.

"We thought you knew him," Bernie replied.

Libby leaned forward. "We definitely did," she said, an earnest look on her face.

"I wish I had," Benson told her. "He sounds

like an interesting man, a man I could have done business with, but to my regret I didn't have the pleasure of making Mr. Zalinsky's acquaintance."

Libby furrowed her brow. "Are you sure?"

"Of course, I'm sure," Benson said. "I just said that, didn't I?"

"Does the name Louis Zebb ring a bell?" Bernie asked.

"No. Should it?" Benson asked.

"He used that name too," Libby informed him.

Benson raised an eyebrow. "That's a bit unusual, isn't it?"

"Maybe you forgot you knew him," Libby suggested helpfully. "You must meet lots of people in the course of a day."

"I don't forget people," Benson told her, a note of irritability creeping into his voice. He raised his hand and smoothed back his hair.

"That's a good skill to have," Libby remarked. "I wish I had it."

Benson made a show of looking at his watch. "Now, if we could get back to your investment strategy. I think you'll find that a balanced portfolio might suit your needs better in the long run than investing in art. Let me explain my thinking to you."

But instead of answering Benson, Libby turned to her sister. "I'm sure I heard Erin right."

"Evidently you didn't," Bernie replied. She turned to Benson. "You do know Erin, though, don't you?"

"Which Erin is that?" he asked, a slight catch notable in his voice. "I know a lot of women named Erin. It's a popular name."

"This is the one you were engaged to," Bernie said sweetly.

Benson licked his lips. The smile on his face was gone. His eyes narrowed slightly. He looked from one sister to the other and back again. "You're not really here to talk about investments, are you?"

"Not really," Bernie confessed.

"And the three million dollars?"

"A complete fabrication," Libby told him. "As is Aunt Pearl."

Benson started to get up. "I don't know what you people want, but I don't have time for this kind of nonsense. My secretary will show you out," he said.

Looking at Benson, Libby wondered what he'd be like if his façade cracked. She had a feeling she wouldn't want to be around to see it. She put out her hand. "Wait. This will just take a few minutes. We have a few questions we want to ask you."

Adam Benson swept his hand around his office. "In case you haven't noticed, I'm a busy man."

Libby made a point of looking around the office too. "Funny, but you don't seem that busy to me right now," she observed.

Benson glared at her. Libby glared back. A

minute went by. Then he laughed. "Okay. You win on sheer gall. So I'm going to ask you why would I possibly give you or your sister any more of my time, especially after you lied your way in here?"

"Because you're curious about why we're here," Libby suggested.

"I'm not," Benson assured her.

Now it was Bernie's turn. "Okay then. Because you're a kind, compassionate soul."

Benson raised an eyebrow. Bernie took that as a sign to continue.

"I have a friend who's been arrested for murdering Zalinsky, and we," Bernie pointed to her sister and herself, "don't think he did it."

Benson made a *pffft* sound of dismissal with his lips. "Of course, he didn't do it! Which you know through some sort of feminine intuition."

"If you want to believe that, that's fine with me," Bernie told him, ignoring his sarcasm, which only annoyed Benson more.

"This is very sweet and touching, but risking my standing as the kind, compassionate soul that I am, so what? What does this man's murder have to do with me?" Benson asked. "Why would I possibly care about him?"

"We just want to ask you about Erin," Libby said.

"Erin?" Benson repeated. He blinked twice, then got control of his face.

"The one you were engaged to," Bernie said helpfully.

"Ah, yes, that one."

"You mean there are others?" Bernie asked.

Benson didn't answer her question. Instead he brought his palms together and touched his fingertips to his lips. "Been doing a little digging, have you?" he asked pleasantly.

"We didn't have to dig very far," Bernie told him.

"I bet." Benson adjusted his tie. "Here's the story. We were engaged and then we weren't, and now you know everything there is to know."

"Not quite," Libby said.

"Then the rest will have to remain unknown."

"I beg to differ," Bernie said.

Benson brought his hands down and looked at Bernie with frank curiosity. "And why should I talk to you about her? You have no official capacity in this matter."

Bernie took a sip of coffee and put her cup down. "I'm glad you asked. You should tell us what we want to know, because that way we won't tell people how you lost our three million dollars for us. Social media is a hard force to combat."

"The imaginary three million dollars?"

"Quite so," Bernie said, imitating his earlier phrase.

"That's absurd," Benson told her. He looked at

Bernie and smiled. "No one will believe you, and if you do that, I can sue you for defamation of character. I can tie you up in court for years to come."

"Maybe you can, but it won't do you much good," Bernie agreed. "Because by that time the seed will be planted and your business is . . . dare I say it . . . fragile. You really can't afford bad word of mouth, and I will make sure it's all over social media."

"That's blackmail," Benson protested.

Now it was Bernie's turn to smile. "I prefer to call it negotiating a deal. You tell us what we want to know, and we won't say anything about you to anyone. No. I amend that. We will only say good things."

Benson thought for a moment. "Oh what the hell," he said. "I suppose I can spare another few minutes. Now there's a relationship I'd prefer not to revisit," Benson declared, as he sat back down.

"We heard that Zalinsky took Erin away from you," Libby said.

Benson laughed, a laugh that seemed genuine to Libby. "Who told you that?"

Libby mentioned the twins.

"Your informants left out a couple of things," Benson told Libby and Bernie. "First of all, I was the one who kicked Erin out. No one took her away from me."

"Why?" Bernie asked.

"Why did I kick her out?"

Bernie nodded.

"Simple. Because I caught her fooling around with this guy named Jason. Guy with lots of tattoos and one of those awful ponytails." He shook his head. "I forget his last name. It was some sort of Italian meat."

"Pancetta," Libby supplied.

Benson snapped his fingers. "Yeah. That's it," he said. "I guess she went from him to the Russian."

"Are you sure?" Bernie asked.

"No. I'm not sure that she went from Jason to the Russian, but I am sure that she went from me to Jason. That I can tell you. For God's sake, I found them in bed together. I was devastated."

"You don't seem that way now," Libby observed.

"That's because I'm not." Benson looked rueful. "In retrospect, getting rid of Erin was a good thing, one of the best things that could have happened to me, although I didn't think so at the time. Obviously." He looked at his watch again. A Patek, Bernie noted this time. "And now, ladies, I think our minute is just about up. I have a conference call I have to get ready for."

"One more question," Bernie asked. "Actually, two."

Benson frowned. "Yes?" he said. His manner was not encouraging.

Bernie gestured toward the blue-and-white pottery, the Tang horses, and the scrolls. "Who got you interested in these?"

"Erin, if you can believe it. And your second question?"

"Have you ever heard of a company called Art Unlimited?"

Benson shook his head. "No, I haven't. Why? What do they do?"

"I think they rent out art."

"That's a lucrative market these days," Benson observed as he pressed a button on his desk. "Come back when you have some money to invest," he told them.

A moment later, his secretary came in and ushered Bernie and Libby out, walking them to the elevator, then standing there to make sure they left.

"Do you think Benson is telling the truth?" Libby asked Bernie as the elevator door closed.

"About Erin and Jason?"

Libby nodded.

"Yeah, Libby. I think Adam Benson is." The elevator door opened, and they stepped out into the lobby. "Erin should have stuck with Benson," Bernie noted.

"Yup," Libby agreed.

Bernie switched her tote to her left shoulder.

She really had to stop putting so much stuff in it. "Finding out that your meal ticket—your meal ticket for whom you gave up a good thing—is leaving you could make you unhappy enough to kill," she said.

"It would make me want to do that," Libby observed.

"Me too, Libby. Me too."

Chapter 25

It was around nine o'clock that evening. Libby was sitting on the sofa in Marvin's living room feeding Petunia the Pig bits of the crackers she was eating while she regaled Marvin with the story of her and Bernie's meeting with Adam Benson and listened to the wind blowing in the branches of the large spruce tree outside. According to the weather reports, a storm was coming, and it was coming soon.

"Jason Pancetta," Marvin said, repeating Jason's name while he absentmindedly scratched Petunia's ample rear end. She had managed to position herself between the two of them.

"What about him?" Libby asked.

"Nothing. I'm just not surprised at what you're telling me." Marvin stopped scratching Petunia for a moment because his hand was tired. She oinked and butted his knee with her behind. Marvin sighed the sigh of the imposed upon and resumed his task.

"You know him?" Libby asked, surprised.

"Yeah. Kinda. We went to high school together for a little while."

"Not the hoity-toity Hecht Academy?" Libby asked, using the school's unofficial name. It was the only private, secular school in the area. Marvin's father had sent him there because he was convinced his son would meet a better class of people, which would eventually translate into better business for the funeral home.

Marvin frowned. He preferred to forget those days. "Yeah. God, that was an awful place," he recalled. "You were lucky you went to public school. Anyway, Pancetta moved away in his junior year. Everyone said he had to."

Petunia bumped Libby's knee with her snout, and Libby fed her another piece of cracker. "That's it," she told the pig. "No more."

"Those words aren't in Petunia's vocabulary," Marvin informed Libby.

"Maybe you should put the crackers away," Libby suggested. "She's getting really big," she added.

"I know. She weighs fifty pounds already, and she still has some growing to do."

"I thought Vietnamese mini potbellied pigs were supposed to weigh thirty pounds."

"They do in Vietnam because they're starving. Here they get to be about one hundred pounds. At least. Maybe more. The vet suggested I put her on a treadmill."

Libby giggled at the thought. "Maybe you should buy her a membership at Gold's."

"He was serious."

"Sorry," Libby said apologetically, since she'd

been the person instrumental in convincing Marvin to take her. "She's just so cute."

"Yes, she is," Marvin told Libby as he got up, took the box of crackers, and put it in one of the kitchen cabinets, much to Petunia's chagrin. "Bigger means more to love," he said from the kitchen.

Libby grinned. Even though she knew that Marvin didn't care that she was twenty pounds overweight it was still good to hear it. Even indirectly. Not that she was sensitive or anything on the subject. Yeah. Right. "Okay," she said to Marvin when he and Petunia returned to the living room. "Tell me why Jason moved away."

Petunia, disgruntled, walked over to her bed near the fireplace, while Marvin plopped down on the sofa next to Libby.

"I'm assuming general bad behavior," he said in answer to Libby's question.

"Meaning?"

Marvin shook his head. "I don't really know. I didn't run with his crowd."

Petunia circled around three times, lay down, got up, came over to the sofa, and jumped up between Libby and Marvin.

"I think she's a tad jealous," Libby observed.

"Or she's holding us up for more crackers," Marvin suggested.

"That too," Libby replied.

"I'll tell you one thing, though," Marvin said as

he scratched Petunia's flank. "Jason really liked the ladies."

"Unlike you?" Libby teased.

"Oh, I liked them alright." Marvin gave a sad smile as he remembered his high school years. "But the girls didn't like me. No one wanted to go out with the undertaker's son. They said I was creepy. Either that or they wanted to make out in a coffin."

"So?" Libby asked when Marvin stopped talking. "Did you?"

Marvin held up a finger. "Once. We were just getting started when my dad came in."

Libby put her hand over her mouth. "Oh dear," she said. Marvin's father wasn't a nice man.

"'Oh dear' is right." Marvin shook his head, remembering. "It was all over school the next day."

"I'm sorry," Libby said, leaning over Petunia and giving Marvin a hard kiss on the lips. Marvin smiled. "They had no idea what they were missing."

Marvin's smile grew even bigger. "Seriously?"

"Absolutely," Libby told him. She gave Marvin another kiss, and Petunia snorted indignantly, jumped off the sofa, marched over to her bed, and proceeded to lie in it with her back facing Libby and Marvin.

"That'll show you," Marvin said to Libby.

Libby laughed. "I guess so." She and Marvin

snuggled for a minute. "So," she finally asked. "Would Jason be upset if someone took his girl away from him?"

"Well, he would have been back in the day," Marvin replied immediately. He didn't have to think about the answer. "He had a big ego and a real mean streak going when he was challenged."

"Maybe he's grown out of it," Libby posited.

Marvin shook his head. "Maybe, but I don't think so. In my experience, people don't grow out of that kind of thing with age. They just get better at hiding it."

"Do you happen to know how Jason ended up working for Zalinsky?" Libby asked.

Marvin sat back and told her the story. As Libby listened, she started to wonder about something that Adam Benson had said.

"Jason's going to be fun to talk to," Libby noted when Marvin was done speaking.

"Well, like I said, he does have a temper."

"He seems so nice too."

"So did the Green River Killer," Marvin pointed out.

Libby laughed, "Let's not exaggerate here." She clicked her tongue against her front teeth. "I wonder where he's working now. Or if he's working."

"I saw him behind the counter of the Quick Fill over by Fairmont a couple of days ago," Marvin was telling Libby when her phone rang.

Libby looked down. "Just a sec. Let me get this," she told Marvin. "It's Bernie."

"I need you to get back to the house, and I need you back here now," Bernie told her. Then she hung up before Libby could ask why.

"So much for a peaceful evening," Libby observed as she stood up and began looking around for her sandals. One of them seemed to have disappeared.

Five minutes later, she located it in Petunia's bed. Evidently, the pig had found something else to nibble on. "We should have kept the crackers out," Libby said sadly as she contemplated her shoe, or the lack thereof.

Chapter 26

I escaped," Casper Cumberbatch declaimed as Libby and Marvin walked through the door of her flat a few minutes later. He, Clyde, and Bernie were milling around the coffee table.

"No, you didn't, Casper," Sean's friend Clyde said.

"I was being metaphorical," Casper informed him.

"You were being inaccurate," Clyde said.

"Consistency is the hobgoblin of little minds," Casper retorted.

If Clyde were an eye-rolling kind of guy, that's what he would have done, but he wasn't, so he didn't. Instead he folded his arms across his chest and glared at Casper. He was good at glaring, almost as good as her dad, Libby reflected. It probably came from spending thirty years on the police force. She had a feeling she was in for a long evening as she looked from Casper to Clyde to Bernie and back again.

"Does anyone want to tell me what's going on?" she asked.

"You want the short version or the long version?" Clyde inquired.

"Let's start with the short version and work our way up to the long one," Libby told him.

Clyde nodded. "I was going to ask Sean if Casper could stay here, but it turned out your dad was out with Michelle," he explained.

"Hunh?" Libby frowned. "I don't understand."

Clyde repeated himself.

"You were going to ask *my* Dad to harbor an escaped fugitive," Libby repeated. She was so shocked she couldn't think of anything else to say.

"Things aren't quite as they seem," Clyde informed her.

"So few things are these days," Bernie said dryly, unfolding her arms. She wasn't too happy either.

Libby ignored her sister's comment. "Meaning?" she asked Clyde.

Clyde shuffled his feet. "Ah . . . I could explain better if I had a little something to eat," he said, having the good grace to blush at his request.

"If it comes to that, I wouldn't mind a bite to eat either," said Casper, who wasn't under that constraint.

"Count me in," Marvin added. Although he'd come along for the ride, he was never one to turn down Libby and Bernie's cooking.

Libby looked at Bernie, and Bernie looked back at her.

"I suppose," Libby said grudgingly. "I'll see what I can rustle up."

In fact, Bernie realized as she accompanied her sister down the stairs, she wouldn't be adverse to a snack either. It had been a trying day and an even more trying evening.

Ten minutes later, Libby and her sister were back upstairs with a tray laden with a pitcher of sweet strawberry/lemon lemonade, a fruit salad composed of locally grown honeydew, cantaloupe, watermelon, and mint, ginger snaps, semolina pine nut cookies, madeleines, and four pieces of carrot cake that hadn't sold that day.

Clyde beamed when he saw the food. His wife wasn't a good cook—actually she was a terrible cook—and since Michelle had come on the scene he wasn't over at Sean's as much as he once was. "I miss this," he said, then blushed again. "I didn't mean . . ."

Bernie laughed. "Don't worry. I know what you mean. I do too."

Libby, who was still peeved, didn't utter a word. Instead, she took a piece of carrot cake and started eating. It was good. No. It was great. She was a good baker, even if she had to say so herself. After a few bites, she realized she felt a lot better. Carbs. The universal balm for the soul.

After everyone had eaten Clyde started to explain. "Casper was never under arrest."

Libby stopped eating. "Casper's friend told us he was!"

"He did," Bernie seconded. "I was there."

Casper swallowed the rest of the pine nut cookie he was eating and fixed Libby and Bernie with a reproachful gaze. "Well," he said, "you would have known Jeremy wasn't telling the truth if you'd come to visit me in jail because I wouldn't have been there."

"I couldn't come visit you," Bernie replied. "Prisoners are just allowed visits from immediate family and legal counsel."

"But you could have tried," Casper said mournfully. "No one even tried."

Libby put her fork back on her plate with a clang. "I don't understand."

"I asked Jeremy to call," Casper said.

"And may I ask why?" Libby said to Casper.

"It was a ploy to flush out Zalinsky's killer, the person who's trying to frame me," Casper said.

"And how was your being arrested going to do that?" Marvin asked.

"Because," Casper explained, "then he'd relax and do something that would tip his hand."

Bernie looked at Clyde. "And you're alright with this?"

"I wasn't consulted," Clyde told her. "Casper initiated this."

"I was just thinking outside the box," Casper explained. "Obviously no one else was doing anything. Someone had to take the initiative."

"You're seriously saying that?" Bernie said, thinking about everything she and Libby had done.

Casper looked abashed. Bernie glared at him for a moment before turning to Clyde. "Why didn't you let us know?" she asked.

"I did," Clyde replied.

"When?" Libby demanded.

"As soon as Casper told me what he'd done. I called here, but your dad was taking a shower, so I told Michelle what was going on. I just assumed she would tell your dad and he would tell you." He looked from Bernie to Libby and back again. "Was I wrong?"

"Evidently." Bernie took a deep breath and let it out. "She probably just forgot," she said.

"Right," Libby said, chiming in. "I'm sure that's what happened."

"It's possible, Libby."

Libby rolled her eyes. "You don't really believe that, do you?"

"I'm trying to take the high road here," Bernie told her. She turned to Casper. "So where have you been staying?" she asked.

"He's been staying with me," Clyde answered for him.

Bernie raised an eyebrow.

Clyde held up a hand. "I know. I know. But Lucy strongly, very strongly suggested it when he heard what Casper had done."

"Why would he do that?" Libby asked. "That seems very un-Lucy-like to me."

"Because at least that way he knows where Casper is, but my wife's sister is coming for a surprise visit, so I'm trying to find another place to park Casper."

"I'm not a car, you know," Casper complained.

"Why can't he go back to his house?" Libby inquired.

"Obviously, because someone is trying to kill me," Casper informed her.

Bernie's eyes widened. "Did something happen that I don't know about?" she asked.

"The note, the threatening note I got," Casper reminded her.

"Basically," Clyde explained, "if by some chance Lucy is wrong and Casper didn't kill Zalinsky and the person who killed Zalinsky does kill Casper, Lucy doesn't want it on his hands. It would make him look bad in the papers."

"So Lucy's doing a Pontius Pilate thing?" Bernie asked.

Clyde nodded. "Exactly. Which is why I was hoping he could stay with you."

"Not unless he wants to sleep on the couch," Bernie said.

"Why not just put me in the dumpster and let me sleep there," Casper cried, flinging his arms out.

"That would work," Bernie told him. She was not feeling charitably inclined at the moment.

226

"Didn't you think about where you'd stay when you decided to do this?"

"I can't think of everything," Casper told her.

Libby rubbed her forehead with her fingers. "I'm getting a headache."

"I already have one," Bernie told her.

Something occurred to Libby. She turned to Clyde. "How did you get in if Dad wasn't here?" she asked him.

Bernie stepped forward. "I let him in."

"But I thought you were hanging out with Brandon."

"I was, Libby."

"And," Libby prompted.

"I got a call from Michelle telling me she was taking Dad to Prompt Care," Bernie replied. "So naturally I ran home."

Libby put her hand to her heart. "Oh my God," she said. "What happened? How bad is it? Why didn't you tell me?"

Bernie ate a piece of watermelon. "Don't worry. He's fine. He had a splinter in his finger."

"A big splinter? A giant splinter?"

"A little splinter."

Libby gave her sister a puzzled look. "I'm losing track here. Why take him to Prompt Care in that case?"

"Good question. You'll have to ask Michelle that. Anyway, I was just about to leave when Casper and Clyde showed up.

"I wonder where they are," Bernie said, looking at her watch.

"Me too," Libby said in a strangled voice. Actually she hoped that her dad and Michelle took a while to get back home. She needed time to calm down. Otherwise she knew she was going to say something awful to Michelle.

"What about me?" Casper said.

Everyone in the room looked at him.

"What about you?" Bernie asked.

"Where am I going to stay?" he asked plaintively.

"You could try your house," Libby repeated.

"You want me to die?" Casper asked, looking stricken.

"Do I have to answer that?" Libby replied. "Anyway," she continued, "don't you have a place in Dumbo?"

"I sublet it," Casper said. "And how am I going to see if anyone comes to the house if I'm in New York City? That was the whole reason for my doing this. I've got all my stakeout stuff in the car."

Libby held up a hand. "Just stop." Then she noticed Bernie looking at Marvin speculatively.

"No," he said.

"I haven't said anything," Bernie pointed out.

"You don't have to. I'm not taking him in," Marvin said.

"You have two extra bedrooms," Bernie pointed out.

"I don't care. You just told me someone is trying to kill him," Marvin complained. "What if the killer comes to my house? What about me? What about my safety?"

"No one is trying to kill Casper," Bernie said. "He's exaggerating."

"All very well for you to say," Casper grumped. Everyone ignored him.

"What about the note you were talking about?" Marvin demanded.

"You know," Bernie said, "even if someone is trying to kill Casper—which they're not—they're not going to know he's in your house."

"Have you no compassion?" Casper cried. "No regard for human life?"

"Not really," Marvin replied.

"You know you don't mean that, Marvin," Clyde said as he took the last madeleine and proceeded to eat it. "Excellent," he said, sitting back.

"I'm not making things up, you know," Casper said. "Really, I'm not. I am scared."

Bernie studied her friend for a minute. Maybe he was frightened, after all. It was hard to tell what was real and what wasn't with him. "Okay," she said, "tell us why you're scared."

Casper took a sip of his strawberry lemonade. "I already told you. I think someone is trying to kill me."

"But you haven't told me why you think that," Bernie said.

Casper swallowed. "The note."

"There's something else going on here," she said.

"Even I can see that," Marvin added.

Casper didn't say anything. Bernie locked eyes with him, then reached over and took his hands in hers. They were cold and clammy. "If you want us to help you, you have to let me know what's happening," she told him.

"I know," Casper said, his voice so low Bernie had to strain to hear.

Bernie waited.

Casper licked his lips, pulled his hands out from under Bernie's, and rubbed them on his pants. He started to say something, stopped, and started again.

"Go on," Bernie encouraged.

Another minute passed. Then Casper asked if he could speak to Bernie alone.

"Sure," Bernie said, and she and Casper went downstairs, leaving everyone else wondering what Casper had to say.

Chapter 27

Neither Casper nor Bernie said anything when they came back upstairs a few minutes later.

"So?" Libby said, but Bernie just shook her head, and Casper said he'd said everything he was going to say, and that was that.

After ten minutes of waiting for Casper or Bernie to speak, Marvin decided it was time to go home. It was getting late, tree branches were bowing in the wind, and flashes of lightning were zigzagging across the sky. It looked as if it wouldn't be long before the storm arrived, and anyway Petunia was waiting for him. Clyde got up at the same time as Marvin. They were joined by Casper, and the three men trooped down the stairs together.

"What if Petunia doesn't like me?" Libby could hear Casper asking Marvin as they walked down the stairs.

"She likes everyone," Marvin had reassured him. "Especially if you feed her." Then she'd heard the door close behind them.

Libby watched another flash of lightning streak through the sky. She turned and was about to ask her sister what Casper had told her when she heard the downstairs door open again and the sounds of a familiar tread coming up the stairs.

A moment later, Sean walked through the door.

"Dad, how's your finger?" Libby asked. Given what Bernie had said, she'd expected him to have a big gauze-and-tape concoction of some sort wrapped around his hand, but she couldn't even see a little Band-Aid.

Sean chuckled. "Oh, it's fine. You know how women get."

"No, I don't," Libby snapped. She resented being put in the same category as someone like Michelle.

"Where is Michelle?" Bernie asked, trying to shift the conversation to a more peaceable tone.

"She went home. She has a lot to do at the shop tomorrow. Opening day isn't that far away." He looked at his daughters. "You're coming, aren't you?"

"Absolutely," Bernie answered for both her and her sister.

It took Libby a lot of effort, but she remained silent. Sean looked around. "Who was here?" he asked.

Bernie told him a condensed version of the story.

"Interesting," Sean said when she was through. "I thought Cumberbatch was under arrest too. I'm surprised Clyde didn't tell me."

Libby started to say something, but Bernie beat her to it. "Clyde said he told Michelle. I guess she forgot to tell you," she said, trying to be tactful.

Sean scratched his head. "Maybe she told me and I forgot," he suggested, although it was apparent to Bernie that he was saying that to try and convince himself.

Libby was about to say "Doubtful," when Bernie kicked her in the shin. Hard. Harder than she had intended. Libby gasped.

"Are you alright?" Sean asked his daughter.

"She's fine," Bernie answered for her sister. "She twisted her ankle on the way up the stairs."

"You did?" Sean asked.

Instead of answering, Libby picked up the tray and stomped downstairs to the kitchen.

"She looks okay to me," Sean noted.

"The pain comes and goes," Bernie told him.

Sean looked Bernie in the eye. "Really?"

"Really," Bernie replied, although her father always knew when she was lying.

"So are you going to tell me what's the matter with Libby?" Sean asked after he'd stooped down to say hello to the cat, who'd just emerged from his bedroom. "What's going on here?"

"Take a guess," Bernie replied.

Sean shook his head. "I don't know. I don't have a clue."

Bernie put her hands on her hips. "Yeah, I think you do," she told him.

Sean looked at his younger daughter and sighed. When he'd walked in the door, he'd been looking forward to a bit of chitchat with his daughters, a light snack, petting Cindy, maybe talking a little about what was going on with the Casper Cumberbatch case, and going to bed. That was clearly not happening. Instead he'd walked into a domestic quagmire.

"Tell me what's going on," he pleaded, although a part of him, the part he was blocking, knew exactly what was going on. He just wasn't ready to confront it yet. He was hoping that if he ignored the situation, things would sort themselves out without any help from him. After all, willful blindness was a strategy that had worked for him before.

"Think about it," Bernie said.

"Can I get something to eat while I'm thinking?" Sean asked as Bernie turned and went out the door. He sighed as he heard his daughter going down the stairs. He hoped she'd heard him, but he wasn't sure she had.

Chapter 28

By the time Bernie walked into the kitchen, Libby was done with the dishes and was starting in on the dough for the morning's cinnamon rolls. Bernie watched her sister measure out a little warm water, add the sugar and yeast to it, and set it aside to proof.

"I don't want to talk about Dad," Libby told her sister, briefly looking up.

"That makes two of us," Bernie replied. What was the point?

Libby measured out the flour and sugar and added those to the mixing bowl. "So what did Casper have to say to you?" Libby asked.

Bernie told her.

Libby's eyes grew wide. "He did what?" she repeated, all thoughts of her dad flying out of her head. She couldn't believe what Bernie was telling her.

"You heard what I said," Bernie told her.

"Oh wow," Libby exclaimed.

Bernie handed Libby the melted butter, the warm milk, and the eggs. Her sister put them in the bowl.

"Exactly," Bernie said.

Libby looked at the water, sugar, and yeast mixture. It had begun to bubble. She added the mixture to the bowl as well and turned on the mixer. The clank of the bread hook as it mixed everything together filled the room. She listened to it as she thought about what her sister had just told her. Now everything made a little more sense.

Libby watched the bread hook go around and around. When the flour, yeast, milk, eggs, and butter had formed a ball, she turned the machine off, lifted up the dough hook, disentangled the dough from it, turned the twenty pounds of dough onto the prep table, and began kneading. The motion and the silky feel of the dough in her hands usually soothed her. But not today.

"So let me get this straight," she said to Bernie. "What you're telling me is that Zalinsky dies, and Casper steals the teapot and hides it in his house, then someone comes into his house and steals the teapot from him, and then Stan . . ."

"We don't know it was Stan," Bernie interrupted. "He was being sarcastic."

"No, he wasn't."

"Yeah. He was."

"Fine. Then an unnamed third person comes into Casper's house looking for the teapot, can't find it, so he or she leaves a note on Casper's dining room table implying that they know what Casper did, and now Casper's afraid they're going to come back for the teapot, and when they find out Casper doesn't have the teapot"—Libby made a

slitting motion with her finger across her neck—
"good-bye Casper."

"That's pretty much it," Bernie said. She got out
three baking sheets and buttered them. Then she
went to the fridge, got out a pound of butter, and
put it in a heavy pot that she put on the stove on
very low heat to melt. While that was happening,
she mixed together the cinnamon and sugar.

"That sounds way too complicated to me,"
Libby said. "Kind of like something out of a
thirties movie."

Bernie sighed. "It does, doesn't it?"

"Okay, back to Stan. You say he was being
sarcastic when he said he left the note, but I think
he did that to throw us off," Libby said.

"And I think you're imputing a level of
sophistication to him that he doesn't have."

"Maybe I did overreach," Libby allowed after
a moment had gone by and she'd reviewed what
had taken place in her head. "When I think about
it, Stan . . ."

"Or George aren't the kind of people to resell
that teapot," said Bernie, finishing her sister's
sentence for her. "Steal a couple of tires maybe,
but something like this. I can't see them for it. At
least, I can't see them planning The Blue House
caper."

"Neither can I," Libby admitted. "Which means
we're back to where we started. The Blue House
caper. I like that."

"Thanks."

Libby took a piece of dark chocolate from the bowl on the prep table, popped it in her mouth, and went back to kneading the dough. Chocolate helped her think. It was a scientific fact.

Bernie took a piece too and stood there enjoying the sensation of the chocolate melting on her tongue. For a moment it was quiet in the kitchen, the only sounds those of their dad running water in the upstairs bathroom sink and the rain pattering on the windows.

Libby stopped kneading, moved the scale closer to her, and began cutting off and weighing pieces of dough. Meanwhile, Bernie took the butter off the stove and brought it and the sugar-cinnamon mixture over to the prep table. She dipped her pinky in the butter. It was lukewarm. Just the right temperature.

Bernie picked up a rolling pin and began rolling out the pieces of dough Libby had cut into strips. When she had done a third of the dough, she painted the strips with butter and coated them with the sugar-cinnamon mix, wound them into circles, and slid them onto the baking sheet. When she was done with the first sheet, she put it in the cooler and started on the second sheet.

"So maybe Zalinsky's murder was about the teapot, after all," Libby mused as she scraped the last of the dough out of the mixing bowl with a spatula.

"Maybe," Bernie agreed. "Maybe Zalinsky was just collateral damage. Although," she added, "it doesn't feel that way."

"No, it doesn't, does it?" Libby agreed as she put the bowl and the spatula in the sink. "I know I'd be pretty pissed if I'd killed someone to get the teapot only to have it go missing," she observed.

Bernie closed her eyes and visualized the note lying on Casper's table. " 'Don't think I don't know what you did. Be careful or you're next,' " she repeated. "If I were Casper and I'd done what he did, I'd be scared too."

"What does he have to be careful about?" Libby asked. "It seems to me he's already done what he did."

"True," Bernie agreed.

Libby flicked a piece of dough off her shirt. "One thing is for sure," she said. "Casper's definitely out of his depth."

"For sure," Bernie said. "Way, way out. Just the idea of him surveilling the house." She shook her head at the thought. Then she frowned. Casper wasn't turning out to be the best in the communication department either. She was wondering what else she didn't know about him as she went back to making the cinnamon rolls. She filled the second baking sheet, while Libby finished the third.

"Did Casper say what he was planning to do with the teapot?" Libby asked as she put the last tray in the cooler. The lower temperature slowed down the rising of the dough so that the rolls would be ready to bake first thing in the morning.

Bernie placed the bowls and the pans in the sink and cleaned off the prep table. "He said he was planning on selling it."

"To whom?" Libby asked.

Bernie shrugged. "Casper didn't know. He told me he hadn't gotten that far yet. He said taking it was a spur-of-the-moment decision. He said he thought of all the money Zalinsky owed him and the way he'd treated him, and he just grabbed it and stowed it behind the curtain and came back for it later."

"So someone knew Casper had taken it. But who?" Libby asked.

"I'm thinking the same person who killed Zalinsky."

"Not necessarily," Libby observed. Then she said, "I wonder if Erin and George were looking for the teapot in Zalinsky's house?"

Bernie shook her head. "Judging by the conversation we overheard, they seemed pretty intent on finding the backpack."

Libby started tapping her fingers on the sink.

"What are you thinking?" Bernie asked Libby.

"That the teapot is worth a lot more money than the backpack," Libby answered.

"True. But the contents of the backpack are easier to dispose of," Bernie reminded her.

"Also true," Libby conceded. She fell silent for a moment, then said, "As I see it, the question is: when did Casper take the teapot? Did he take it while Zalinsky was in the back, or did he take the teapot after Zalinsky was killed?"

"It had to be after," Bernie said, "when everyone was running around like lunatics."

"Unless he had an accomplice," Libby suggested. "Then he could have gotten it right when the lights went out."

Bernie shook her head. "That implies Casper knew what was going to happen when Zalinsky grabbed the teakettle, which implies Casper caused it to happen."

Libby wiped her hands on a kitchen towel. "That's my point, Bernie."

"You're wrong," Bernie told her. "Casper couldn't plan something like this. Take advantage of, yes; set in motion, no."

"So you keep saying."

"Hey. There's a world of difference between fantasy and reality." Bernie waved her hands in the air for emphasis. "That's like saying the guy who writes a book about a serial killer can be one. Anyway, Casper's too nervous to plan and commit a murder," Bernie told her sister. "Every little thing freaks him out, and he literally faints at the sight of blood."

Libby thought over Bernie's answer for a moment. "He *is* a nervous Nellie," she conceded.

Chapter 29

Libby walked back to the prep table and sprinkled some flour on it.

"What are you doing?" Bernie asked, looking over her shoulder.

"Drawing a map of the theater. Obviously."

"Silly me. I thought you were starting on the chocolate chip cookies."

"That comes next."

While Bernie watched, Libby blocked out the stage, the backstage area, and the kitchen with lines of flour. Then she took a handful of the large seventy-percent dark-chocolate chips she was going to use to make the cookies and laid them out according to where everyone was at the time of Zalinsky's death.

"See," she said. "This is you and me," she pointed to two of the chocolate chips, "and these are George and Stan." And she went on naming everyone else who had been there.

"I hate to say this," Bernie said as she studied the diagram Libby had created, "this is a lovely work of art and all, but it was pitch-black in the theater at that time. We know where everyone was supposed to be; we just don't know where they actually were. Anyone could have been anywhere."

Libby sighed. "You're right. This is pointless." And she picked up Zalinsky's avatar and ate him. "Here, have one," she told Bernie, sweeping the rest of the chocolate chips into her hand.

"Thanks," Bernie said, taking several. "Let's hope that in real life everyone meets a better end."

"Let's hope so indeed," Libby said as she ate another chocolate chip. They were really quite good, and she liked the fact that they were made in Brooklyn. Then as she was putting another one in her mouth, something occurred to her. "Remember the person who bumped into me when I was carrying out the tray of pierogies?"

"I thought you bumped into him."

"That's not the point."

"Okay. What about him?" Bernie asked.

"Well, I thought it was a techie, but now that I think about it, I'm wondering if it couldn't have been Jason Pancetta."

"Why are you saying that?" Bernie asked.

Libby shook her head. "I'm not sure. I think it was the voice, plus he was the same size as Jason . . ."

Bernie interrupted. "That's not much to go on."

"You didn't let me finish. I also have this vague recollection of seeing the flash of something metal. Something round."

"The March Hare's pocket watch?"

"That's what I'm thinking. After all, it was

pinned to his vest. I think you should look Jason Pancetta up on the Internet, and we'll see what we can find."

"Why don't you?"

"Because you're better at it."

"Only because you don't do it."

"I will," Libby promised.

"When?" Bernie demanded.

"Soon."

"We are living in the twenty-first century, you know."

"You do it faster."

"You would too if you did it more often."

"How about if I separate the eggs for the macaroons while you do that?" Libby suggested.

"Fine," Bernie said, bowing to the inevitable and going into the office. She came out ten minutes later. Jason Pancetta didn't have a large presence on the Internet, but what she'd found was suggestive. "Remember what Adam Benson said about Jason and Erin?" she asked Libby.

"Yes."

"Well, what he didn't say was that Jason worked for the same firm Adam did before he quit, after which he went to work for Zalinsky. I wonder why he'd abandon a perfectly good job to work as an errand boy for the Russian?" Bernie mused.

"Something tells me it wasn't for career advancement," Libby surmised as she covered the bowl full of eggs whites with plastic wrap. The egg whites had to be refrigerated for three days before they could be used for macaroons. "Interesting that Adam Benson, Erin, Jason, and Zalinsky all knew each other back in the day."

Bernie nodded. "Isn't it, though?" she said. Then she took out her phone and texted Adam Benson. Not that she expected an answer, which was good because she didn't get one. "We should run everything we have by Dad," Bernie said, putting her cell down. Their father had a knack for clarifying things. "It would be interesting to hear what he has to say."

Libby squared her shoulders. "You can if you want to. I'm not going to."

"Don't be like that," Bernie urged.

"Be like what?" Libby asked.

"Like this."

"This meaning?"

"Pissy, Libby."

"Maybe I am," Libby answered, "but that's the way I feel right now."

"You're acting like you're two."

Libby stuck her jaw out. "So what if I am?"

Bernie sighed. There was no arguing with her sister when she got like this. "You know you're just like Dad," she told her.

"No, I'm not," Libby protested.

"Yeah. You are. You're just as stubborn as he is."

"He needs to apologize."

"You're going to wait a long time for that."

Libby shrugged. "Maybe. We'll see. But I'm not going up to ask him for help."

"Fine," Bernie said. "Don't. I will."

Libby folded her arms across her chest. "And while we're on the subject, I'm not going to the opening of Michelle's store either. There's no reason why we have to be there."

"Good luck with that!" Bernie told her.

"I'm not," Libby repeated.

"I think you are," Bernie told her. "Otherwise life around here is going to be total hell. In any case, that's a ways away."

"Two and a half weeks, to be exact," Libby told her.

"More like four or five the way these things go." Bernie reached in the bag of chocolate chips, grabbed a handful, and ate them. Normally she wasn't an emotional eater, but she was making an exception in this case. "Fine. How about we forget about Dad and Michelle for now and concentrate on finding Jason and talking to him?"

"Works for me." Libby dipped into the bag again. At this rate, she noted, there wouldn't be enough left for the cookies. "Okay then. Moving along. On the business front, how do you feel about using something like quinoa flour to make the chocolate chip cookies?" Libby asked as she swept the remains of the white flour into the wastepaper basket with the edge of her hand.

"We could try," Bernie said, although she had her doubts about how the end product would taste, but people were entranced with quinoa right now, so it was worth an attempt.

"We'll try them out on Dad," Libby suggested, having thought over what Bernie had said and decided that peace might be the better alternative. "If we can get them by Dad, we can get them by anyone." Their dad was a conservative eater. He didn't like change.

"Good idea," Bernie replied, refraining from further comment. In the meantime, she'd decided she was going to ask their dad to find out if Stan and George had any priors, something her sister didn't need to know. As Bernie was about to turn off the light, she noticed that Libby had put some lemon squares on a plate, one of their dad's favorites.

"In case we get hungry," Libby explained, even though Bernie hadn't asked her to bring food upstairs.

Bernie smiled. Maybe domestic harmony was about to be restored after all. At least until the next bit of Michelle drama. In any case, it was nice to end the day on a positive note. Especially this day. Now, Bernie thought, if the storm would just blow itself out, they'd be all set.

Chapter 30

The next day it took Libby and Bernie until early in the afternoon to track down Jason Pancetta. Well, that wasn't exactly true. They really didn't track him down. It was more like they bumped into him. He was going into The Blue House while Bernie and Libby were coming out. They'd just finished trying to talk to Magda and spectacularly failing at that endeavor when Pancetta brushed by them.

"Hello," Bernie said, noting that Pancetta was carrying a takeout bag from McDonald's and wearing aviator-style sunglasses, black cargo shorts, a T-shirt proclaiming *Drink Is Good,* and flip-flops. Not exactly going-to-work clothes, Bernie thought, as she caught a whiff of suntan lotion coming from him. The smell made her want to go to the beach. Heaven only knows, it was hot enough for it. Unfortunately, the storm had arrived and departed without cooling anything down.

Pancetta looked up, startled. "Yes," he said, removing his earbuds from his ears.

"What a coincidence," Bernie said. "If you're looking to talk to Magda, she's not in a very good mood."

"She's never in a good mood, and I'm not."

"Not what?" Bernie asked.

"Not here to talk to Magda."

"So what are you here for?" Bernie asked.

Jason scowled. "Not that it's any of your business, but I came to pick up my baseball hat."

"Are sure you're not picking up a teapot?" Libby asked him apropos of nothing.

Jason scrunched up his face. "What are you talking about?" he asked Libby.

Libby waved her hand in the air. "Never mind. Forget it. We need to talk."

"We are talking," Pancetta pointed out.

"She means about what happened the other night," Bernie explained.

"Then she should say what she means," Pancetta observed.

"And mean what she says," Libby couldn't resist adding.

Jason shook his head. "You're talking like a crazy lady."

"And you're talking like a crank," Libby told him.

Jason shifted his McDonald's bag to his other hand. "You'd be cranky too, if you didn't get paid."

"What makes you think we have?" Bernie said to him.

"As far as we can tell, no one has," Libby said. "From what I understand from Hsaio, Zalinsky has no money in his bank accounts. None."

"He would if someone sold all that art stuff Zalinsky has," Pancetta observed. "Then there'd be plenty of cash."

"I don't think so," Libby told him.

"What do you mean?" Jason demanded. "Do you know how much that stuff is worth?"

"If you own it," Bernie said.

"And Zalinsky was renting it," Libby said.

Jason blinked. "Get outta here!"

"Seriously," Libby said. She'd gotten a call from Clyde that morning informing her that Art Unlimited had called the Longely police department wanting to know when they could pick up their stuff.

"Except for the teapot," Bernie said. "Zalinsky owned that. Too bad whoever took the teapot won't share."

"They will if I find it," Jason growled. "You'd better believe that."

Looking at him, Bernie did. "So who do you think took it?" she asked.

"How would I know," Jason replied.

"Just askin'," Libby said. She snapped her fingers. "Hey. I have an idea. It could even be you. You could have it."

"I could," Jason replied. "But I don't. Now if you'll excuse me," he continued before Libby could reply, "I'd like to get my hat and have my lunch."

Bernie pointed to Jason's bag. "Is that it?" she

250

asked as she watched a yellow butterfly fluttering around a black-eyed Susan, one of many that had been planted in front of The Blue House. She didn't remember them being there before, but maybe she just hadn't noticed.

Unlike the black-eyed Susans, the storm had flattened the petunias in The Blue House's flowerbeds and splashed mulch out onto the newly growing lawn. It was just a couple of weeks since Zalinsky had died, but speedwell was taking hold in the grass, and deadly nightshade was growing in the flowerbeds. It wouldn't be long, Bernie reflected, before the place began to look abandoned. The town was going to have to come to a consensus on what to do with The Blue House, and sooner would be better than later.

"No. I got it to feed the geese," Jason told her. "Of course it's my lunch. Why? Do you have something to say about it?"

"Why would I?" Bernie asked. She brushed a small leaf off her pale blue T-shirt. Today she'd paired her top with a vintage white linen skirt and white espadrilles. It was the perfect outfit for a summer afternoon as far as Bernie was concerned.

"Because of the place you run," Pancetta told her. "You know, everything there is organic this and locally sourced that."

Bernie laughed. "I was just going to say I like Mickey Dee's apple pies. Of course, I liked them better when they fried them. The ones they bake, not so much."

Jason smiled despite himself. "It's true. Fried was better."

"Sadly, healthier is not always tastier," Bernie observed.

"Maybe we could sit outside and you could eat your lunch while we talked," Libby suggested, gesturing to a bench in front of The Blue House.

"I already told you, I have nothing to talk about," Jason replied. He used his forearm to wipe off the beads of sweat on his forehead.

"How can you say that when you don't know what we want to discuss?" Libby asked.

Jason gave her an incredulous look. "Of course I know what you want to talk about. I'm not an idiot, you know. You're helping out our erstwhile director, never mind that he's a thief and a liar . . ."

Bernie interrupted. "But not a murderer."

Pancetta ignored her and went on with what he'd been saying. "You want to talk about Zalinsky, and I have nothing to say about him."

"Fair enough." Bernie smiled. "I could see why you would feel that way. I'd be embarrassed too, if I were you." Earlier in the day, she'd managed to have an interesting conversation with Adam Benson's assistant, Hillary John, about Jason Pancetta. It had turned out that the information Bernie had found on the Internet had been correct. Pancetta had worked for Smith and Miller too. Talking to. Hillary, it had been obvious to Bernie that Jason had been engaged in some non-kosher activities at the firm, but what they were Hillary wouldn't say, and Jason had either been forced to quit or had been fired.

"Why would I possibly be embarrassed?" Pancetta demanded, attempting to keep his face expressionless and failing.

Bernie enlightened him. "You know," she said, "your losing Erin to Zalinsky, and then his making you work for him like he did." Bernie could see Jason's knuckles whitening as his grip on the takeout bag tightened. "I wouldn't want to relive that either. What did he have on you that made you stay?" Despite her best efforts, Bernie hadn't found anything on the Internet when she'd gone back to it. That didn't mean there wasn't anything there. It just meant she'd run out of time to look. "Did you stay because you were hoping to win Erin back? Or was Zalinsky blackmailing you because he knew about something you'd done?" Given what she'd learned about Zalinsky, she was betting on the latter scenario.

Splotches of color appeared on Jason's cheeks. "He didn't have anything on me," he snarled.

"That's it, isn't it?" Bernie said, thinking about

what Hillary had told her about Jason being let go from Smith and Miller. "What did you do that was so bad?"

"I didn't do anything," Jason protested.

"Did you kill somebody?" Libby asked.

Jason laughed. "You got me. I killed the president of Smith and Miller and threw his body in the Hudson River because he was about to complain to the SEC about his losses."

Bernie looked him up and down. "I don't see you for a violent crime." And she didn't. "I see you as a lover, not a fighter."

Jason smirked and puffed out his chest. "That's right, baby. Anytime you want a demo I'll be happy to oblige."

"Thanks, but no thanks." Bernie studied him some more. "I see you as more of a white-collar–crime kind of guy. A schemer." She could tell from the expression on Jason's face that she was getting warmer. "Embezzlement?"

"You want me to tell you about the misunderstanding?" Jason asked her.

"It would be nice," Bernie allowed.

"But we've already established I'm not a nice guy." Jason moved a step closer to her. "So how about this? How about talking to me when you find the damned teapot. I might feel a little more inclined."

"Fair enough," Bernie said. "I do have one more question, though."

Jason rolled his eyes. "I'll say this for you: you are persistent."

Bernie curtsied. "I try. We talked to Adam Benson."

"Ah," Jason said, frowning slightly. "Good old Adam. Now there's a blast from the past."

"You two worked in the same firm."

"You know we did," Jason told Bernie. "Is that your question?"

"No. My question is why did Erin leave him for you?"

Jason grinned. "Why do you think?"

"Sex?" Bernie said. "Or money?"

Jason's grin grew larger. "If there's one thing I know, it's my ladies."

"So you were her backdoor man?" Bernie asked.

Jason shrugged. "Everyone has a talent."

Bernie thought about Erin for a moment. She saw her as cold and calculating, a woman moved by money, not sex. "But you had to be making money too," she said, musing out loud. "Probably a lot. Otherwise Erin wouldn't have looked at you."

"Let's just say we satisfied each other's needs," Jason said, miming sex with his hands.

"I'm puzzled," Libby said, jumping into the fray. "If that's the case, why did Erin leave you for Zalinsky?" she asked.

Jason flushed. His jaw muscles tightened. "It wasn't her choice."

"Really? People always have choices," Libby said.

"What world are you living in?" Jason snapped.

"Obviously not yours," Libby snapped back.

Bernie raised an eyebrow. "Is that what Erin told you? That she didn't have a choice?"

"No. That's what I know," Jason said, and he stormed off toward the parking lot.

"Hey, you forgot to get your hat," Libby called after him.

"You're going to need it for Zalinsky's funeral," Bernie added.

Jason didn't answer. Instead he raised a middle finger.

"Oh dear," Bernie said while she watched him getting into a Jeep. "Maybe he didn't hear us," she suggested.

"Somehow I doubt that," Libby replied.

"I do too," Bernie remarked as she watched Jason zoom out of the parking lot and onto Seeley Road. A minute later he'd gone around the curve and was out of sight.

Libby bent over and took a pebble out of her loafer. "I have to say he's rather touchy about Erin," she observed when she straightened up. She fanned herself with her hand. Bernie was right. She should have worn a sundress instead of Bermuda shorts and a polo shirt—a dark red polo shirt at that.

"He certainly is," Bernie agreed. "Or maybe

he's getting crabby because that bald spot on the back of his head is getting sunburned. We should give him his hat back."

"Yes, we should. We wouldn't want him to get skin cancer or anything like that," Libby replied.

Bernie put her hand to her heart. "Heaven forefend, Libby. Heaven forefend."

Libby looked at the expression on her sister's face. "You have a plan, don't you?"

"I'm not sure you'd call it that," Bernie said modestly. Then she smiled and told Libby what she had in mind.

Chapter 31

But why would the teapot be in The Blue House?" Libby asked Bernie when her sister was through talking. The longer Bernie talked, the more faults Libby found with her sister's notion. Her plan seemed quixotic at best, disastrous at worse.

"Can you think of a less likely place?" Bernie asked.

"Yeah. Timbuktu."

"We can't look there, but we can look here," Bernie said, pointing to the structure.

Libby shook her head at her sister's logic or lack thereof.

"And if it's not there," Bernie continued, "we can cross The Blue House off our list."

Libby widened her eyes. "List? What list? Do we have a list?"

"I'm speaking metaphorically," Bernie informed her.

"Ah. How can I not have gotten that?" Libby asked.

"Sarcasm does not become you," Bernie told her.

"Neither does the heat." Libby fanned herself with the edge of her hand to make her point. "The Blue House is like a sauna."

"Such a delicate flower," Bernie observed.

"At least, let's wait for a cooler day."

Bernie put her hands on her hips. "You mean to tell me that you're going to be put off by a little heat with Casper's life hanging in the balance?"

Libby snorted. "Let's not overdramatize here. Casper is fine."

"For now," Bernie said. "But if we don't solve this, he'll be going to jail."

Libby waved her hand in the air. "Now is what counts." She went on. "And have I mentioned the fact that in my humble opinion looking for the teapot is going to be like looking for a . . . ?"

"A needle in a haystack, to use another well-worn phrase," said Bernic, finishing her sister's sentence for her. "And yes, you have. Several times."

"Plus there's Magda," Libby continued, undcterred by her sister's adversarial stance.

"What about her?"

"Shouldn't we tell her what we're doing?"

"Why would we?" Bernie inquired as she watched a cicada land on the grass in front of her, its wings glinting in the sun.

"So she won't call the police or think we're a burglar and shoot us."

"She won't know we're there, and she doesn't have a gun."

"What if she does hear us and she does have a gun?" Libby argued. "What then?"

"Then we'll just have to be very, very quiet," Bernie told her.

"We should tell her," Libby argued.

"No, we shouldn't!" Bernie told her.

"Why not?"

Bernie transferred her glance from the cicada to her sister. "Obviously, because she could be the one who took the teapot. She could be the one who killed Zalinsky."

"Even if you're right," Libby said. "Why do we have to do this now? Why can't we wait till she's gone? It would be easier."

"And we're going to get in how?"

Libby went silent. They'd given their key to Magda, and the place was still alarmed.

Bernie rubbed her hands together. "So are we going to do this or not?"

"I guess," Libby said with a notable lack of enthusiasm.

Five minutes later, they were inside The Blue House. Bernie quietly closed the side door behind her. It shut with a soft thud, blocking out the afternoon sun. They'd come in that way because Magda had a clear line of sight to the front door.

"I don't see how Magda can stand this," Libby observed as she held up her hair to cool off the back of her neck, then pulled out her polo shirt to let the air circulate.

"She dressed for it," Bernie observed.

Libby let the dig go by. "God, I hope they get

the money to fix the air-conditioning because it's even hotter in here than it is outside."

"Told you you should have worn something cooler," Bernie couldn't resist pointing out as she blinked her eyes to get used to the dim light.

Libby just grunted. She stood there for a moment, fanning herself. "Where to?" she asked Bernie. "This is your party. You pick."

"Stage and backstage area first," Bernie said because those were the areas that were the farthest from where Magda was sitting. "Then the rest of the space."

The thick beige carpet muffled their footsteps as they walked down the side corridor. At ten feet in, they took a left, walked twenty more feet and took a right. The place seemed huge with no one in it. It was quiet, dead quiet, tomb quiet, in contrast to when Zalinsky had been alive. Then the place had been full of people running about, excited people busy having meetings, willing the future into existence. Now, except for Magda, no one was here.

"I wonder if Zalinsky is going to haunt this place," Bernie mused. "Or maybe he already is."

"What an odd thing to say," Libby told her.

"Not really. After all, this was his baby," Bernie said running her fingers along the wall. Who was going to pay the bills for the place, she wondered, and how long would the lights stay on if no one did. It would be a shame to see a space like this go to waste. "He did die here, and ghosts *are* tethered to places."

Libby couldn't get her sister's words out of her mind as she walked next to her. She was sure it was because her sister—damn her—had suggested it, but she kept thinking she saw something out of the corner of her eye, and when she turned around nothing was there. She would be very glad to get out of there.

"What's the matter?" Bernie asked as she and Libby neared the backstage area.

"Nothing," Libby lied.

"Because you're looking a little spooked."

Libby glared at her sister. "Let's just do what we came to do and get out of here." She blinked the sweat out of her eyes. "I feel as if I'm going to dissolve into a puddle."

"Do you think the g—"

Libby held up her hand to stop her. "Don't go there."

"Just sayin'," Bernie replied.

"Well, don't," Libby snapped. Being backstage was creeping her out anyway, without thinking that Zalinsky's ghost was looking over her shoulder.

"He could be a helpful ghost," Bernie went on. "Maybe he wants to help us get the teapot back."

"And maybe you should shut up," Libby hissed.

"Fine," Bernie said. "If that's the way you want it."

"It is," Libby said. "It definitely is."

"You take the right side, and I'll take the left," Bernie said.

At which point they got to work. They looked under and around the curtains, they went through the prop area and down into the areas underneath the trap doors. They lifted up the floor panels and examined the areas between the floodlights, then they opened up the cabinet drawers and moved the chairs.

"Hey," Libby cried, as she picked up one of the cushions on the chair, "look what I found."

Bernie came over. She stared down at the pair of white gloves that had been underneath the cushion. "Wasn't Zalinsky looking for those?"

"Oh yes," Libby said. "Remember? He was running around, accusing everyone of stealing them."

"Maybe he wasn't wrong," Bernie said, studying them. "Maybe someone did." She indicated the gloves with a nod of her chin. "Somehow I have the feeling these didn't get under the cushion by themselves."

"Maybe someone hid them to annoy him," Libby suggested.

"Possibly," Bernie said as she picked up the gloves and slowly turned them over. They were white cotton. But they felt funny. She ran her fingers over them. They were lined, which was unusual for cotton gloves. She turned the gloves inside out. They were indeed lined with a thin layer of rubberized material. She showed the lining to Libby.

"Odd," Libby said.

"Suggestive," said Bernie as a glimmer of an idea began to occur to her. She closed her eyes and tried to picture the scene in the kitchen when she'd run in and found Zalinsky on the floor. "He was wearing gloves onstage."

Libby nodded. "Yes, he was."

"I wonder where he got them from," Bernie mused.

"He must have had an extra pair," Libby suggested.

Bernie grunted.

"What are you thinking?" Libby asked.

"I'm thinking you should call Marvin," Bernie replied.

"And why should I do that?"

Bernie explained.

"It seems far-fetched," Libby said of Bernie's idea.

"It is," Bernie agreed. "But it's possible. Do you want to call Marvin, or should I?"

"I will," Libby said. "Although he's not going to like this," she predicted.

She was right. He didn't. But he agreed to it nonetheless.

"When?" Bernie asked after Libby lowered her phone.

"Maybe tonight. Maybe tomorrow," Libby told her. "Depends on when everyone clears out."

"I guess that'll have to do," Bernie told her as she took photos of the inside and outside of the gloves, then put them back where Libby had found them. She had been going to give them to Clyde but had decided to leave them where they'd found them and show Clyde the photos instead.

"Now what?" Libby asked as she watched her sister.

"Now we go through the lounge, the changing rooms, and the kitchen." Especially the kitchen, Bernie thought. She definitely wanted to see the kitchen.

Libby groaned. "I'm getting light-headed," she complained.

Bernie rummaged in her bag. "Here," she said. "Drink this." And she handed her sister a flask of homemade lemonade.

"Is there anything you don't have in there?" Libby asked, referring to Bernie's tote as she opened the flask and gulped it down.

"You're one to talk," Bernie answered. "Feeling better?"

Libby had to admit she did, which was a good thing because they were coming to the tricky part. While the stage area was away from where Magda was presently ensconced, the lounge, the dressing rooms, and the galley kitchen were not. Now they'd be in close proximity to Magda, or at least close enough so that Magda would be able to hear them moving around if they weren't very quiet, especially since there were no other sounds in the building, not even the hum of the air-conditioning unit.

Libby reflected on that as she and Bernie walked down the hallway to the lounge. When they got there, Libby took a deep breath, grasped the handle of the door to the lounge, and pulled. The door creaked as it opened. Libby cursed under her breath. She and her sister stood there waiting for Magda to come, but she didn't, and after a minute they went inside.

Everything looked the way it had the last time they had been in here, Libby thought. The sofas and the chairs were in the same places; the coffee table was still littered with paper coffee cups and crumbs from the muffins everyone had been eating before they'd gone onstage; rose petals still marked the spot where Zalinsky had thrown the vase with Erin's flowers.

Looking at the lounge, Libby couldn't help thinking about everyone gathered here the evening before the performance. One of those people had killed Zalinsky. They were moving closer to the how, but not to the who. Everyone had hated him, but who had hated him enough to take things one step further? Libby thought back to that night. Had anyone been acting strangely? Had anyone said or done anything that indicated they were planning on killing someone? She shook her head. If they had, she hadn't seen it.

But one thing was for sure. No one in that room had been happy. No one in that room had wanted to be there. Everyone there was there under duress. Certainly she and Bernie were. Libby closed her eyes and pictured the scene. She could see Erin's fury when Zalinsky had thrown the vase with her flowers on the floor and told her to clean it up, and she could hear Casper cursing Zalinsky under his breath. Then there'd been the Holloway boys in a major sulk over their costumes and Magda with her blood-red fingernails sitting by herself, looking as if she'd like to rip someone's heart out and eat it, and Hsaio looking as if she wanted to disappear into the sofa.

Libby was trying to remember exactly what everyone had said when Bernie poked her in the ribs. "Are we going to do this or what?" she asked her sister.

Libby startled. "Sorry," she said, and she got to work.

Fifteen minutes later, she and Bernie were through searching. They'd covered every inch of the space, and Libby felt reasonably sure that unless Zalinsky's teapot was buried under the floor or secreted somewhere in the walls, it wasn't there. She was on her knees, having just finished looking under the sofa, and was thinking about how she and Bernie were going to handle the dressing rooms and the galley kitchen, and that maybe they should have started with the kitchen because that, after all, was where everything had begun, when she heard a noise.

Libby turned around and saw Magda standing in the doorway.

It took Libby a second longer to see the gun Magda was holding in her hand and a second after that to realize that it was pointed at her and her sister.

Chapter 32

*T*his, Libby thought, *is not good.* She turned to her sister. "Don't worry, you said," Libby told Bernie, imitating Bernie's voice. "She won't have a gun, you said. She'll never hear us, you said."

"So I was wrong," Bernie replied. She had just finished looking under the chairs in the corner. "So shoot me."

"I have a feeling that could be arranged," Libby retorted.

Bernie tsk-tsked. "That's not nice."

"But true," Libby exclaimed.

Bernie sniffed. "Hopefully not."

"Don't you two ever shut up?" Magda exclaimed, taking a step into the room.

"It's a sister thing," Libby explained.

"Makes me glad I'm an only child," Magda told her.

Bernie nodded toward the gun. "How about lowering the weapon?"

"And why should I be doing that?" Magda asked Bernie.

"Because it's not as if we're strangers," Bernie answered. "You know who we are."

"Precisely," Magda said. "And anyway, how do

I know you're not here to do something awful?"

"Like what?" Libby demanded.

Magda shrugged.

"Then at least put the safety back on," said Bernie, who had noticed that it was off. "Accidents can happen."

Magda smiled brightly. "*Da.* They can. They happen all the time in America. Now what are you two doing here?" she asked.

Libby said the first words that came to her. "Looking for a charm bracelet."

"My charm bracelet," Bernie said to Magda. "I loaned it to her, and now she can't find it. Can you . . ."

Magda interrupted before Bernie could finish. "This is a stupid story you are telling me." She waved the gun around. "You think maybe I am a stupid person?"

"Not at all," Bernie quickly replied. "Frankly, I wouldn't believe it either." She turned to Libby. "See," she said, "I told you we shouldn't have snuck in here like this. I told you Magda would be angry. I told you we should tell her what we were going to do."

"No, Bernie, I told you that."

"No, you didn't, Libby."

"Yes, I did, Bernie. I told you Magda looked like the type who might have a gun."

"And you were right, Libby," Bernie told her sister.

"Stop this . . . this . . ."

"Bickering," Bernie said, supplying the word.

"Yes, bickering," Magda said.

"Fine," Bernie told her. "I'm just surprised, is all. You just didn't strike me as the type," she pointed to the weapon, "to have one of those."

"It is Zalinsky's," Magda informed her.

"So I don't owe you a dollar after all," Bernie told Libby. "We bet," she explained to Magda, even though she and her sister hadn't.

"Was Zalinsky's," Magda corrected herself. "He keep it in the drawer for just in case."

"In case what?" Libby asked. She'd gotten up off her knees. At least Magda hadn't objected to that.

"In case people, bad people, come to visit. Of course."

"Of course," Bernie said, also rising. She brushed her legs off. "Were there a lot of those?"

"He said there were going to be," Magda replied. "Myself, I did not see them. But he always talk big."

"Talk big?" Libby asked.

Magda explained. "He always make things bigger than they were."

"He exaggerated?" Bernie asked,

Magda nodded. "*Da.* That is the word I am looking for."

Libby indicated the gun with a nod of her head.

"Maybe you should put that down. Your arm looks like it's getting tired."

Magda scowled.

"Or not," Libby told her.

"Did Zalinsky ever find his gloves?" Bernie asked, changing the subject. "I know he was looking for them before the performance."

"Such a fuss about nothing," Magda said, nodding in remembrance.

"Good thing he had another pair," Libby observed.

"No. He find his pair right where he leave them," Magda said.

"Interesting," Bernie said.

"This is not interesting," Magda snapped, the color rising on her face. "This is just stupid."

Bernie decided a change of subject might be beneficial. "Have I told you I love the new you," Bernie said to Magda, going for disarming—both literally and figuratively. And it was true. Looking at her again, Bernie realized that Magda had blossomed since Zalinsky's death. She had a new look, a younger, more fashionable one, one that Bernie was sure had cost a fair amount of money to achieve.

For openers, Magda had gotten a makeover. She'd abandoned her bright red lipstick for a softer shade of pink and dialed down the black eyeliner to a more flattering shade of brown. She'd cut her bangs and changed the color of her hair to a pretty auburn and caught it up in a loose bun on the top of her head. Tendrils escaping from the bun framed her face.

Then there were her clothes. They were different too. They were funkier, Bernie decided. More flattering. Softer. Definitely more expensive. Magda was wearing a loose-fitting, yellow and blue, pin-striped, knee-length dress that looked like an old-fashioned house dress, but Bernie had seen it featured in *Vogue*. If she remembered rightly, the dress had cost somewhat over four hundred dollars. And then there were Magda's shoes. Platform sandals. Bernie had seen them in Bloomingdale's for three hundred dollars. Not bad for a working girl.

"I love the dress," Bernie said.

"Good for you," Magda replied, but she lowered the gun a little.

"And the shoes. Were they expensive?" Bernie asked, encouraged by Magda's response. "Did you get them at Barney's or in Little Russia?"

"None of your business," Magda told her.

"I seem to be getting a lot of that lately," Bernie remarked ruefully.

"Maybe that's because you're sticking your nose in where you shouldn't," Magda replied. "I could have shot you," she added, but then, to Bernie and Libby's relief, she put the gun on the end table by the sofa.

"We wouldn't want that to happen," a relieved Libby observed.

"I go for the lighter firearms myself," Bernie wisecracked. "Easier to carry around in my tote."

"You have gun?" Magda asked.

Bernie shook her head. "I don't like them very much."

Magda considered Bernie's answer as she reached up and fingered the gold chain she was wearing around her neck. "I thought all Americans like guns."

"Not me," Libby said.

"Or me," Bernie added.

"I do not like them either," Magda confided. "They're too obvious."

"What do you mean?" Bernie asked.

"The gun goes bang. Someone dies. You see this," Magda replied.

Bernie nodded encouragingly.

"I think other ways of killing people, less . . ."

"Obvious ways," Libby said supplying the phrase Magda was looking for.

"*Da*. Less obvious ways are better."

"Like what?" Bernie asked. "If you were going to kill someone, how would you do it?"

For a moment, Bernie thought Magda was going to answer her question, but instead she said, "You are smarty-pants people, then you

274

must figure it out. You must leave now. I have work to do."

"Your boss is dead," Bernie observed. "How much work could you possibly have?"

"Enough," Magda said. "I told you this when you were here before."

"I'm surprised the police didn't take Zalinsky's computer," Bernie said.

"They took the ones from his house and his office, not the one here," Magda informed her.

"How come?" Bernie asked.

Magda shrugged again. It seemed to be her gesture of choice. "I do not know. You have a problem with this?" Magda demanded.

"No. My sister was just asking a question," Libby said.

"You and your sister are busy"—Magda hunted around for the correct word—"mouses."

"Bees," Bernie corrected. "The phrase is a busy bee."

"Actually, we're just here to get Jason Pancetta's hat," Libby said.

"This is another lie," Magda stated.

"Why would I lie?" Bernie asked.

"You still have not told me why you are here," Magda said.

"I think you know," Bernie told her.

"I do not," Magda said.

Bernie clicked her tongue against her teeth. "Magda, Magda. Now you're the one who is telling fibs." Bernie turned to Libby. "Of course Magda knows why we're really here."

"How could she know?" Libby demanded.

"How could she not?" Bernie replied. She pointed at Magda. "She's not dumb. Maybe she found it already. In fact, given her new clothes, shoes, and hairdo, I think that's a definite possibility. No, I'm figuring that's a reality." Bernie smiled at Magda. "I'm figuring you didn't ask us what we were looking for because you've already found it."

"Did you?" Libby asked Magda. "Just tell us if you did."

Magda looked from Bernie to Libby and back again. "Vhat you two are talking about?" she asked, her Russian accent getting even thicker.

"The teapot, of course," Libby said. "The two-million-dollar teapot. What else would we be looking for?"

"You don't have to pretend," Bernie told Magda. "We know you know that Casper stole the teapot."

"I didn't," Magda said, although Libby and Bernie could see from the way she was blinking her eyes before she got control of herself that she did in fact know.

"That's funny," Bernie said. "I was positive that you knew and that you know that someone took the teapot from him."

Magda rebuttoned the top button of her dress,

even though it hadn't come undone, to give her hands something to do. "And you think that maybe this person is me?"

"Why not?" Bernie said. "You had access, and you have a motive. I have to say," she indicated Magda with a nod, "you're putting the money to good use. You look really, really good."

Magda picked up the gun. "So what you are saying is that I kill Ludvoc and then Casper steal the teapot and I take it from him and hide it back here. This is what you think? This is the reason you are here crawling around on your hands and knees?"

Bernie turned to Libby. "See, Libby," she said, "I told you Magda was smart."

"And why are you thinking this?" Magda asked, waving the gun in their general direction. "Someone is telling you?"

"No one told us anything," Bernie said hastily. "We're just guessing. But if you put the gun back down and if you haven't sold the teapot, perhaps we can help," Bernie said.

"That's right," Libby seconded. "That way your kids won't have to go to a community college . . ."

Magda interrupted. "Why you say this about my children?" she demanded. "You think they are stupid too?"

"Not at all," Libby said. "We know that they're very smart. It's just that colleges cost money, lots of money."

Magda stood up straighter. "They will get big scholarships and go to an important school."

"I'm glad to hear that," Libby went on. "The only reason I'm saying that is because I heard that Zalinsky had promised to pay for your kids' college education and then he reneged."

Magda glared at Bernie and Libby. "He was not a good man."

"No, he wasn't," Bernie agreed. "I wonder what happened to all his money."

Magda lowered the gun. "I do not think he had any," she confided. "I think he fool everyone."

"But he had to have money to pay for this," Libby waved her hand around, indicating The Blue House. "Not to mention his house. And his art collection."

Magda shook his head. "I think he use money that wasn't his. I think he borrow lots and lots of it."

"And you know this for a fact?" Bernie asked.

"I know he was getting lots of calls," Magda replied, echoing what Hsaio had told them. "Everyone wanted their money. They all say things about going to court, but Zalinsky, he just keep telling them everything will be fine, and he's working on getting their money to them."

Libby turned to Bernie. "Well, that would explain the go bag."

Magda looked at Bernie and Libby. "What is this go bag?" she asked.

"He was getting ready to get out of town," Libby explained, "and take the teapot with him. It was his insurance policy. He just didn't count on being dead, but then who does?"

Bernie turned to Magda. "So did you find the teapot?"

Magda made a dismissive noise. "If I find the teapot, why I still here? Explain this."

"Because leaving would make you look suspicious," Libby replied.

"And there *are* your new clothes," Bernie said.

Magda raised her gun again. "So I take some money from Ludvoc's account. So vhat? He owe me."

"I thought you just told us Zalinsky didn't have any money," Libby said to Magda.

"He have some, a little."

"How little?" Libby asked.

Magda smiled, but didn't reply.

"Maybe we can help you out," Bernie said, deciding to try a different tactic. "Maybe Libby and I can help you find a buyer for the teapot for ten percent—assuming, of course, that you have it."

"Twenty, Bernie," Libby said. "We'll do it for twenty percent."

Magda's eyes widened. "I thought you are finding out who killed Ludvoc for your friend."

279

Bernie gave a casual shrug. "I am. We are. But hey, this is America. Who's to say you can't make a couple of bucks in the process. Right?"

"Right," Magda said, lowering the gun for the third time. "You leave," she told Bernie. "You leave now."

Bernie and Libby both nodded.

"With pleasure," Libby said—and, boy, did she mean it.

This time the sisters left through the front door. As they were going out, they passed Magda's office. Bernie's eyes widened when she saw what was sitting on Magda's desk. Judging by it, she figured that the money left in Zalinsky's account wasn't so "little" after all.

Chapter 33

"Wow," Bernie said once they'd gotten outside. "That's certainly interesting."

"The gloves?" Libby asked, glancing at her sister after she'd scanned the sky. It had gotten cloudy and looked as if it was going to storm soon. Again. First, they'd had no rain, and now it was raining every day. It felt as if they were in the middle of monsoon season. Okay. Slight exaggeration.

"Those too, but I was referring to the Birkin," Bernie replied.

She took a deep breath, taking in the odors of grass and the tang of the Hudson River and thinking about how nice it was to be out of the suffocating heat of The Blue House. She didn't know how Magda stood it. The building had been constructed with air-conditioning in mind. Without it, there was no air movement at all.

Libby brushed a mosquito off her polo shirt. "The Birkin? What the hell is a Birkin?" she asked. "It sounds like a disease. You know, she came down with a bad case of Birkinitis."

Bernie rolled her eyes. Libby's lack of sartorial knowledge never failed to amaze her. "The handbag on Magda's desk."

281

"What about it?" Libby tried to remember it, but she couldn't.

Bernie redid her ponytail. "Only that they're impossible to get. Magda probably paid at least ten for it."

"Dollars?"

Bernie snorted. "Thousand."

Libby's eyes widened. She couldn't conceive of someone spending that kind of money on something like that. "You're kidding."

Bernie shook her head. "Not at all. And that's if she got it used. New they go for between fifteen and twenty-five. They're the holy grail of bags. Of course, she could have rented it."

"Rented?"

"Yeah, rented. As we know, you can rent pretty much anything these days," Bernie said, thinking of Zalinsky's car and the artwork in his house and office. "There are sites in Japan where you can rent a pet for a day."

Libby sniffed. "That's terrible."

"Agreed," Bernie answered.

Libby turned to her. "Do you think Magda was telling us the truth about where her newfound wealth came from?"

"I don't know," Bernie answered. "She could have pilfered from Zalinsky's account. Or she could have found and sold the teapot. She would know who to sell it to. After all, she had access to Zalinsky's correspondence."

Libby bit her lip.

"What are you thinking about?" Bernie asked as she cut across the lawn to get to the van. The long grass brushed against her calves as she walked. She gave a wide berth to a stinging nettle, one of several, that was in her path. A rumble of thunder sounded in the distance. A zigzag of lightning cleaved the sky to the east. A dark cloud hovered overhead. The storm was moving faster than Bernie thought it would.

"I'm thinking wc should go get some more coffee," Libby said. "We have about a two-day supply left."

"Yeah, we should," Bernie agreed. "We can do that on the way back." She could feel the temperature starting to drop and the wind pick up. A moment later she poked Libby in thc ribs.

"Hey," Libby cried. "That hurt."

Bernie pointed to the front of The Blue House. Magda was coming out and trotting to her car. Hcr hcad was down, and she was talking on her cell, looking neither to her left or her right.

"Now, there's someone in a hurry," Bernie observed. "I wonder who she's talking to."

"Maybe she just got a call from one of her kids," Libby hypothesized.

"Or maybe we spooked her," Bernie said.

"Maybe," Libby said.

"Maybe she's going to get the teapot or talk to the person who has it," Bernie posited.

283

"Let's assume that what you're saying is true—which I have my doubts about. Why wouldn't she just pick up the phone?" Libby asked her sister.

"Because some things are better to talk about in person."

"Who do you think she's going to talk to?" Libby asked.

"My money is on Jason. After all, we didn't see his hat there."

"Not that that means anything," Libby pointed out.

"No, it doesn't," Bernie told her. "Still, it would be interesting to see where Magda goes."

"Well, it wouldn't hurt," Libby agreed as she scratched her upper arm. It itched. Probably a bug bite, she decided, looking at the welt.

The sisters looked at each other and by common consent turned and hurried toward the van. By now Magda was at her vehicle and had the door of her car open. A moment later, Bernie and Libby reached their van. Magda still hadn't looked up as Bernie and Libby opened Mathilda's doors. They paused for a moment as the heat flowed out of the van.

"We should get one of those silvery things that you put on the windshield to stop the van from getting hot," Libby observed.

"Yes, we should," Bernie agreed. For some reason, they kept on talking about getting a sun visor, but they never did. By the time they got around to it, it would be fall.

Chapter 34

The van was still too hot when Libby and Bernie got in. Libby winced as the hot leather seat cover touched the back of her leg. "Damn," she said.

Bernie didn't say anything. She was focused on watching Magda. Magda closed her car door, started up her engine, and drove out of the parking lot. Bernie watched her take a left onto Clarke before following.

"She'll probably see us," Libby noted as they reached the main road. "It's not as if we're inconspicuous."

"If she does, she does," Bernie said, turning onto Clarke as well.

She followed, careful to keep a three-car-length distance between the van and Magda's car. As Bernie drove, she noticed that their van was pulling to the right. "I think we need to get the alignment checked," she told Libby.

"We did last month," Libby reminded her.

"Then they didn't do a very good job, because it's off again."

"Lovely," Libby said as she fanned herself with the edge of her hand. It might be cooling off outside, but it was still hot as hell in the van.

Magda made a sharp left onto Cliff Street, and

Bernie followed a moment later. "Well, she's not going home because this isn't the way to her house," Bernie remarked.

"Maybe she's got an appointment," Libby suggested.

"We'll see," Bernie said. "Doesn't Jason rent a place around here?"

Libby scratched at her bite again. "Yeah. I think he does."

Bernie grunted and concentrated on her driving. "You know," she said a moment later. "I think I can make a strong case for Magda killing Zalinsky."

"You can do that for everyone else as well," Libby replied.

"A stronger case then. Magda had access to his accounts. She was his personal assistant. She knew what he was doing. Maybe," Bernie hypothesized, "she was syphoning money off from his accounts and he caught her and threatened her."

"With what? Jail?"

"No," Bernie said. "You don't threaten someone with jail if you're running a scam. You threaten them with bodily harm . . . or you threaten their kids . . . if the money isn't put back."

"That would be a good motivator," Libby said. "Especially if he threatened her children. It would make me want to send him off to a better place."

Bernie slowed down slightly. She didn't want Magda to spot the van. "The teapot would be an added bonus for her."

"But when she goes to get it, it's not there," Libby said. "So she had to have seen Casper taking it."

"And maybe Jason did too." Bernie turned the wheel to keep the van from drifting to the right. "So they joined up. They probably looked through The Blue House, but it wasn't there, so they assumed it was in Casper's house."

"But it wasn't there either," Libby said.

"Because someone else had taken it," Bernie surmised. "But they didn't know that. They thought that if they came back and left a note, that would spook Casper into retrieving the teapot."

"Casper's house sounds like Grand Central Station," Libby reflected.

"Jason knows Adam Benson," Bernie said.

"And Adam strikes me as the kind of guy who wouldn't mind buying something like that under the radar," Libby observed.

"In fact," Bernie added, "it wouldn't surprise me if Jason knew a fair number of people in that category. After all, he used to move in those circles."

"He did, didn't he?" Libby said. She glanced up at the sky. It was getting darker outside; the wind was whipping the branches of the oak trees around and pressing down the stems of

287

the Queen Anne's lace and the loosestrife that grew in the ditch that ran parallel to the road. "Of course, Magda could have come into an inheritance. We don't know. This is all conjecture."

"She pretty much told us where she got her money," Bernie objected. "She told us she stole it from Zalinsky."

"She could have done both," Libby said.

"Indeed, she could have," Bernie agreed.

"I'd be tempted if I were her," Libby noted. "Very tempted." Then she pointed toward the sky. "It looks like it's going to rain," she observed, changing the subject.

"Storm," Bernie corrected. "It looks as if it's going to storm." She heard a buzz coming from her phone.

Libby reached over, got it, and read the text message. "It's a flood warning," she informed her sister.

"Terrific," Bernie said.

"Maybe we should go back," Libby suggested.

"We'll be fine," Bernie said automatically, her mind on the road in front of her. She was straining to see Magda's Hyundai, which had just gone around a curve. Cliff Road was a series of curves, but there were no cutoffs until Ashcroft Corners, so Bernie was fairly confident she didn't have to worry about losing Magda for another mile or so.

"What about the ditches?" Libby asked.

"What about them?" Bernie said.

"They're going to fill with water."

"We're almost at Ashcroft," Bernie told her sister, and then the heavens opened up. The rain came down in horizontal sheets. It thrummed on the roof and the windshield. The windshield wipers fought a losing battle with the rain, and the world vanished into a watery haze.

Bernie turned the wipers on as high they could go. It didn't help. She cursed under her breath as she leaned forward, trying to see the road ahead of her. But she couldn't. As she came around the curve, she spotted the taillights on Magda's car, two blurry red circles, but then they got farther and farther away until they were gone altogether. Now nothing was in front of them. There was nothing to navigate by. Bernie slowed down, and then she slowed down even more. The van was pulling more and more to the right, and she had to fight to keep it on the road.

"We should pull off to the side," Libby suggested.

"There is no side," Bernie answered without taking her eyes off the road.

"Can't we stop somewhere?" Libby asked.

"Like where?" Bernie demanded. The only place to pull off would be someone's driveway, and the stretch of road they were on now was all woods. "We can't stop in the middle of the road. Someone could smash into us. No. We have to keep going."

Libby didn't answer because she knew Bernie was correct.

"At least we're not on Forest," Bernie said, her voice lost in the roar of the storm. Forest was a dirt road, really little more than a country lane that became sludge when it rained. The county had been promising to pave it for the last ten years, and each year they'd pushed it down on their to-do list.

"If we weren't following Magda, we'd be home by now," Libby commented.

"But we are," Bernie replied. Then she didn't say anything else. She was too busy concentrating on keeping Mathilda on the road. It was getting harder and harder. Aside from not being able to see and the fact that the road was slippery, the car kept pulling to the right. Two minutes later, she said, "I think there's something wrong with Mathilda's right side."

"What?" Libby asked.

Bernie just grunted. She leaned forward, trying to see the curve in the road. She knew it was close by, but she didn't know how close. God, what she wouldn't give to have another vehicle in front of her. A moment later, the van lurched and leaned toward the right. Bernie wrestled with the steering wheel, but it was too late. The van began to slide. *This is like steering an elephant,* Bernie thought.

"Bernie," Libby screamed as the van began tipping, "do something!"

"I'm trying," Bernie yelled back as she turned into the slide. *We're going into the ditch,* Bernie realized, as the van tipped some more.

After what seemed like hours but was actually just a minute, Mathilda came to a shuddering stop. She was lying on her right side, half in and half out of the ditch. Bernie looked over. Libby was fumbling with her seat belt as water came bubbling up through the crack in the door.

Chapter 35

It was two hours after the accident, and Bernie and Libby were sitting in the waiting room of the Ogleebee Repair Shop, waiting for Mathilda to get a new tire. Bernie had called Sid Ogleebee immediately after she and Libby had climbed out of Mathilda's window. He'd raced over with his tow truck and found the two sopping-wet sisters huddled together by the side of the road next to the van. Miraculously, no one had been hurt. Well, maybe a little bruised, a little shaken, but that was the extent of the damage.

"Damn ditches," Sid had grumbled as he got ready to winch Mathilda out of the ditch. "Every time it rains, I get to pull someone out on this curve. It's a miracle no one's been killed yet."

"Tell me about it," Bernie was saying to Sid when Brandon arrived. She'd called him a few minutes after she'd called Sid.

He'd taken Bernie and Libby to their flat, where they'd changed into something dry, then dropped them off at Sid's repair shop on his way to work. Bernie had expected to have to explain to her dad what had happened—she had her story all ready—but she didn't have to tell him because he was out with Michelle, a fact that made her feel both relieved and sad at the same time.

Bernie was thinking about that and about how she and Libby weren't seeing much of their dad these days as she looked around the room they were sitting in. It was not a thing of beauty, but then neither was the garage it adjoined. The room looked to be about twelve feet by twelve feet, and that was a generous estimate. A layer of grime covered everything.

The counter was piled high with auto parts manuals, as were the shelves in back of the counter. There were two patched chairs to sit in as well as a hot plate sporting burnt coffee, a bowl full of stale powdered donuts, and a two-year-old, tattered copy of *People* magazine on a small side table. So much for the amenities. In better times, Libby and Bernie would never have touched the donuts or the coffee, but now they were glad to have them. Actually, they were ecstatic, neither one having realized until they started eating how hungry they were.

"We must be in shock," Libby told Bernie as Sid walked in the room, carrying one of Mathilda's tires in front of him.

"I don't believe it," Bernie said to Sid when she heard what he had to say.

Sid didn't reply. Instead he pointed to the gash in the deflated tire that had been the cause of the crash.

Libby brushed a scattering of powdered sugar off the front of her polo shirt, came over, and examined the gash Sid had indicated. "Maybe a nail did it."

"That would be a puncture," Sid said. He wiped his hands on a rag that he stuck back underneath the counter. He'd been a mechanic for twenty-five years and was pretty good at figuring out what was what. "You'd see a hole."

"A piece of glass?" Bernie hazarded. "That would make a cut, right?"

"Not that kind of cut," Sid informed her.

"Why not?" Bernie demanded.

"Because these sides are even," Sid explained with as much patience as he could muster. He was a taciturn man who preferred the company of cars to people, especially female people, most of whom made him nervous. "Someone slashed this tire with a knife." He pointed to the cut. Then he moved his fingers a little farther up to the second cut. "Twice. Trust me, this wasn't made by a piece of glass in the road."

Libby looked at where Sid was pointing, and then she looked at Sid's face and the one milky eye and the other one that worked. "There's no possibility you could be wrong, is there?" she asked.

Sid shook his head again. "None. I've been in this business a long time, and I know a knife cut when I see it."

"Could we have had a blowout?" Libby asked.

"You could have if you'd been going faster," Sid told her. "So in this case the rain was a good thing."

Libby swallowed. She felt slightly sick to her stomach thinking about what might have happened.

"I'm betting on Jason having done this," Bernie said. She didn't feel queasy, she just felt really, really angry.

"Possibly," Libby replied. She put her hands together and touched the tips of her fingers to her lips while she thought. "He had plenty of time when we were inside."

"Yes, he did," Bernie agreed. "And he was pissed at us."

"He wasn't that pissed," Libby objected. "Annoyed, yes. Furious, no."

Bernie put her hands on her hips. "Then who else could it be? Some random stranger?"

"Maybe. Or it could have been one of the Holloway brothers or Erin," Libby suggested.

Bernie snorted. "Because they were just passing by, saw Mathilda, and said, *Hey what the hell? Let's teach Bernie and Libby a lesson?*"

"It's possible," Libby insisted.

"So is New York City being swallowed by a tidal wave."

"It could happen," Libby countered. "Global warming."

"Well, there's only one way to find out," Bernie continued.

"About the tidal wave?"

"About Jason."

"A Ouija board?" Libby hazarded.

"I was thinking more of going the direct route and asking him."

"Oh goody!" Libby clapped her hands together. "What a super idea. I'm sure he'll say, *Yes. I did it. I cannot tell a lie.*"

"So what would you suggest?" Bernie asked.

"I'd suggest we let the police deal with this."

Bernie frowned. "How did I know you were going to say that?"

"Maybe because it's a good idea."

"I don't think so," Bernie said. "Now we have the element of surprise. Jason won't be expecting us. We might actually find something out."

"She's right," Sid put in.

Libby glared at him. "Thanks for your input."

"Well, Bernie *is* right," Sid said, choosing to overlook Libby's sarcasm. "Besides, the cops won't do anything. They never do."

Libby took a deep breath and let it out. Then she smiled. "Sid," she said, "have you forgotten that at the moment, we don't have a vehicle?"

"Not a problem. You can borrow my old junker," Sid told Libby.

Bernie grinned and thanked him.

"We can wait for Mathilda," Libby said.

Sid clasped his hands together and cracked his knuckles. Libby cringed at the sound.

"That's going to take a couple of hours. At the very least. I have to send out for tires."

"We don't want to wait," Bernie said before Libby could say anything.

Libby turned to Bernie. "Aside from everything else, we don't know where Jason is," she said.

"Nothing ventured, nothing gained," Sid chirped.

"I think I liked you better when you didn't say anything," Libby told him. Sid's face fell. Libby felt as if she'd shot a puppy. She immediately apologized. "It's the aftereffects of the accident," she explained.

"Maybe you have PTSD," Sid said in a worried voice.

"Yeah, that would be it," Bernie told Sid as she dragged Libby out the door.

"The keys to the Civic are in the ignition," Sid yelled after them.

The junker, a dented, rusted 1990 green Honda Civic, sat in the corner of the lot. The keys, as promised, were in the ignition. "So, are you coming, or do you want me to drop you off at the shop?" Bernie asked Libby as she got into the car.

"Coming, I suppose," Libby said with a notable lack of enthusiasm. Even though she really didn't want to, she was going along to make sure that

Bernie didn't get out of hand. Paying five hundred dollars for a new set of tires was bad enough. She didn't need to be laying out money for Bernie's bail as well.

The sisters spent the next hour and a half driving around Longely. They started out at Jason's apartment, but his car wasn't in the parking lot, and his roommate didn't know where he was or when he was likely to come home. Next they went to where Marvin had said he'd seen Jason working. His shift didn't start until eight that evening.

"We can always come back if we have to," Bernie said to Libby as they drove over to the apartment Magda was renting.

But Jason wasn't there. Neither was Magda, for that matter. Libby sighed.

Bernie glanced at her sister. "Don't say it," she told her.

Libby whipped her head around. She'd been staring at the scenery. "Say what?"

"What you were thinking."

"You don't know what I was thinking," Libby protested.

"Yeah, I do," Bernie told her. "You're thinking that this is turning out to be a waste of time."

"You said it, I didn't," Libby replied before she went back to looking out the window.

Bernie made a right at the corner of Ash and Dupont and started down Willow Street. Recess and The Waterhole, two bars Jason liked to frequent, were there, just two blocks apart. Unfortunately, Jason's vehicle wasn't in either of the establishments' parking lots.

Maybe Libby was correct; maybe this was going to be a waste of time, Bernie couldn't help thinking as she called Casper to see if he had any suggestions as to Jason's whereabouts. He didn't.

"Let's try the park," Bernie said to Libby after she'd hung up. "If he's not there, we'll go back to the garage."

"Works for me," Libby replied. She had been thinking about the list of things she and Bernie had to do.

Turned out that Jason wasn't in the park, or if he was, Bernie and Libby didn't see him among the crowd of dog walkers, joggers, and mothers with small children taking advantage of the sunshine.

"You win," Bernie said to Libby as she climbed back into the Civic's driver's seat.

For once, Libby had the grace to say nothing. Bernie started the Civic up and drove out of the park and onto Main Street. She had just turned the corner when Libby pointed to a man walking into the Best Serve Super Mart.

"I think that's Jason," she said.

Bernie jammed on her brakes and made a U-turn in the face of oncoming traffic. "Let's find out, shall we?" She drove into the strip mall and stopped in front of the store. Sid's junker made a clunking sound as she turned off the ignition.

"I hope that wasn't the bumper," Libby said as they got out. The bumper was tied on with rope.

"If it is, we'll just tie it back up," Bernie said. She looked around. Jason's Jeep Wrangler was sitting over to the left, next to the street light. "I do believe our guy is here," she said, gesturing to Jason's vehicle.

"It looks that way," Libby told her.

Bernie nodded and headed into the Best Serve Super Mart with Libby tagging along behind her. Bernie scanned the aisles. Jason wasn't in the bread or cereal aisle. He wasn't by the ice cream freezers or buying soup or cold cuts. Finally, she spotted him standing in front of the beer cooler to the far left. He was lost in thought, trying to decide which beer to buy. He'd just reached in and gotten a six-pack of Coors when Bernie sidled up to him.

Chapter 36

C oors," Bernie said. "That's like drinking warm piss. Surely you can come up with something better."

Jason turned to face her. "Well, hello to you too."

Bernie made a slight curtsey.

"I might have known you'd like the overpriced, overhyped yuppie beers."

"No. I just like things with a little bit of taste," Bernie told him.

Jason shifted his weight from his right to his left foot. Looking at him, Bernie had the same thought she'd had when she'd seen him earlier in the day. That he'd gained weight. That he looked bloated and unhealthy. "Boy," he told her, "I get to talk to you twice in one day. First you criticize my lunch choice, and now you don't like my beer. Jeez, how much can a man take?"

"I didn't realize you were such a sensitive flower," Bernie said.

"I am," he replied. "Can't you tell?"

"It's written all over you."

"So to what do I owe the pleasure?" Jason asked as he closed the cooler door.

"I guess this is just your lucky day," Bernie told him.

Jason laughed. "Well, I won't go that far."

"I would," Bernie said. "Just be happy we're not going to the police."

Jason looked puzzled. "Why would you do something like that?"

"Because of what you did," Bernie told him, figuring she might as well throw out a line and see what happened.

"Which was?" Jason asked her.

"You know," Bernie told him.

"Actually, I don't," Jason responded. He turned, reached back in the cooler and took out another six-pack. "Better to be on the safe side," he told Libby and Bernie, cradling the two six-packs in his arm as if they were babies.

The sisters ignored the comment. They stared at Jason, and he stared back. He didn't seem intimidated, Libby decided. But then why should he? It wasn't like they were two tough guys with guns. She wished they were. It would make things a lot easier.

Bernie took a step forward. "You know you're a lousy liar," she told him.

"That's what my ex told me when she caught me with my secretary," Jason replied. "So are you going to tell me what this is about or not? Because if you're not, I have things to do."

"We were nearly killed." Bernie poked him in the shoulder. "And it's your fault."

Jason took a step back. "Hey, don't touch me,

that's number one. And number two, tell me what you're talking about or get out of my face."

Libby stepped in between them. "My sister is talking about the fact that you slit one of the tires on our van and we crashed in the ditch."

"I'm sorry to hear that," Jason said, although he didn't look as if he was. "But why the hell do you think I did it?"

"Simple," Libby said. "Because it happened while we were at The Blue House and you were around."

"Just because I was there doesn't mean I did it," Jason objected.

"Au contraire, mon ami," Bernie told him. "The odds are great that you did."

Jason shook his head. "Give me a break. Anyone could have seen your van from the road. It was in the public parking lot, for friggin' sake. Why would I do something like that?"

"Exactly," Bernie said, going around Libby. "That's what we want to know. Aside from almost killing us, it's going to cost us five hundred dollars for a new set of tires. This does not make my sister or me happy. I'm thinking you should pay for the new tires."

Jason snorted. "Good luck with that. I don't have an extra five hundred, and even if I did, why would I pay you for something I didn't do? You've definitely gone over the edge."

"Have I?" Bernie said. "Well, let me tell you what I think happened."

Jason made a rude noise.

Bernie ignored him and kept talking. "I think you wanted to keep us from following you or Magda."

"And why would I care if you did or didn't?" Jason asked.

"Because either Magda was bringing you the teapot or you were bringing her the money from selling it."

Jason looked at Libby. "What is your sister smoking?" Then he turned back to Bernie before Libby could answer. "Okay. Here's the deal. Stay away from me with your crazy theories or else . . ."

"Or else what?" Bernie demanded.

"Or else I'll get a restraining order against you and your loony sister."

Bernie laughed.

"You think that's funny?" Jason asked.

"Yeah, I do," Bernie replied.

"Just tell us about the teapot and we'll leave you alone," Libby said in a reasonable tone of voice.

"And Zalinsky's gloves," Bernie added. "Did you take them?"

"I don't have the friggin' teapot," Jason yelled. "I don't know about the teapot. And I don't know anything about any goddamned gloves."

A lady who was reaching into the next cooler for a carton of Coke put the carton in her cart and hurriedly moved down the aisle away from them.

"Just tell us what you do know," Libby urged.

"Are you friggin' deaf? I already told you I don't have a clue. Talk to Erin," Jason screamed. "If you have questions about the teapot, talk to her, and leave me alone or so, help me God, I will get that restraining order."

"What's Erin going to tell us?" Libby couldn't help herself from asking.

"Do I look like a psychic to you?" Jason snapped as he pivoted and stalked off.

"Told you we were wasting our time," Libby said to Bernie as she watched Jason walk up to the cashier.

Bernie took a strand of hair that had come loose from her French knot and twirled it around one of her fingers. "I'm not so sure about that. I'm not so sure at all."

"Really. Then tell me what did we find out aside from the fact that Jason has bad taste in beer?" Libby challenged.

"We found out that Jason has a bad temper and poor impulse control."

"Aside from that," Libby asked.

"Not that much," Bernie admitted. "But that's enough."

Libby rubbed her forehead. She could feel

another headache coming on. It was the heat and this case that were doing it to her. "So do you still think Jason slit our tire?" she asked.

"Yeah, I do," Bernie replied. "Who else could it be?"

"Just about anyone, unfortunately," Libby replied.

Chapter 37

L ibby was quiet on the drive back to the garage. "What are you thinking about?" Bernie finally asked her after five minutes had gone by.

"I'm just thinking about the case and what we've found out so far," Libby told her.

"Me too," Bernie said. "In one sense we know a lot, and in another sense we know nothing."

Libby tapped her fingers on the Civic's dashboard. "That's true." She began to summarize. "We suspect that Zalinsky was running some sort of scam and that that scam was about to come crashing down, which is why he was getting ready to get out of Dodge."

Bernie picked up the narrative. "Which meant his income stream was drying up. Which is why Hsaio was about to get thrown out of her apartment and Zalinsky wasn't going to pay for Magda's children to go to college. And then," Bernie continued, "Zalinsky was throwing Erin out for a younger model, blackmailing Jason, who'd been sleeping with Erin, not to mention giving Casper a really hard time."

"And let's not forget George and Stan," Libby added. "Zalinsky bought their business and ruined it and them and their family."

"While forcing them to be in his play," Bernie said. "The coup de grâce."

"He was just an all-around nice guy," Libby observed.

"True. A real prince among men," Bernie said. "The question becomes: Who didn't want Zalinsky dead?"

"His creditors," Libby said. "If he died they couldn't get their money back."

"As opposed to the cast," Bernie observed. "He was worth more to them dead than alive."

"Which is why," Libby continued, "the person who took the teapot from Casper is probably the same person who killed Zalinsky."

Bernie stopped at the corner to let an old lady with a walker cross the street. "I'm thinking that's the case. The note on Casper's dining room table was angry, threatening."

Libby nodded. "Agreed."

"Ergo the writer was."

"Obviously," Libby said, thinking that a piece of cheese and a cucumber did not lunch make. Maybe she'd be less irritable if she had eaten more.

Bernie continued. "Which means that the person who wrote the note had expected to get the teapot, and he didn't. That's the reason he was angry. Why did he expect to get the teapot? Because he knew that Zalinsky was going to be dead, and the only way he'd know that is if he or she was the one who hotwired the teakettle. The only problem was that when he went to get the teapot the teapot wasn't there."

"Which leads us back to the same question again," Libby said as she bent over to refaste her sandal. "How did Zalinsky's killer know that it was Casper who took the teapot?"

Bernie slowed down again for a calico cat that looked as if it was going to run across the road. "I thought we agreed. He had to have seen him take it."

"Then why didn't he get the teapot back from Casper immediately?" Libby challenged.

Bernie sped up again as the cat changed its mind and scurried under a parked car instead. "Maybe he didn't want to confront Casper and risk being fingered; maybe he couldn't follow him and see where he left it—or he did, but by the time he got back there, Casper had already taken the teapot to his house."

Libby straightened up. "So then he goes to Casper's house to look for the teapot, only he can't find it, so he writes this note in essence telling Casper that he'd better get the teapot back or else."

"But why leave the tin of tea?" Bernie asked, thinking out loud. "There had to be a reason."

Libby shook her head. She didn't have a clue. "If the killer wrote the note, then who took the teapot from Casper?"

"I don't know," Bernie said. "But obviously the killer didn't know that someone had stolen the teapot from Casper."

"He wouldn't exactly broadcast that fact, would he?" Libby said

"Well, I certainly wouldn't," Bernie replied. "Poor Casper. He's certainly having a rough time."

"He is, isn't he?" Libby said. She took a drink of water from the bottle in the cup holder next to her and made a face. The water was warm. "I wonder what Dad would say about the tea."

Bernie shook her head. She couldn't even surmise.

"Too bad he's not around to ask," Libby observed tartly.

"Yes, it is," Bernie replied softly. For the last two weeks, Sean had been spending most of his free time with Michelle. "I miss our talks," Bernie said.

"Me too," Libby admitted. "A lot. It's not the same."

"No, it isn't," Bernie agreed.

The sisters were quiet for a moment.

"I'm still having trouble believing Casper took that teapot," Libby said, breaking the silence.

"I know. He's hardly a master criminal," Bernie replied.

"No. He's a klutz, and yet he managed to steal the damned thing," Libby said.

"I guess he got lucky," Bernie said.

"Not really," Libby said. "Not when you consider what happened afterward. He should have put it back," she added.

"Given everything that's happened, I bet he wishes he had. But once he had it, I think it would have been easier to hide it. Putting it back—now, that would have taken nerve. Would you have put it back?"

"Yes," Libby said.

"Seriously?"

Libby hedged. "I like to think I would."

"Me too," Bernie said, "but I'm not so sure I would have had the guts to do that." Bernie clicked her tongue against her teeth while she thought. "It could lead to all sorts of unpleasant consequences, especially with Zalinsky dead."

Libby took another sip of water. She needed some chocolate in the worst way. "Well, even without stealing the teapot, Casper is still their number-one suspect."

"True," Bernie said.

"Wait," Libby cried. "I know who did it. An alien."

Bernie laughed. "Now why didn't I think of that?" She furrowed her brow as another idea occurred to her. "You know," she said as she stopped for a red light, "maybe we should be talking to some of the galleries down in the city that specialize in Asian art and see if they've been offered the teapot for sale."

"It couldn't hurt," Libby said. "Maybe we'll actually turn something up."

"Maybe," Bernie said. "I guess we'll have to trot out our fancy clothes and pretend to be better off than we are."

"That's not going to take a lot," Libby replied. Then she added, "Maybe Hsaio can help us get a list together."

"Call her," Bernie suggested.

Libby did. Hsaio said she could and she would.

"Good," Libby said, settling back in her seat. A minute later, she reminded her sister that they needed to pick up some coffee on the way back to Sid's garage, after which she turned on the radio. Neither of the women spoke for the rest of the trip.

Chapter 38

M arvin gave Libby a baleful look. It was seven-thirty at night, and Libby, Bernie, and Marvin were standing in the rear of Marvin's dad's funeral home. The loading dock was empty, as were the parking spots in front. No one was there. Death, as Bernie had quipped when they'd pulled up, had taken a holiday. This, of course, was the reason Marvin had called.

"I shouldn't be doing this," Marvin said for the fourth time. He'd gotten a bad case of cold feet in the interval between his conversation with Libby and the sisters' arrival.

"Yeah, you should," Bernie told him.

"Easy for you to say," Marvin shot back. "You're not the one who's going to get in trouble."

Libby put her hand on Marvin's arm. He was wearing a short-sleeved, button-down shirt, and his skin was warm to her touch. "You're not doing anything wrong," Libby said. "And anyway, your dad isn't going to know. He's not here."

"He always knows," Marvin said gloomily.

"But you're helping to solve a crime," Bernie said, not bothering to argue Marvin's point.

"And you know what my dad's opinion of that is," Marvin retorted.

Bernie did know. He disapproved of her and

her sister's activities. He thought crime solving was better left to the police, an opinion he was not shy in sharing.

"Look," she said. "All we want to see are the gloves and shoes Zalinsky wore. It's not like we're asking to see his body."

"That's it?" Marvin asked.

"That's it," Libby said. "I already told you that."

Marvin remembered that that was true. He had a tendency to inflate things.

Libby raised her hand. "I swear. It'll just take a minute."

"Two at the most," Bernie said.

"Then we can get a beer at RJ's," Libby said. After the day's events, especially given what she'd found out when she picked up the coffee, she needed a drink.

"And you'll tell me what this is about?" Marvin asked.

"When we know for sure, you'll know," Libby assured him.

"Think of it this way," Bernie added. "The faster we solve this, the faster Casper will be out of your house."

Marvin grinned. As far as he was concerned, that couldn't be fast enough. Not only did Casper never shut up, he never picked up after himself. "You wanna come in, or do you want me to bring the stuff out?" he asked.

"Out," both Bernie and Libby said simultaneously. They both knew it was silly, but they didn't like to go in the back, where the bodies were kept.

Marvin shrugged. "Alrighty then. I'll be back in a few."

While Libby and Bernie waited for Marvin to reappear, they watched three seagulls fishing for food in the dumpster behind the funeral home.

"It always surprises me when I see them so far from the ocean," Bernie noted.

"We're not that far from the river," Libby reminded her. She heard a door open and turned around.

Marvin was coming out holding Zalinsky's gloves and shoes in his hands. He handed the gloves to Libby and the shoes to Bernie. "What are you looking for?" he asked.

They showed him.

"It's right there," Bernie said, pointing. "If you know where to look."

Marvin's eyes widened. He never would have thought of that.

A half hour later, Marvin, Bernie, and Libby were sitting at RJ's nursing beers, eating pretzels, and watching the Longely baseball team get drunk. There was a lot of arm wrestling and high fiving and trash talking going on. Evidently, they'd just won a game against the neighboring town— a rare occurrence.

"So," Brandon said to Bernie in a quiet moment, "you want to fill me in on how you came to this conclusion?"

Bernie ate a couple of pretzels and took a sip of her Blue Moon. In the summer, she liked wheat beer, with its golden color and its bubbles. "You sound as if you think I'm wrong."

"I didn't say that. I just want to know how you arrived at your conclusion," Brandon reiterated.

"Okay." Bernie took another sip of beer, then ate the orange slice and rested the rind on her napkin. "First there's the teakettle in Zalinsky's kitchen. It's the exact same electric kettle he used at the theater."

"So?" Brandon said. "Maybe, he liked the model."

"Maybe," Bernie replied. "But I'm almost positive there was something weird about the handle. Anyway, why would he have an electric teakettle when he didn't have any tea in the house?"

Brandon planted his elbows on the bar. "That's the basis you're using to say that Zalinsky substituted a hot-wired teakettle for the regular one himself?"

"It's the only thing that makes sense. I think that the police will find that he used the one in the kitchen to practice on."

"And why would he do something like that?" Brandon asked.

"To provide a distraction so an accomplice could steal the teapot."

Brandon shook his head. "I don't know about this."

Bernie leaned forward. "What about his gloves?"

"What about them?" Brandon asked.

"They had a rubberized lining in them. Why would he do that otherwise?"

Brandon had to admit he couldn't think of an answer. "So what you're saying," he said slowly, "is that his accomplice double-crossed him."

Bernie nodded her head vigorously. "Exactly. His accomplice hid the gloves he was supposed to wear and substituted another pair, a pair that had a cut in them. And then someone very carefully took off the soles of the shoes he was wearing, hollowed out the heels, and put pieces of wire in them."

Bernie took another sip of her beer. "The new gloves had a cut in the lining, so when Zalinsky grabbed the teakettle handle, the cut would open up and put him in contact with a live wire. And bingo. Zalinsky was gone."

"And the shoes?" Brandon asked.

"Insurance," Libby said.

Brandon crunched down on a pretzel. "What was Zalinsky going to do with the teapot?"

Bernie shrugged. "Sell it, I imagine, so he could get out of town for a while. Everything was about to be revealed."

"From what you said, he could have left without it," Marvin observed. "He had money. He had a passport."

"I'm guessing he couldn't resist one last scam," Libby said. "He was greedy—the kind of man who never has enough."

It was an assessment Brandon agreed with. "So who killed him?" he asked.

"I wish I knew," Libby said.

Chapter 39

I don't want to talk about it," Sean said, surveying the expression on the faces of his two daughters. "This has nothing to do with me."

"But Dad," Libby protested.

"You always make too much of things, Libby," Sean told her, cutting her off.

"No, I don't," Libby said. She took a deep breath, trying to calm herself down. It was nine at night, and she, her sister, and her dad were standing in the living room of their flat having a discussion.

"Why don't you ask Michelle?" Sean suggested, although on second thought he wasn't sure that was such a good idea either. "She's the one you should talk to. I'm sure she'll have a good explanation."

"For buying our brand of coffee and chocolate and sugar?" Libby demanded. "For asking what kind of flour we use in our brownies?"

Sean sighed a long, deep sigh and carefully lowered himself into his armchair. All he wanted was a little peace. The moment he was sitting, the cat jumped up onto his lap, circled three times, and plunked herself down. Sean automatically began to pet her, his fingers feeling the silky soft fur beneath them, reflecting as he did that it was hard to imagine life without her. Cindy purred contentedly. Let Michelle say what she would, Sean thought, this cat belonged inside.

"Surely, other people buy those things too," Sean told his eldest daughter—pleaded with her really.

"According to Mike, she asked him what brands we used."

Sean kept stroking the cat. "Didn't you tell me Mike liked to cause trouble?"

"That was me," Bernie informed him. "And that was when Mike told Libby and me that Conroy's was relabeling the butter he was selling."

"Which wasn't true, if I recall," Sean said. He relaxed a little and sat back in his chair, feeling he'd scored a point.

"But this is different," Libby informed him.

"How so?" Sean asked, not that he really wanted to know. "Maybe Mike is lying."

"Why would he?" Libby demanded. "He has nothing to gain."

"Maybe he's just one of those guys who likes to start trouble," Sean posited. He knew his hypothesis was lame, but it was the best he could come up with at the moment.

Libby made a can-you-be-serious gesture with her hands, then put them on her hips, always a bad sign. "That I doubt. Michelle just wants to copy our recipes."

"Now you're being paranoid," Sean told her.

"Really?" Libby began tapping her foot on the floor. "Then why did she name her shop after ours."

"The names are similar, Libby. They're not the same. And I already explained that was my fault. Michelle asked me if you'd mind, and I said you wouldn't. I should have been paying more attention," Sean added ruefully. "She'd change the name, but it's too late now. The sign has already been made. So if you want to blame anyone, blame me."

"Of course, I don't want to blame you," Libby said, but Sean looked at Libby and knew from the tightness in her jaw that she wasn't mollified.

He sighed again, a longer deeper sigh. He'd known this was going to be difficult; he just hadn't realized how difficult it was going to be. After all, Libby and Bernie weren't like this when he'd been seeing Inez. In fact, they'd been encouraging. Sean rubbed his chin with the thumb of his left hand. Could they feel this way because Michelle was so much younger? Was that it?

"Maybe," Sean suggested to Libby, "you should take Michelle choosing a similar name to your shop as a compliment."

"Maybe we should," Bernie said, trying to broker peace. Not that she didn't feel the same way that Libby did; she was just determined to take a different path. She believed that harping on Michelle would drive her dad further into Michelle's arms, so she ignored Libby's glare and changed the subject to something she knew her dad would like to discuss. "Do you mind if we talk about the case?" she asked him.

"By all means," a relieved Sean replied.

Libby didn't say anything. She grumped over to the sofa, sat herself down, and sulked. Bernie ignored her and started talking. She was in the middle of telling their dad about what had happened to their van and discussing why Jason might or might not have been the perpetrator when the downstairs door opened and Bernie heard the clop of heels coming up the stairs.

"I hope I didn't interrupt anything," Michelle trilled as she opened the door a second later and came inside the flat. She gestured with her chin to the white box she was carrying. "I just came by to drop off some sugar cookies."

"You're not interrupting anything at all," Bernie said sweetly. "We were just talking about the case."

"Oh yes, the case." Michelle gave a little laugh. "I understand you two are at a standstill."

Libby roused herself. "And who told you that?"

Michelle's smile got brighter. "Marvin."

"Where did you see him?" Libby asked, feeling something ugly begin to stir in her belly.

"Oh, he was buying a salad at Whole Foods. He's really quite delightful," Michelle said, giving Libby her full-on-charming smile. "You're lucky to have him."

"I know," Libby replied, forcing a smile, while what she really wanted to say was don't talk to him, don't look at him, don't even think about him. But she didn't. Even she knew her reaction was over the top.

Michelle waved in Sean's direction. "Well, don't let me stop you. I know Sean is anxious to hear the progress you're making—he told me so yesterday, didn't you, dear?" At which point she walked over, planted a kiss on the top of Sean's head, then put the box of cookies on the side table next to Sean's armchair. "A snack for later," she told him. "You two have been so busy," she explained to Bernie and Libby. "I know he misses seeing you and eating those special treats you make him. Not, of course, that I could take your place."

"That's not exactly what I said, Michelle," Sean informed her as she perched on the arm of the chair Sean was sitting on.

Michelle did a pretend pout. "You know you did, sweetie." She turned to Bernie and Libby. "Your dad is so adorable." Then before Libby or Bernie could say anything, Michelle added, "You're coming to my opening, right?"

"We wouldn't miss it for the world," Bernie

replied. "So sorry we have to go now," she added, grabbing Libby by the hand before her sister could say anything.

"Are you going detectiving?" Michelle asked.

"That's exactly what we're doing," Bernie said as she dragged Libby toward the door.

"Oh, that sounds so exciting," Michelle squealed. "Maybe you'll let me come with you sometime."

"We'd love to," Bernie said.

"It's funny how things work out," Michelle said to Bernie as Bernie was closing the door to the flat.

Something in Michelle's voice made Bernie open the door again.

"Meaning what?" Bernie asked, sticking her head into the room.

Michelle waved her hand in the air. "I feel bad."

"Bad about what?" Bernie asked.

Michelle contrived to look guilty, "All the problems you're having."

"How's that your fault?" Bernie asked in her nicest voice.

Michelle let out a nervous giggle. "Well, Ludvoc asked me if I wanted to cater his soirée, and I said no. Thank God. Otherwise, I would have been the person involved in the mess you're in."

Bernie and Libby both stepped back into the room.

"You never said you knew Zalinsky," Bernie said to Michelle.

"Oh dear," Michelle replied, contriving to show remorse. "I'm so sorry. I thought I did."

"No, you didn't," Bernie replied.

Michelle wrinkled her forehead. "Are you sure?"

"Of course, she's sure," Libby said. She was about to make an extremely unpleasant comment when Bernie laid a restraining hand on her arm, so she just scowled instead.

Michelle reacted by looking even more contrite.

Sean patted her knee. "I'm sure you didn't do it on purpose," he said to her.

Michelle sniffed and gave him a grateful smile. "Of course, I didn't. And I didn't know, know Ludvoc, if you know what I mean. I'd just talked to him a few times."

"Where?" Libby said sharply.

"At a couple of receptions at the Asia Institute."

"What were you doing there?" Libby demanded.

"It's not like I was born in a barn," Michelle snapped, her hurt feelings forgotten for the moment. "What do you think I was doing there?"

Bernie took a step toward Michelle. "That's not what my sister meant," she said in a soothing voice.

Michelle harrumphed, but Bernie noticed she had relaxed her shoulders, a sign that her level of hostility had gone down.

"I went to school with Lucy Chin. She's the curator there," Michelle explained when she saw the blank looks on Bernie and Libby's faces.

Bernie and Libby exchanged glances.

"Do you think she would talk to us?" Bernie inquired of Michelle, even though it killed Bernie to ask her father's girlfriend for a favor.

Michelle's smile returned, broader than ever. "I'm sure she would if I asked her to." She bent over and opened the box of cookies she'd brought, took two out, and offered one to Bernie and the other to Libby. "I'll be very interested to hear what you think of these," Michelle purred.

Libby smiled as she accepted one—even though she didn't want the cookie and she didn't want to smile. *She has us right where she wants us,* Libby thought as she took a bite. Then she got even unhappier because the ginger-flavored shortbread fan really was very good. Better than hers and Bernie's, in fact.

Chapter 40

As it turned out, Michelle proved to be as good as her word about arranging a meeting. A day later, Bernie and Libby found themselves in Lucy Chin's office at ten in the morning, drinking tea out of bone china cups and nibbling on whole wheat apricot biscuits. The Asia Institute didn't open until eleven on Thursdays, so the only sounds the sisters heard were the hum of the floor polisher on the hardwoods outside Lucy Chin's office, the rumble and honking of the traffic on Park Avenue, and the quiet comings and goings of guests in the upstairs bedrooms.

The building, a three-story, white limestone affair, had been built in the days of the robber barons, the days when families were large and the staffs that cared for them even larger. The mansion had belonged to one of New York's wealthier families; over the years, it had gone through various incarnations as a variety of embassies, libraries, and private clubs for alums of the Ivy League. Now, as the members-only Asia Institute, it was all plush carpeting, dark wooden floors, cream-colored plaster walls, high ceilings, and subdued lighting. The former ballroom had been turned into a library with floor-to-ceiling book-shelves, comfortable armchairs, and reading tables, while the dining room and the kitchen had been updated, and the garden had been filled with Japanese plantings.

The Institute sponsored art exhibitions, lectures, and trips to various overseas destinations, as well as providing a quiet place for its members should they wish to conduct business meetings there. The bedrooms on the second and third floors, eight of them, all with private bathrooms and canopied king-sized beds, could be reserved for visiting out-of-town guests and were frequently full during the holidays.

As Bernie admired the slender white vase filled with a few yellow blossoms on Lucy Chin's desk, she couldn't help thinking that Zalinsky must have felt out of place in the quiet, hushed atmosphere. He was too loud, too big, too boisterous. If Bernie felt ill at ease here, she couldn't imagine what Zalinsky had felt.

She wondered if his experiences here had been the impetus behind the building of The Blue House. She thought maybe they were, that he'd built the art center as an I'll-show-you kind of thing, a gauntlet flung down to the culturally elite.

"Nice flowers," Bernie said as she took a sip of her tea.

Lucy Chin smiled. "The color is pretty, don't you think?"

Bernie and Libby both nodded.

"What are they?" Bernie asked.

Lucy Chin shook her head. "I have no idea. The florist brings a new arrangement twice a week." She leaned forward. "Although he did warn me not to eat them or use them to make tea. He said they were quite toxic." She gave a little laugh. "Who would eat flowers?"

"Well, they did in the Middle Ages," Bernie said. "And some people still do. Like rose petals in a salad, for instance. Or nasturtiums."

"I much prefer looking at them," Lucy Chin replied. She re-crossed her legs. "So what do you think of the tea you're drinking?" she asked, changing the subject.

Bernie didn't think much of it, but she was hardly going to say that. "Interesting," she said instead. "I've never tasted anything like it."

"I'm not surprised," Lucy Chin said. "It's not to everyone's palate."

"It's"—Bernie searched for a neutral word to describe the taste—"earthy."

"What kind of tea is it?" Libby asked, wondering how much of it she had to drink to be polite.

"It's called pu-erh tea. It's from China's Yunnan province," Lucy Chin answered. "I get it from a purveyor out in Flushing. It has a multitude of health benefits."

"I've never heard of it," Libby said.

Lucy Chin nodded her head as if Libby's comment reconfirmed what she already knew.

"You're not alone. A lot of people haven't," Lucy Chin told her. "It's extremely rare and expensive because it's post-fermented."

"Post-fermented?" Libby repeated.

"The tea is fermented for varying amounts of time after the tea leaves have been fried and rolled. It's a very difficult, exacting process," Lucy Chin explained, seeing the puzzled look on Libby and Bernie's faces. "It takes years to master the technique."

"Is that like the yellow tea Zalinsky drank?" Bernie asked.

"Hardly." Lucy Chin frowned at Bernie's lack of knowledge. "You don't drink much tea, do you?"

"No, I don't," Bernie admitted, feeling as if she should.

"Well, *that* tea is in a completely different category." Lucy Chin raised her hand. "But enough about tea. We could spend all day talking about it. Michelle said you wanted to know about Ludvoc," she said, using Zalinsky's first name. She took a delicate nibble of her biscuit.

Looking at her, Bernie reflected that she was probably one of those ladies you see on Fifth Avenue sauntering along, looking cool and collected, never mind that it's a hundred degrees. Lucy Chin would look elegant wearing a potato sack, Bernie decided. Even though Bernie was wearing her Missoni and her Prada sandals and had felt good leaving her flat, she now felt dowdy and fat and sweaty.

Bernie stole a look at Libby. She didn't seem to care, but Bernie didn't want to think about the impression her sister, in her Bermuda shorts and polo shirt, was making on Lucy Chin.

Bernie nodded. "Did you know him well?"

"Really hardly at all," Lucy Chin said.

"Well, anything you can tell us would be appreciated," Libby told her.

"I'm afraid you've made the trip down from Longely for nothing then. I don't have much to say about him," Lucy Chin said, resting her biscuit on the edge of her saucer. "He was only here for the receptions, and our conversations were superficial at best. He and his girlfriend . . ."

Bernie leaned forward. "Girlfriend?" she asked.

Lucy Chin corrected herself. "Fiancée, I think. In any case, she was wearing a rather large engagement ring."

"Was her name Erin?" Bernie asked.

Lucy Chin shook her head. "I don't recall."

"Magda?" Libby queried.

"Sorry, that doesn't ring a bell."

Libby leaned forward too. "What did she look like?"

Lucy Chin thought. "I think maybe Russian. Good posture. Dark hair. Lots of jewelry. Lots of makeup. Expensive dress. Nothing out of the ordinary."

"Anything else?" Libby asked.

"Not really." Lucy Chin took another sip of her tea. "All these Russian women look the same to me. You know, I like to chat with everyone at our events," she added, "but since they are usually quite well attended, all I have a chance to do is say hello and move on."

"Did Zalinsky want to join the Asia Institute?" Libby asked.

Lucy Chin laughed at the absurdity of the idea. "That's not how we do things here. This is a private club. You can't join. You have to be sponsored and voted on by the members."

Libby smoothed down the collar of her polo shirt. Even though Bernie hadn't wanted her to wear what she was wearing, Libby was glad that she had. At least she was comfortable, which was more than she could say for her sister in her four-inch heels and tight silk sheath. Why Bernie had insisted on wearing something like that in the city when the temperature was supposed to top one hundred degrees was beyond Libby.

"And would anyone have sponsored him?" Libby asked, picking up on Lucy Chin's tone.

"Probably not," Lucy Chin said, dismissing the idea with a wave of her hand. "And even if someone did, Ludvoc probably wouldn't have gotten all the votes he needed. It has to be unanimous."

"And why do you think he wouldn't have been voted in?" Bernie asked.

Lucy Chin took another sip of her tea and put the cup down. "Because," she replied, "to put it bluntly, he wouldn't fit in here. Most of our members are on a certain economic and social level."

"And Zalinsky was a self-made man," Bernie observed.

Lucy Chin nodded. She fingered a strand of pearls around her neck.

"But he was interested in the arts," Libby pointed out.

"From what I could tell by the tenor of his conversations," Lucy Chin replied, "he was mostly interested in acquiring pieces of art," she made the word *acquiring* sound like a dirty word, "whereas our members are interested in deepening their knowledge and appreciation."

"Are you referring to Zalinsky acquiring the clay Yixing teapot?" Bernie asked.

Lucy Chin nodded. "Just so. Because he wanted to brew his tea in it, he was willing to pay an exorbitant amount of money."

"So then other members of the Asia Institute wouldn't want it?" Bernie asked.

"Of course they would," Lucy Chin answered. "It's a masterpiece."

"Then I don't see what the difference is," Libby said.

"What I mean," Lucy Chin said in a tone that made it clear that Libby's question was too obvious to merit a reply, but she was going to explain anyway because that's the type of person she was, "is that there are people who are collectors, and then there are people who just want stuff because it confers a level of respectability on them. No one who is a member here would have purchased that teapot and treated it the way Ludvoc did."

She sniffed. "Using something like that as a stage prop, in a production of *Alice in Wonderland*, no less. Ridiculous. Trying to garner publicity with it. Absolutely unacceptable." The corners of her mouth turned down. "No one who had any true feeling for the teapot would have done something like that." Lucy Chin's voice rose and wobbled with indignation. "No one."

"What would they have done?" Libby asked.

"Well," Lucy Chin replied, "I'll tell you what they wouldn't have done. They wouldn't have turned the teapot into a media circus, for one thing. They would have treated the teapot with the respect it merited. They wouldn't have bragged about how much money they'd spent on it so that that was the only thing people thought about when they saw it."

Lucy Chin took a deep breath and got hold of herself. Then she took another sip of her tea and put the cup down gently on the saucer, which was sitting on top of a black lacquered table, which Bernie assumed was hundreds of years old.

"He was one of those people," Lucy Chin declared, "who thinks that money can buy anything. But it can't. It can't buy taste or education or good character." She waved her hand around her office, gesturing to the scrolls on the walls and the glass case full of blue-and-white pottery. "I like to think that I and the members of the Asia Institute are custodians of these things. That we are people who will guard them, who will find a safe resting place for them so they may be enjoyed by the generations to come."

"And you don't think Zalinsky wanted that?" Bernie asked, thinking of the artwork she'd seen in his house.

Lucy Chin favored her with an amused glance. "Not at all. I think Zalinsky wanted to acquire art because it was what rich people do. I think Zalinsky was all ego. I think he fancied himself smarter than anyone else. You evidently knew him. Do you think I'm wrong?"

"No. I'd have to agree with your assessment," Bernie allowed, thinking back to the play.

There had been no detail that was too small for Zalinsky not to have meddled in it. The whole play, the whole art center was a tribute to his ego. Sometimes when egos clashed, people got upset. Very upset. So was Zalinsky's murder about colliding egos, or was it about money? Bernie still didn't know. As she pondered the questions, she took another sip of her tea. It might be rare, but she sure wasn't enamored of the taste. She guessed at heart she was a coffee person.

"Is Adam Benson a member here?" Bernie asked, the idea having suddenly occurred to her.

"Yes, he is," Lucy Chin replied. "Why are you asking?"

"No particular reason," Bernie answered. "We were in his office. He has some nice pieces on display."

"He's building a stunning collection," Lucy Chin agreed as she looked from one sister to another and back again. "I take it we're through here?" she said as she started to rise.

"Well," Bernie replied, "we wanted to know about Zalinsky, of course, but we'd also like to know about the teapot."

An annoyed expression crossed Lucy Chin's face, but she sat back down. "Ah yes," she said. She tapped her fingers on the glass. They were long and elegant and adorned with the perfect emerald and diamond ring—not too small and not too big. "The famous Yixing teapot." She paused and Bernie and Libby waited. "What about it?" she finally said.

"I guess we'd like to know," Libby said, "if you know of any people who would be interested in acquiring it."

Lucy Chin glanced at her cell phone and back at Libby and Bernie. "I heard it was stolen."

"You heard correctly," Libby replied.

Lucy Chin nodded. "What is your interest in finding it?"

"We think its disappearance might have something to do with Zalinsky's death."

"I see," Lucy Chin said. She took another nibble of her biscuit. "I assume we're talking about acquiring the teapot through nontraditional channels."

"That's one way of putting it," Bernie said.

Lucy Chin smiled a frosty smile. "I think I can say with one hundred percent confidence that our members would never have anything to do with that sort of thing."

"It must be nice to be so confident," Bernie said.

"Yes, it is," Lucy Chin said, choosing to take Bernie's comment at face value. She looked at her cell phone again.

"Is this a bad time?" Libby asked her.

Lucy Chin shook her head again. "Sorry," she said. "I was just thinking."

"About what?" Bernie asked.

"The teapot. Zalinsky," she said, then fell into another silence.

Bernie and Libby waited.

"Why do you think he paid so much?" Bernie asked.

"Because he wanted it," Lucy Chin said, "and he was a man who got what he wanted." But the expression on her face told Bernie that there might be more to the story than that.

"Any other reason?" Bernie asked quietly.

"One hears rumors," Lucy Chin replied.

"Like?" Libby said encouragingly.

"About Ludvoc," Lucy Chin said after another moment had gone by. "His honesty. Or lack thereof."

"I've heard those too," Bernie said. "But I don't see what that has to do with the teapot."

"If it were stolen," Lucy Chin said slowly, "you would get insurance money, and then if you were the one who was responsible for the theft, you could resell the teapot to a collector. Or even better, you could copy it and sell it to multiple collectors. They wouldn't know they'd bought a fake because they're doing something illegal and aren't apt to check. So you would get paid over and over again. Well worth the two-million-dollar investment."

Bernie leaned forward. That would explain Zalinsky's thinking. "Are you saying Zalinsky did that?"

"I'm not saying anything at all," Lucy Chin told her. "Some other people are, though."

"Would someone actually do something like that?" Bernie asked.

Lucy Chin laughed. "They most certainly would. We have our sharks in our world just like every-one else. Only they tend to be a little politer."

"Not necessarily," Libby said, thinking of how Zalinsky had ended up.

Lucy Chin got up. "And now I really must go," she said.

"Are you sure you don't remember what Zalinsky's fiancée looked like?" Bernie said as she rose.

"Positive," Lucy Chin answered. Libby and Bernie were halfway to the door when she called them back. "We take pictures of our events. If I have the chance, would you like me to go through them and see if I can find Zalinsky and the woman he was with?"

"That would be fantastic," Libby assured her. "Absolutely fantastic."

"And I think I can give you that list of people you were asking for before," Lucy Chin said.

As Bernie watched, Lucy Chin walked over to a desk that was butted up against the far wall, picked up a fountain pen, uncapped it, and began to write on a piece of thick, white stationery, the pen making a scratching sound as she wrote.

"Here," she said, straightening up. She handed the list to Bernie. "I hope this helps."

"Can I ask you why you've changed your mind?" Bernie inquired.

Lucy Chin smiled. "Because everything is about money these days, and I'm tired of it. Good luck." And with that she walked out into the hallway and held the door for Libby and Bernie.

Chapter 41

L ibby and Bernie walked out of the Asia Institute and into the muggy heat of a New York City summer. Their ears were assaulted by the sounds of taxis honking as the vehicles navigated the traffic on Park Avenue.

"So we were right about Zalinsky planning to steal the teapot," Bernie said as she watched people fanning themselves with magazines and newspapers as they walked along, trying to keep to the buildings' shadows. Even the impatiens planted in the medians on Park Avenue looked as if they were wilting in the heat.

"It makes sense," Libby agreed. "Not that that always means anything."

"True," Bernie said.

A nanny hurriedly pushed what Bernie knew to be a five-hundred-dollar stroller across the street. A small boy on a scooter wearing shorts and a T-shirt struggled to keep up with her. Clearly they were on their way to Central Park, as were the three British tourists next to them discussing whether they should go to the zoo or the lake. Then the light changed, and the cars started zooming by again in a scrum of traffic.

"I hope Lucy Chin finds those photos," Libby said. "I bet it's Erin."

"I bet it is too," Bernie agreed. "She certainly fits the description. Heaven only knows, if anyone had a reason to kill him, she did. I know I would want to if I was in her shoes."

Then Bernie leaned against the wall of the Asia Institute and unfolded the paper Lucy Chin had given her. The ink was a bright blue. The paper felt creamy in her hands. She studied the writing. It was beautiful. A lost art. They didn't even teach cursive in school anymore. A pity, she thought, as she studied the list of art dealers Lucy Chin had given her.

There were ten names on the list. Four of them were small galleries scattered on the Upper East Side, one was located on Columbus Avenue on the West Side of town, and the remaining five were in the West Village.

Bernie thought about the best way to approach them. She could only see one way, and she didn't think that Libby was going to be that enthusiastic when she told her. Oh well. Bernie sighed. It was going to be a long, hot day, and she was not in the mood. Especially because she was going to have to deal with Libby first—Libby, whose default position was always no.

"I don't want to go into Bloomingdale's," Libby whined.

Bernie and Libby were standing on the corner

of Fifty-Ninth Street and Lexington Avenue breathing in the exhaust fumes from the buses and cars driving by.

"There is no way people will believe you're in the market for the teapot looking the way you do," Bernie pointed out. She'd been saying the same thing to her sister for the last ten minutes and had gone from tactfully hinting to baldly stating.

"Rich WASPs would look the way I do," Libby told her.

"True," Bernie replied. "But you're not tall and blond and thin."

"You're saying I'm fat?" Libby asked.

"Don't start," Bernie warned.

Libby frowned. "Fine. We can call them."

"No, we can't," Bernie argued. "We want to see their faces so we can gauge their reactions. That's the whole point of the exercise."

"If you want to see their reactions, you go right ahead and see them. I'm going home," Libby told her sister, putting her hands on her hips. "If you ask me—which, by the way, you haven't—this is a stupid idea anyway. What are we going to do? March into these places and say—oh, hello, I'm looking for a stolen two-million-dollar clay Chinese teapot? Do you happen to know where I could find one?"

"That's not exactly what I had in mind," Bernie told her.

"Fine. Then what do you have in mind?" Libby challenged.

Bernie smiled what she hoped was a smug smile. "I'm hoping to spread the word that we're in the market for the teapot."

"And then?"

"If someone calls, we can work backward and find out who took it."

Libby took a couple of steps back so she and her sister were out of the pedestrian flow. She studied the store windows in front of her. They were featuring fall clothes already! How depressing. Where had the summer gone?

"And once more I ask," she said to Bernie, "why should they tell us anything?"

"For the money," Bernie said. "They'll want the money."

"So this is essentially a sting operation?"

"Yeah, Libby. You can call it that."

Libby, however, noticed the defensive tone in her sister's voice and decided to push things a little further. "What are you going to tell them when we meet them?" she asked, then added, "Exactly."

Bernie made a dismissive motion with her hand. "Don't worry."

"I'm not worried," Libby retorted. "I'm just asking."

Bernie would have answered her sister's question if she'd known exactly what she *was* going to say. But she didn't. However, she was confident she'd come up with something once they got to where they were going. She found she did best when she was improvising.

Instead she put her hand over her heart and said, "I'm deeply, deeply wounded and insulted by your lack of trust."

"Ah hah," Libby cried, jabbing her finger toward her sister and feeling vindicated. "Just as I suspected. You have no idea what you're going to say once we get into those places, do you? *If* we get into those places," she added.

"Of course, we'll get in. They're public places. And I will have an idea by the time we get there," Bernie promised. "When have you ever known me not to come up with something?"

Libby snorted. "It's the something that worries me."

"It's air-conditioned in Bloomie's," Bernie cooed, trying another approach.

Libby reached up and wiped a drop of sweat out of her eye. All she wanted to do was go home, jump into a cool shower, and have a large iced coffee. "I don't care." She moved to let a woman carrying a parasol go by.

"You need a new dress anyway," Bernie told Libby.

"I can buy it online," Libby snapped.

"We can get some of the chocolates you like," Bernie murmured in her most seductive voice.

344

"No," Libby said again. But Bernie could tell from the slight hesitation in her voice that her sister's resolve was weakening.

Bernie smiled and widened her eyes. "We can get an iced coffee. That'll help get the taste of Lucy Chin's tea out of our mouths."

"It was pretty bad," Libby admitted. "The biscuits weren't too great either."

"No, they weren't," Bernie allowed. "You know," she began, "we'll just have to come back down here again to do this if we don't do it today. And we don't really have the time. For one thing, we have the Kings' party coming up, and then there are the four bar mitzvahs."

Libby thought about everything she and Bernie had to do in the coming weeks and caved. "Alright," she said. "But let's make this fast."

"We will," Bernie promised.

"And I don't want to spend a lot of money either."

"We won't," Bernie swore.

Libby stared into her sister's eyes. "I mean it."

"Me too," Bernie replied, although clothes that she considered cheap Libby considered prohibitively expensive.

A half hour later, the sisters left Bloomie's with Libby sporting a black linen mid-thigh shift that Bernie had found on the sale rack at seventy percent off, a pair of gold sandals, a small gold clutch, and a new pair of sunglasses, while Bernie had scored a five-ply black cashmere sweater, a pair of red-rimmed leopard-print ballet flats, and a Burberry scarf.

"We did good," Bernie said, indicating the shopping bags she and Libby were carrying.

"I feel ridiculous," Libby groused to her sister while Bernie stepped out into the street to hail a cab.

"You look great," Bernie assured her before she put her fingers in her mouth and let out a loud whistle. A cab stopped, and the sisters hopped in. "Stop fidgeting," Bernie told Libby after she'd given the cabby the address of the first place on the list.

Libby gave her skirt another tug anyway. It was way too short, in her opinion. Way, way too short.

Chapter 42

Aston's, the first stop on Bernie and Libby's list, was located on Madison Avenue two blocks down from the Carlyle Hotel. Everything about the place screamed money, from the window display of old Greek and Roman coins, to the Roman torsos on pedestals dotted around the floor, to the muted lighting, cream-colored walls, and thick, light-gray carpeting.

But then, given the neighborhood, what else would it be, Bernie thought, as she gazed at the man sitting behind a desk, a desk Bernie was sure was extremely valuable. The man was slender and tanned, the kind of tan you get at the Hamptons, not at your local tanning salon. He had a full head of carefully barbered silver hair and bright-blue eyes. In spite of the heat, he was wearing a light-gray suit, a periwinkle shirt with French cuffs and gold cuff links, and a dark-navy Italian silk tie. He looked comfortable, and in charge.

"Can I help you?" he asked, looking up from his phone.

"Perhaps," Bernie replied. She took a couple of steps toward him, took a couple of deep breaths, mentally crossed her fingers, and began her spiel. "I'm really embarrassed," she said, "to ask this, but I don't know who else to turn to, and Lucy Chin from the Asia Institute told me you might be able to help me and my sister." Bernie stopped talking and indicated Libby, who was standing slightly behind her. "You are Mr. Aston, aren't you?"

The man sat up straighter and folded his hands on the desk. His fingers, Bernie noted, were long and slim, the nails carefully cut. "Indeed I am," he said, nodding his head slightly.

Bernie smiled her best smile and approached the desk. "This is just so embarrassing, Mr. Aston."

He leaned forward. "Wycliff. Call me Wycliff. Now suppose you tell me what this problem of yours is."

So Bernie did. She gestured toward Libby. "You might have heard about Ludvoc Zalinsky's death."

Wycliff shook his head. "Horrible. Simply horrible. Such a loss. A brilliant collector. So young too."

Bernie couldn't tell whether Wycliff Aston was being sarcastic, so she opted for neutral. "So I was told," she said. "I'm sure you heard about the teapot he purchased from Sotheby's."

Wycliff nodded his head graciously. "I have indeed. I was at the auction when he bought it. Excuse me, his representative did. Everyone wondered who the purchaser was, considering the price that was paid. The purchase made quite the stir."

"You think Zalinsky paid too much for it?" Bernie asked, genuinely curious.

Wycliff shrugged. "Not if he wanted it badly enough. Over the years, I've found that price is set by desire, not by intrinsic worth. If I had to guess, I would say that Zalinsky was satisfied with his purchase. From what I'm told, he certainly could afford it."

"So you think the teapot was real?" Libby asked, introducing a new wrinkle into the conversation.

"Well, given the price, I certainly hope it was. I haven't heard anything to the contrary. Is that what this is about?"

Bernie took another step forward. "It could be. From our point of view, it would be nice if it was a copy."

"Really?" Wycliff leaned forward. Bernie could tell she had him hooked as he cocked his head and waited for the explanation.

"Here's the thing," Bernie said, approaching Wycliff. She placed her hands on his desk, leaned over, and lowered her voice to a whisper. "My sister gave the teapot away to a friend," she said, counting on the gallery owner not having heard about Casper and the teapot. "She didn't know what it was."

"Oh dear," Wycliff said gravely. "That *was* a major error." If he thought Bernie was lying, he didn't show it. "So why doesn't your sister ask her friend to return it?" he asked.

"She has. I have. Unfortunately, her friend has a stand at the Thursday evening flea market at the Longely train station. She sold it. For cash. To someone in the antiquities business. And no, she doesn't know to whom. We've already asked."

"Nice find for that someone," Wycliff remarked dryly.

"Isn't it, though?" Bernie said. "Unfortunately, the executors of Zalinsky's estate want the teapot back. They're being quite strident about it."

"I imagine they would be," Wycliff said. "I can see your problem. What I'm unclear about is where I come into this fiasco."

"We would like you to put the word out that we'd like to buy it back," Bernie said.

"How do you know it's not sitting in someone's kitchen being used to brew Lipton's tea at this very moment?" Wycliff asked.

"We don't," Libby answered. "We're just hoping that's not the case."

"I bet you do," Wycliff said. He leaned back in his chair and looked Bernie up and down. "How much are you willing to pay?"

"As much as we have to," Bernie quickly responded.

"Really?" Wycliff said. "If you'll pardon me for saying so, you don't look like someone who has access to that kind of money."

"We have access," Bernie told him. "And naturally, there will be a finder's fee."

"Naturally," Wycliff said gravely. He leaned further back in his chair, clasped his hands together, turned them inside out, and stretched. "I'll see what I can do," he said after a minute had gone by. "But I'm not too optimistic."

Bernie smiled again. "That's all I ask."

"Do you think he knows anything?" Libby asked Bernie when they were back out on Madison Avenue.

Bernie shook her head. "But maybe he knows someone who does."

"Personally, I still think this is a waste of time."

"You may be right," Bernie admitted, "but this way we close off some of the loopholes. And you have a new dress."

Libby couldn't say anything because it was true, not that she had wanted a new dress. But she did need one. Even she couldn't argue about that. The sisters spent the rest of the day imparting their message to the people on Lucy Chin's list. Midway through, Bernie decided that Libby might have been correct after all and they'd embarked on a fool's errand. But then they got to the next-to-last person and heard something interesting.

Michael Cotton dealt antiquities out of the first two rooms of his ground-floor apartment on Jane Street. Bernie had always loved the West

Village, fantasizing at sixteen that she would buy a brownstone when she got older and live in it. She felt that dream come alive again as she looked around Michael Cotton's shop. The place called to her. It seemed like the kind of place that would welcome you home at night, a place that would be cool in the summer and warm in the winter.

"If it were me," Michael Cotton said, handing them two large glasses of water that he'd gotten from the kitchen, "I wouldn't be drinking out of that teapot. That's all I'm sayin'," he told Libby and Bernie when they told him what they wanted. Then he told them why he'd said that. "I'm not saying it's true, but why take chances?" He pursed his lips. "On the other hand, it could be a complete fabrication. People love to make up stories on the basis of no facts at all."

"Where'd you hear this?" Bernie asked as she took a drink of the water he'd offered them. It tasted delicious. She hadn't realized how thirsty she was until then.

Michael Cotton shrugged. "At a party in Dumbo."

"Do you think we could talk to the people you heard it from?" Libby asked.

Michael Cotton laughed. "I don't remember their names, if I ever knew them. Too much booze. It was that kind of party."

"Thanks anyway," Bernie told him as she finished her water.

She kept thinking about what Michael Cotton had told them as she and Libby caught the 6:15 Metro-North train to Longely out of Penn Station.

They were in the tunnels underneath Penn Station when Libby turned to Bernie. "Cotton's story. Do you believe it?"

Bernie bit her lip. "It seems far-fetched."

"Yes, it does," Libby agreed. "But why would someone make something like that up?" she asked.

"I think because it's exciting. If you have insider information"—here Bernie made air quotes with her fingers—"it puts you at the center of attention."

The sisters were silent for a moment, then Libby said, "That story you told everyone about the teapot."

"What about it?" Bernie asked.

"It has more holes than a wedge of Swiss cheese."

"It doesn't matter," Bernie replied.

"How so?" Libby asked as the train began to move again.

"Because greed always wins."

"You don't really believe that, do you, Bernie?" Libby asked.

"Yeah, Libby. With a few exceptions I kinda do," Bernie replied.

Chapter 43

Sean sat in his armchair petting Cindy and intently listening to his daughters' theory of how Zalinsky was killed. "That could work," he said when Bernie and Libby were done. He chuckled. "Talk about being hoisted on your own petard."

"What is a petard anyway?" Libby asked.

"A petard is a small bomb," Sean explained. "Being hoisted by your own petard literally means being blown up by your own bomb."

"He was double-crossed," Bernie said.

"I said literally. The expression is a metaphor," Sean told her.

"Sorry. It's been a long day," Bernie explained, running her fingers through her hair. It needed a wash, but she was too tired to do it tonight. Maybe in the morning.

"Evidently. How did the day go?"

Libby and Bernie told him. They saved what Cotton had said for last.

"Humph," Sean said. "Interesting story."

"Isn't it, though?" Libby observed.

"Yeah. Why kill Zalinsky twice?" Bernie asked. "That makes no sense."

Sean shrugged. "Maybe because whoever was

doing it wanted to make sure that Zalinsky was really dead. Maybe he or she was afraid that the hot-wired teakettle wouldn't be enough. That the gloves wouldn't work."

"There could have been two people," Libby suggested.

Sean raised an eyebrow. "Neither one knowing what the other one was doing? Seems unlikely."

"Maybe they were working in concert," Bernie suggested.

"They probably were. Or," Sean said, "Cotton could be wrong. It could be a baseless rumor. Heard lots of those in my time."

"I know," Libby said. She and Bernie had heard her dad's stories.

It was nine o'clock at night, and it was just Libby, Bernie, Sean, and the cat in the flat, a rare event these days. They were sharing a late supper of old-fashioned beet borscht, a simple green salad dressed with lemon juice and olive oil from California, a store-baked baguette with butter from a nearby farm, and a dessert of local peaches, a simple but satisfying meal, as they watched lightning arc across the night sky.

There'd been flash flood alerts on the TV and on Libby and Bernie's cell phones again. Even if there hadn't been, they could feel yet another storm coming. The humidity was dropping, and the wind was picking up. The curtains

355

billowed, and both open windows began to bang against the sills.

"Double death," Bernie murmured as she got up to shut them.

Sean laughed. "Sounds like the title of a dime novel."

"It does, doesn't it?" Bernie agreed. "Only now that novel probably costs eight bucks."

"Or more," Sean said.

"But it is suggestive," Libby observed.

"It certainly is," Bernie agreed. "If it's true."

"There is that. Even if it is true, I don't think there's any way to prove it," Sean said after he'd eaten a little more borscht. "I'm not sure that a tox screen would work. Zalinsky is embalmed."

"Surely they . . ."

"By 'they' you mean Lucy?" Sean asked.

Bernie nodded. "He could do something if he wanted to," Bernie said. "There have to be ways to test for poisons even at this late date."

"I'm sure there are," Sean told her. "But . . ."

"But what?" Libby asked, interrupting.

"I think 'if they wanted to' is the operative phrase here," Sean said, finishing his sentence. "Lucy has one homicide method. He doesn't need two. That would just complicate things for him. Makes it harder to prosecute. Especially poisons. They're slippery buggers. Anyway, the lab is probably backed up. It usually is." Sean patted his stomach. He was getting full. "On the bright side, you girls have come up with a working theory. So that's good."

"True. But we still don't know who double-crossed Zalinsky," Bernie pointed out.

"You're closing in, though," Sean said, cheer-leading.

"Not fast enough," Bernie noted.

Libby put a spoonful of sour cream on top of her borscht and stirred. She watched the white cream swirl into the ruby-red borscht, turning it a pretty pink. "I assume Lucy still likes Casper for this?"

Sean cleared his throat. "You said it. I didn't."

Bernie groaned. "I bet he's not looking at anyone else."

"You know he's not," Sean said. "Once Lucy gets someone in his sights, that's it! Just pure laziness, if you ask me." He sat back and crossed his arms over his chest. "You know what I think," he said.

"What?" Bernie asked.

"I think you need to forget about the teapot for the moment."

"But you said to concentrate on it," Libby cried.

"I did, and doing that provided one part of the equation," Sean replied. "But I don't think it's going to provide the second part, the who-done-it part of the equation."

"Why?" Bernie asked her dad as she took a bite

of bread. She decided it had integrity. The bread's crust had a satisfying crunch to it beneath her teeth, not like some of that stuff you found at the supermarkets these days.

Sean took a breath. "Because no matter how much I try, I don't see the teapot as the primary motive for the murder. At least in this case."

Libby smiled a cat-ate-the-canary smile. Bernie glared at her.

"Don't say it," she warned her sister.

"Don't say what?" Libby asked, all pretend innocence.

"What you were going to say."

"I wasn't going to say anything," Libby protested.

Sean smiled. God help him, but he liked hearing his daughters bicker. He hadn't realized how much he'd missed it.

Bernie turned back toward her father. "Explain," she said.

"Happy to," Sean replied.

He'd been doing a lot of thinking about the Zalinsky case one way or another while Michelle had been dragging him around to this and that store. He had been beginning to feel like a piece of flotsam bobbing around in the water, and he'd found that thinking about the case helped him pass the time and prevented him from yelling something not nice while Michelle argued with the contractors or debated whether she

358

wanted the walls of her shop painted eggshell or cream or maybe robin's-egg blue. Like he cared.

Sean ate a little more borscht. He'd forgotten how good it was—sweet and smooth, with just a little bite from the black pepper Bernie had put in—and began. "Like I said, I think that Zalinsky was killed for more personal reasons. I don't think that the motivation for the crime was the stealing of the teapot. I think stealing the teapot was a secondary benefit. The primary crime was killing Zalinsky. Whoever did this really hated Zalinsky's guts and wanted to make sure he was very, very dead."

"Yeah, he wasn't big on making friends and influencing people," Bernie observed. "He was a con man, pure and simple. That even comes down to the bodyguards he hired to guard the teapot. They looked like the real deal, but they weren't. They were actors decked out with pretend vests and toy guns! I think he prided himself on pulling the wool over people's eyes and making fools out of them."

"Which tends to spark an intense desire for revenge in the taken," Sean said.

"Everything he did was for show," Libby added.

"Well, the gun in his go bag and the one at The Blue House weren't for show," Bernie said. "Those were real."

"They certainly were," Libby replied, thinking back to Magda and the pistol.

Bernie broke off another piece of bread from the loaf on the coffee table and began to butter it. If she weren't careful she'd end up eating the whole loaf. Not a good thing since her pants were getting tight, and she was damned if she was going to buy another pair.

"There's too much stuff going on here," Sean noted after he'd put a dab of sour cream on his finger and extended it to the cat, who licked it off.

Bernie looked at him. "What do you mean?"

"Exactly what I said," Sean replied. "This crime is like a big ball of knotted yarn. In order to solve it you're going to have to separate the threads."

"And how do you propose we do that?" Libby asked.

Sean speared a piece of lettuce with his fork and ate it. He'd never liked salads until he'd gotten married and his wife had shown him how good a salad could be if you treated it with respect, and his girls had carried on the tradition. He started talking. "Slowly. Patiently," he said. "When you have this kind of problem, you have to follow the yarn until you can't go any farther, and then you pick another piece and start unraveling that. Eventually you unravel all the knots."

"Very poetic," Libby said. She started eating her salad too. It was carefully composed of butter lettuce, sorrel, arugula, and red leaf lettuce, and dressed with fresh lemon juice and olive oil, with just a sprinkling of Maldon sea salt and pepper. It was excellent, if she had to say so herself. "So what end do you suggest we start with?" she asked.

Sean told them.

Bernie's eyes widened. "I don't believe you," she cried.

"Ask him," Sean suggested. "It's the only thing that makes sense."

"Not to me," Bernie protested.

"Think about it," Sean urged.

"And the note? Did he do that too?" Bernie demanded.

"If my hypothesis is right, then yes, he did."

"You're nuts," Bernie told him.

Sean shrugged. "Of course, I could be wrong."

"You probably are," Bernie said. "About everything."

"There's only one way to find out," Sean told her. "Talk to him."

"Fine," Bernie said as she jumped out of her chair. "I will."

"I didn't mean right now," Sean told her.

Bernie didn't answer. She just grabbed the keys to the van and headed out the door.

"Libby, go with her," Sean urged.

Libby sighed. This was not what she was planning on, but she tore off a piece of bread from the baguette and hurried out the door. Meanwhile, Sean sat back in his seat and reached for the remote. He might as well get some TV in while he could, because when Bernie came back through the door he was going to have to do a lot of handholding, metaphorically speaking. As he turned the TV back on, Cindy stood up, circled three times on Sean's lap, and plopped herself back down. Sean was wondering why she did that as his show came on.

Chapter 44

Bernie banged on Marvin's front door as a clap of thunder let loose. The storm was moving closer. When Marvin didn't answer, she banged on the door again.

"Give Marvin a moment," Libby said. "He's probably in bed."

Bernie lowered her hand and waited, tapping her fingers on her thighs, while tree branches rustled around her.

Marvin's voice floated through the door a minute later. "Who is it?" he asked.

"It's me," Bernie told him. "Let me in."

"What's the matter?" Marvin cried as he opened the door. "Is everything okay?" He was in his pajamas and, as Libby had predicted, had been in bed.

"No, it's not okay," Bernie answered. "Far from it." She stepped inside Marvin's house. "Where's Casper?" she demanded, ignoring Petunia, who was butting Bernie's thigh with her snout.

"In his bedroom," Marvin answered. "Why?"

"I have something to ask him," Bernie replied, pushing past Marvin.

Marvin turned to Libby, who had bent down to pet Petunia. "What's this about?"

"That stupid teapot," Libby answered while she scratched Petunia under her chin.

"Couldn't it wait till tomorrow?" Marvin asked her. "I have to be up early. We have a delivery."

"I know. I'm sorry to barge in like this," Libby said. "My sister is . . . a tad upset."

Marvin rubbed a mosquito bite on his arm. "About what?"

Libby explained as she walked into the living room and sat down on the sofa. She could hear Bernie through the door of Casper's room. "Well, did you or didn't you?" Bernie was demanding. "I need you to answer me now." Libby couldn't hear Casper's reply, but it must have been in the affirmative because the next thing Libby heard was, "So you lied to me again." Then she heard, "Why? I want to know why?"

A minute later, Bernie came out of Casper's room and stormed through the living room without looking at Marvin or Libby, much less saying anything.

Libby jumped up. "Gotta go," she told Marvin. "I'll call you later." She followed Bernie out the door. Her sister didn't say anything on the ride back to their flat, and Libby didn't ask her for an explanation. When they got to the flat, Bernie slammed on the brakes, and Libby was glad she had her seat belt on because otherwise she would have hit the dashboard. By the time Libby had her seat belt off, Bernie was out of the van and pounding up the stairs.

Sean looked at his youngest daughter when she came barreling in and turned off the TV.

"Casper should have told me," she said.

"He was probably scared to," Sean answered. Then he said, "Fool me once, shame on you. Fool me twice shame on me."

Bernie bit her lip. "I guess I deserve that."

"You do, but it's a hard lesson to learn."

A moment later, Libby came up the stairs. Five minutes after that, Casper did the same. He was still in his pajamas, looking disheveled and gaunt. "I'm sorry," he said to Bernie. He was holding a cardboard box in his hands. "I'm really sorry." He went over to Bernie and gently placed the box in her hands.

"Is this what I think it is?" Bernie asked him.

Casper nodded.

"Why don't you sit down?" Sean told Casper while Bernie opened the box. "Do you want something to drink?"

Casper shook his head. He was feeling queasy.

"Eat?"

Casper shook his head again.

"You want some peach pie," Sean declared. "We all want some of Bernie and Libby's peach pie." When Casper didn't answer, Sean said, "I'll take your silence as a yes."

Libby got up and went downstairs to do the

honors. By the time she came back up, Bernie had the teapot out of the cardboard box and carefully placed on the mantel.

"It doesn't look like it would be worth that much," Libby said about the teapot as she set a tray loaded down with peach pie, plates, forks, spoons, and homemade vanilla ice cream on the coffee table.

"It doesn't, does it?" Casper said in a low voice.

Libby dished out the pie and the ice cream, and for a moment no one spoke. They were too busy eating.

"This is really wonderful," Casper said when he was halfway done. Surprisingly, he was feeling a little better.

"Have some more," Sean directed, leaning over, cutting another slice, and plopping it on Casper's plate. "You look as if you could use it."

"Why?" Bernie asked when Casper was finally done eating.

Casper bit his lip and looked down at his plate. "I have all these bills. I thought I could sell it. I told you. But I couldn't. I didn't know what to do with it."

"I get taking it the first time, but the second . . . the whole note and teapot thing . . . ," Bernie said. "Why?"

Casper pressed his lips together and shook his head. "I never should have done it," he said. He didn't have the energy to lie anymore. "I've never done anything like this before."

"And it shows," Sean said. He'd heard all he needed to hear.

"Dad!" Bernie cried.

Sean turned to her. "Well, it's true." Then Sean finished the last of his pie, sat back in his chair, and waited for Casper to speak. When he didn't, Sean put his hands on his thighs and leaned forward. There was a clap of thunder signaling the arrival of the storm. "Do you want to tell Bernie and Libby why you did what you did, or should I?" Sean asked Casper.

"I meant well," Casper said.

"Did you?" Sean asked.

"Yes, I did," Casper told him.

"Do you want to hear what I think happened?" Sean asked. Then he went ahead before Casper said anything. "This is what I think occurred," he told him. "First, of course, you stole the teapot. That was a crime of opportunity. You didn't think it through. You thought you'd be able to sell it quickly. But you couldn't.

"So you had this thing lying around, and I think you were getting nervous that Zalinsky's killer and possibly my daughters were going to figure out that you were the one who stole the teapot, so you decided to stage a diversion, a diversion that would hopefully send everyone off in a different direction. Moving out of your house made everything seem more convincing."

"That's not true," Casper said. "Well, maybe it's partially true."

"Which is it?" Bernie asked.

Casper didn't reply.

"But why did you think that?" Bernie asked him. She didn't understand. "We never thought anything of the kind."

"He did it because he was greedy," Sean said.

"That's not it," Casper said.

"Then what was it?" Sean demanded.

"I was trying to do a good thing," Casper told him.

"How do you figure that?" Libby asked.

When Casper didn't answer, Sean continued. "He wasn't. Casper figured that with you running around, he had more time to sell the teapot. But it didn't matter. He didn't know the right people to sell it to. He was stuck with the thing, the thing that someone else felt belonged to them. Then there were the police. He could have gone to them, but if they found out he had the teapot, they would use it as confirmation that he killed Zalinsky. So he was in a bind, a bind of his own making. Do I have it right, Casper?" Sean asked.

Casper lifted his head up. "Some of it."

"What's the rest?" Bernie asked.

"What's the point?" Casper said. "You won't believe me anyway."

"Try us," Sean said.

"I just thought . . ." Casper shook his head. He looked miserable. "Forget it. I was probably wrong anyway. What are you going to do now? Call the police and turn me in?"

"That's up to my daughters," Sean informed him, deciding Casper looked as if he was going to cry.

"You deserve it," Libby told him.

"But we're not going to," Bernie quickly added, although she would have liked to, given all the trouble he'd caused.

Casper leaped off the sofa and hugged Bernie and Libby. "Thank you, thank you," he said. Then he turned to Sean.

"Not necessary," Sean said, shrinking back in his seat. He held up his hands. "No hugging, please. I don't do hugging. Just sit back down."

"I'm not a good criminal," Casper observed once he was back on the sofa.

"Now that's a massive understatement if I ever heard one," Sean remarked.

"I thought I would be," Casper said mournfully. "I've staged two mysteries."

"Not quite the same thing," Sean was telling him when he noticed that Bernie was looking at her cell. "Can't you put that thing away?" he told her.

"It's Lucy Chin," Bernie replied. "She sent me the photos she promised."

"Let's see," Sean said.

Chapter 45

Bernie got up, went into the bedroom, and got her laptop. The photos would be easier to see on that. She came out a moment later and put the laptop on the table. Everyone huddled around it while she downloaded the file. The first two images showed a large group of fancily dressed people holding drinks and talking. So did the third and the fourth ones.

"I hope this isn't going to be a waste of time," Bernie said as the fifth image came into view.

Casper squinted and pointed to the picture. "Can you make this larger?"

Bernie did, and Casper tapped the screen. "There," he said. Suddenly he was smiling.

Bernie and Libby leaned in.

"What?" Bernie asked. She still didn't see what Casper was pointing to.

"I see," Libby said. A moment later, Bernie did too. It was Zalinsky and his partner. Libby turned to Bernie. "Is he with who I think he is?"

Bernie nodded. "Yeah. He is." She went back to the earlier images. Now that she knew who she was looking for, she could see the couple in the third picture as well.

"I thought he was with Erin," Libby said.

Casper laughed and pumped his fist in the air.

"I was right. I was right all along. I thought I was crazy, but I wasn't."

"About what?" Bernie asked.

"You'll see," Casper said, with a smug smile on his face.

"I wonder if she's who he was leaving Erin for?" Libby mused.

"Even if she was," Bernie pointed out, "I don't see how she could have had anything to do with Zalinsky's death. She wasn't at *Alice*."

"Yes, she was," Casper contradicted. "I saw her there. She was in the audience. First row, last seat on the left."

"But she wasn't backstage," Bernie said. "I would have seen her if she had been."

"Not necessarily. Anyway, he was," Casper said, pointing to a waiter standing off to one side.

"Is that Ivan?" Libby asked, bending even closer. "Ivan the bodyguard?"

"Sure looks that way to me," Casper replied, his smile getting even bigger if that was possible.

"Maybe it's coincidence," Bernie suggested.

"Doubtful," Sean remarked, voicing his opinion. If his years in law enforcement had taught him anything, they had taught him not to believe in coincidence.

Bernie scrolled through more of the photos. There were twenty in all. In the eighteenth image, they found a picture of Alla Feldman, Zalinsky's partner, and Ivan talking off in the corner.

"Those two definitely know each other," Casper observed.

"Really well, judging by the expressions on their faces," Bernie said.

"Agreed." Sean straightened up while Bernie scrolled down to the next photo.

Libby tapped the screen after Bernie had enlarged the photo. It showed Ivan and Alla still talking to each other, only they were standing closer now, almost shoulder to shoulder. "Look at their hands," she instructed. Bernie, Sean, and Casper did. There was no doubt. Alla and Ivan were holding hands.

"That's suggestive," Sean observed.

"Isn't it, though?" Bernie agreed.

Sean turned to Bernie. "What were these shots intended for?" he asked his daughter.

"PR stuff. Lucy Chin said they take them at all their events and archive them," Bernie replied. She rubbed her chin with her knuckles. The name sparked a memory. The flowers, she thought, suddenly remembering what Lucy Chin had said about the flowers on her desk. Then she recalled the photos on the tea shop wall. The flowers were the key. They'd been growing in the garden, right there for everyone to see all along. "You're wrong," she said to her dad. "Remember you said the poison is going to make things harder. It's not. It's going to make things easier."

Then she looked at the grin on Casper's face.

"You knew," she said.

"I suspected," Casper said. He was having a hard time suppressing his glee.

"Then why didn't you tell us?" Libby demanded.

"You wouldn't have believed me," Casper said.

"You could have tried," Bernie told him.

"I tried. I pointed you in the right direction," Casper said.

"No, you didn't," Libby told him.

Bernie held up her hand. "He did," she said, catching on.

Libby put her hands on her hips. "How?" she demanded.

"The tea," Bernie said. "The tea was yellow."

Casper nodded. "Like the flowers."

"Are you crazy?" Libby demanded of him. "How were we supposed to figure that out?"

Casper bit his lip. "You're detectives. You're supposed to detect. I thought you'd get it. I did something like it in the last play I staged."

"Only this isn't a play. This is real life," Libby pointed out. She was having trouble keeping herself from yelling.

"How did you know?" Sean asked Casper before Libby could say anything else.

"I didn't know. I told you: I suspected," Casper replied. There were beads of sweat on his forehead. He took a handkerchief and mopped his brow. "Actually, 'suspect' is too strong a word."

"Well, I'm going to use it anyway," Sean said. "Why did you suspect?" he asked, careful to keep his voice low and reassuring.

"I don't know. I was in Alla's tea shop, and I told her what I was doing. I was staging *Hamlet*, and I was talking about the poison in the ear scene, and she said in Russia they would use a flower, and then I complimented her about her photographs. Later I remembered seeing flowers like that down in South Carolina, where I was directing *Death of a Salesman*, and someone telling me to be careful because they were toxic."

"Yes," Sean said. "But what made you think that Alla had murdered Zalinsky?"

"It was something she said when I was in there buying tea."

"I didn't know you bought tea there," Libby interrupted.

"You had only to ask," Casper told her.

"Go on," Sean urged Casper.

"It was a line of Tennyson." Casper closed his eyes and recited. "'The honey of poison-flowers and all the measureless ill.'"

"She said that?" Bernie asked.

"No, I did," Casper explained. "She responded with, 'That works for me' or words to that effect. Then a couple of days later it just came to me. All the pieces fell into place."

"I don't see how you went from there to her poisoning Zalinsky," Bernie said.

"Because Stan told me she hated Zalinsky," Casper said.

"And how did Stan know?" Libby asked, although she was almost afraid to.

"Because he and Alla were sleeping together," Casper replied.

Bernie thought back to chasing Stan through the parking lot. She'd been right about his going to see Alla after all. "She was sleeping with Stan and Ivan and Zalinsky?"

"She was a busy lady," Casper said.

"I'll say," Libby replied.

Casper continued. "You can see why I didn't want to accuse someone if I was wrong," he said, appealing to Bernie. "The whole thing was so nebulous, and I do have a tendency to invent stuff. I know that. I just thought if I nudged you in the right direction you'd figure it out."

Scan leaned forward. "The important question," he said, "is what are we going to do now?"

"I think I know," Bernie responded.

Chapter 46

The next morning turned out to be one of those perfect late-summer mornings. The rain had washed all the heat and humidity out of the air. It was seventy degrees and sunny at eight o'clock. The sky was cloudless, the trees, grass, and flowers all vibrant colors. It was a glorious day. A perfect day, Bernie thought, as she, Libby, and Casper drove over to Alla Feldman's house. They were all crammed together in the front seat of the van, and Bernie was going over the plan.

It was simple, really. Casper and Libby were going to knock on the door, and when Alla answered, he and Libby were going to tell Alla that Casper had had a change of heart and wanted to give her back the teapot, which he would do for a percentage of the sale price. While they were discussing that, Bernie would slip through the gate, go into Alla's garden, find a sample of the *Gelsemium elegans*, or flower of death, as Bernie had taken to calling it, photograph it, and leave. When she got back in the van, she'd call Libby, at which point Libby would feign an emergency, and she and Casper would head out the door. Then they'd all drive home, and Bernie would give what they'd collected to

Clyde, who would blackmail Lucy into looking at the new evidence. At least that was the plan.

"It'll be fine," Bernie was reassuring Casper as she passed Michelle's new shop. It still had a ways to go, she thought, as she warned Casper not to eat or drink anything Alla offered him.

"Of course, I'm not going to take anything from her. Do I look stupid to you?" Casper demanded.

Bernie wisely refrained from answering.

Casper rubbed his hands together. "In fact, I'm looking forward to this. It's about time Alla got some of her own back."

"Let's just stick to the script," Libby told him.

"I will," Casper told her. "You can count on that."

Libby hoped that was the case. Five minutes later, Bernie pulled up in front of Alla Feldman's house. It was a classic brick colonial, with the window frames and front door painted white. A riot of annuals and perennials bordered the house, while the lawn was a vivid emerald green. If there was a weed anywhere, Bernie didn't see it. Whatever else Alla was, Bernie thought, she was a good gardener.

"Luck," Bernie told Casper and Libby as Libby started to get out of Mathilda. Then Bernie ducked down as Casper and Libby walked up to Alla's house and rang the bell. Bernie could hear the door open a minute later. Bernie couldn't hear what was being said, but a couple of moments after that she heard the sound of the door closing.

Bernie gave it a couple more minutes, then she lifted up her head and peered through the window. Yup. Everyone was inside. Bernie waited another minute before she got out of the van and quietly shut the door. She kept the van between herself and Alla Feldman's house until she was out of range of the front window, after which she quickly followed the brick path that led to the backyard. A stockade fence surrounded the backyard, and Bernie had no trouble opening the bolt on the gate and letting herself in.

For a moment she stood there, overcome by the riot of color. Her first impression was a tangle of plants and flowers and vegetables. It took her a moment to sort things out. A very large vegetable garden was planted in the middle of the yard; to the left of it was an herb garden, and to the right the flowerbeds. Apple, cherry, and peach trees grew around the garden's perimeter, while a variety of houseplants, including a fig tree, sat on the patio absorbing the summer sun.

It was an incredible garden, and Bernie was wondering if she and Bernie might be able to grow their own vegetables—on a modified scale, of course—as she walked toward the flowers. Even though it was late in the season, the bed was filled with sweet alyssum, black-eyed Susans and coneflowers, asters, and heather, as well as petunias, snapdragons, impatiens, and a flower with purple fronds that Bernie didn't know the name of. Morning glories and climbing roses, intertwined with ivy, scaled the fence.

Bernie was thinking that somehow the whole thing worked, that the flowers formed a coherent whole, when she spotted the plant she was looking for. The *Gelsemium elegans* was hanging out in front of a bed of ferns near the stockade fence. The yellow, trumpet-shaped flowers glowed in the sunlight. No one, Bernie thought, would ever think those flowers were as deadly as they were. And yet, eating just half of one of them could kill someone.

She was reflecting on how deceptive appearances could be as she made her way toward it. She took out her cell and snapped ten pictures of the flower, after which she went about the business of getting a sample. She was breaking off a stem when she felt rather than heard someone come up behind her. Before she could turn her head, the person had their forearm across Bernie's neck, cutting off her breathing. She could feel the barrel of a gun jammed against the side of her forehead. *Dumb,* Bernie thought. *Really dumb. The garden shed. I should have checked it.*

"What you doing here?" A man's voice, a voice she recognized as Ivan's, asked her.

She wanted to answer him, but she couldn't, because her vocal cords weren't working.

Chapter 47

L ibby's eyes widened as Ivan opened the sliding glass door that led onto the patio and frog-marched her sister into the middle of the living room.

"Look what I found snooping outside," Ivan declared, throwing Bernie next to her sister and pointing his gun at Libby and Bernie.

Bernie rubbed her throat. "I take it that weapon is real?" she asked, her voice coming out in a croak.

"No. Is fake," Ivan snapped.

"I thought it might be a prop," Bernie replied. "Like at the play. When you were supposed to be guarding the teapot but were actually planning on stealing it."

Ivan straightened up. "You think you're so smart, but you not smart enough."

"I think we can agree on that," Libby said as she watched Ivan grab Bernie's tote with his free hand.

"Looking for something?" Bernie asked as Ivan rummaged through it. "If you want my lipstick, it's in my cosmetic case."

Ivan ignored her and kept rummaging. "Aha," he said a moment later, taking out her phone and holding it aloft. Then he went through the photos on the phone while keeping an eye on the sisters. "Why you taking this?" he demanded, showing Bernie the pictures of the yellow flowers.

"Would you believe I'm submitting them to a gardening magazine as the mystery flower of the month?" Bernie asked him.

Ivan didn't smile. Neither did Alla.

"Not funny," she said.

"I thought it was," Bernie told her. She held out her hand. "Now if you'll give me back my phone, we'll be going. I didn't realize we would be intruding."

"You not going anywhere," Ivan snarled.

"And how are you going to stop us?" Bernie asked him.

"Simple." Ivan nodded toward the gun with his chin. "I shoot you."

"Then you'd have to shoot all of us," Bernie pointed out as she wondered where Casper was.

Ivan smiled. "Why not? I no see problem."

"You're not helping the situation," Libby told Bernie.

"I'm open for suggestions," Bernie replied.

"You two be quiet," Alla ordered.

"I guess you could," Bernie observed. "After all, if you've killed one person, another three probably wouldn't matter. You know, in for a penny, in for a pound. Not that I know this from personal experience, you understand."

381

Alla got up and stood next to Ivan. "Ivan is a hot head. I'm not. Maybe I make you some tea, and we all feel better, yes? Then we can talk."

"No," Libby said. "No tea."

"It's good," Alla told her. "It's special."

Bernie laughed. "That's one way of putting it. You should have stuck with rigging the tea-kettle," Bernie informed her. "The poison was de trop."

Alla wrinkled her nose. "De trop? What does that mean?"

"French words that mean over the top, too much," Libby informed her.

"Told you," Ivan said to her.

"You be quiet," Alla admonished.

"Why?" Ivan asked her. "They no be speaking to anyone."

"You can't kill us," Bernie repeated.

"And why is this?" Ivan asked. "You just said I could."

"That's not what I meant," Bernie told him. "Anyway, think of the labor involved in getting rid of three bodies."

"Not that hard," Ivan said, grinning unpleasantly.

"In any case," Bernie continued, "people know we're here. They'll come looking for us."

"And we will tell them we don't see you," Alla told her.

Bernie decided to change the conversation to a pleasanter topic. "So how long have you been seeing this guy?" Bernie asked Alla, indicating Ivan with a nod of her head.

"Magda introduced us," Alla replied.

"You know Magda?" Libby asked.

Alla nodded. "Yes. She is my cousin. She gave me the idea for this."

Wonderful, Bernie thought. "Was that you in the apartment when Libby and I came to speak to Ivan and Igor?" she asked.

"*Da.*" Alla stroked Ivan's arm. "Ludvoc, he was a bad man. He promised everyone everything, but he didn't have anything to give. He rented everything."

"Except for the teapot," Libby said.

Ivan and Alla both nodded.

"We need to know where it is," Ivan said.

"We are waiting for the short, fat one to come back," Alla said to Ivan. "He will tell us."

"I wouldn't call him that," Bernie protested. "He's very sensitive about his weight."

Ivan ignored her. "Where is he?" he asked Alla. "I thought you said they both come together."

Alla nodded toward the hallway. "He is in the bathroom. He told me he drank too much coffee and he had to go pee because he had a nervous bladder."

"We wait," Ivan announced. Five minutes later, when Casper hadn't come out, Ivan announced that he was going into the bathroom to check.

He handed Alla the gun. "You keep eye on them," he instructed her.

Bernie looked at her sister and nodded imperceptibly. Libby nodded back and started her spiel.

"I told you this wasn't a good plan," she said to her sister. "In fact, this is the epitome of a not-good plan."

"Not true," Bernie replied, taking a step closer to Alla.

"How can you say that?" Libby countered.

"I can and I am," Bernie responded. "The problem with you is that you're too negative."

"Negative?" Libby said indignantly. "You really are crazy."

"Me crazy?" Bernie cried as she slowly inched closer to Alla. "I'm not crazy. You're stupid."

"Are you calling me stupid?" Libby screamed. By now she and Bernie were within an arm's reach of Alla.

"I most certainly am," Bernie told her as she prepared to shove Libby into Alla. She was just about to when Ivan came running back in.

"Casper no there," he yelled. "He go out window. How you be so stupid?"

Alla flushed. "Me stupid?"

"Stupid seems to be the word of the day," Bernie commented as she reached out her hand. She was just about to grab for the gun when she heard a noise. A loud noise. A loud noise that was getting closer. It sounded like their van, Bernie decided. And she was correct. It was their van.

Everyone looked up just in time to see Mathilda speeding over the front lawn. Casper was in the driver's seat, and he had a demonic look on his face. The van was heading toward the house. A moment later, Mathilda tore through the living room wall with a tremendous roar. Alla dropped the gun and ran into the kitchen. Everyone else scattered. Mathilda went a little farther and stopped with a jerk in front of the sofa.

Casper jumped out of Mathilda and ran toward Alla. "Now we're even," he screamed at her as Libby picked up the gun Alla had dropped and turned it on Ivan, who had been stunned into immobility.

"I'll call the police," Bernie said, taking back her phone from Ivan.

"You do that," Libby told her as she watched Casper tackle Alla and bring her to the ground.

"You ruined everything," he growled at Alla. "Everything. Now I'm going to have to go back to dinner theater."

Chapter 48

Three weeks later, Bernie, Libby, Sean, Marvin, and Clyde were gathered at Michelle's shop for its official opening. By now the majority of the crowd had dispersed, leaving the Simmonses, the Simmonses' friends, Michelle's friends, and her staff behind. Thirty people in all.

The opening had gone well, with Michelle giving out free samples of the food she was going to sell, food Bernie and Libby were distressed to see was a lot like the food they were selling. So was the store layout, for that matter. Maybe the colors on the walls weren't exactly the same shade as the ones on the walls of A Little Taste of Heaven, but they sure weren't that far apart either.

Bernie, Libby, Marvin, and Clyde were quietly standing off in the corner discussing Casper's stunt with Mathilda, while Sean was near the display cases chatting with Michelle's friends.

"It's a miracle she's still running," Libby was saying, her eyes darting to her dad and back again.

"No," Marvin said, "it's a miracle you're still alive."

"That too," Libby agreed. "Thanks to Casper. Otherwise we'd be dead."

"Disagree. When it comes down to it, I don't

think Ivan or Alla would have shot us," Bernie said. "I think they would have tied us up and run away."

"As you pointed out, they already killed one person. Why not three?" Libby demanded.

"So did Casper actually bring the teapot over to Alla's house?" Marvin asked, interrupting the conversation. Just hearing about the possibility of Libby or Bernie being killed was enough to make him feel queasy.

Bernie shook her head. "Nope. It was at the shop."

"So where is it now?" asked Marvin.

"The bank has it. I understand it's going to go back on the market again."

Bernie explained.

"Zalinsky bought it with money he borrowed from the National Bank of Florida. He got that money by putting up the apartment building he 'owned'"—Bernie did air quotes with her fingers—"and by using the painting he'd rented as collateral. His fortune was all a house of cards."

"And no one thought to check?" Marvin asked. "I find that hard to believe."

"He forged the provenances," Libby told him. "And anyway, the more it looks like you have money, the less people are tempted to investigate."

"Lucky my father got paid in advance," Marvin observed.

"Yes, it is," Bernie agreed. "I'll say this for

Zalinsky, though. He was a pretty good con man."

"But not good enough," Libby pointed out.

"True," Bernie agreed. "If he was, he'd be in Belize right now, soaking up the sun and planning his next scam instead of six feet under in the Longely cemetery."

Marvin took a sip of water and rested his cup on the wrought-iron table next to the window. "I thought for sure it was Erin that killed him."

"Me too," Bernie replied.

"So why Alla?" he asked.

"Because," Bernie told him, "not only had Zalinsky ditched Erin for a younger model, but he was in the process of ditching Alla as well."

"And Magda," Libby said. "Don't forget about her."

"I don't think I'd have the energy," Clyde commented, speaking up for the first time. "Even when I was younger. Three women. That's too much for me."

"And evidently for Zalinsky as well," Libby said.

"For sure," Bernie agreed. "And if you do do that, here's what you don't do," she said, warming to the topic. "You don't ditch the woman you're using to help you steal something. Especially when that woman knows about poisons and her boyfriend knows about electricity."

"Well, Zalinsky didn't know that," Libby said.

"Evidently not," Bernie agreed. "He wasn't as smart as he thought he was."

"But how did Alla find out about the other woman?" Marvin asked.

"She didn't. Magda did. She listened in on one of Zalinsky's phone calls, after which she started going through his financial statements. She was so upset with what she found that she went to her cousin Alla for advice . . ."

"Which was how Alla found out," Clyde said, finishing Bernie's sentence for her.

Marvin frowned. "But why electrocute the man and poison him at the same time? Why not one or the other?"

Clyde stifled a cough. "According to the statement Alla gave, she wanted to make sure he was dead, dead, dead. She wasn't sure that the shock would do it, so she decided to add an insurance policy."

"Well, she certainly accomplished that," Libby observed.

"And Ivan?" Marvin asked. "How did he figure in this?"

"He was just the poor shmuck who went along for the ride," Clyde said. "Sex is a powerful incentive."

"Speaking of ride, let's not forget our tires," Libby said.

"That was just because Ivan wanted to put suspicion on Jason," Bernie said. "He saw us talking to him and figured we'd suspect him when we came out of The Blue House. Which we did."

"So what's going to happen to Alla, Ivan, and Magda?" Marvin asked. There hadn't been anything in the local paper to date.

Clyde answered. "Magda agreed to testify against Ivan and Alla, so she's probably going away for seven years and will be out in three, while Alla and Ivan will be going on trial for murder two."

"And The Blue House?" Marvin asked.

"Evidently, the town is going to take it over," Bernie answered.

"Well, that's one good thing to come out of this at least," Marvin said.

"True," Libby said.

"And you can't say Zalinsky wasn't a force to be reckoned with," Bernie said.

"Also true," Clyde agreed. He was about to say it was a force he could do without when Michelle clapped her hands.

Everyone turned toward her. She smiled and began to talk. "The first thing I want to do is thank everyone for coming. I want to especially thank Bernie and Libby for being my inspiration." At that point, she gestured to Bernie and Libby, leaving them no option but to smile their thanks, even though that was the last thing they wanted to do. "It's been a long, hard slog," Michelle continued, "but I finally made it, and I hope to see everyone back here soon, and if you like my stuff, I hope you'll tell your friends about this place. I'd really appreciate it."

"We will," one of Michelle's friends called out.

"Definitely," another of Michelle's friends said. Everyone clapped.

"Super," Michelle replied. Her smile grew. "And now I have one more announcement to make. An important one."

Libby turned to Bernie. For some reason, Libby could feel a knot in her stomach, and she could tell from the expression on Bernie's face that Bernie was feeling the same way she was.

Michelle paused again to increase the suspense. Then she said, "This just happened, and I am so happy that I wanted to share it with you immediately. Sean and I have decided to get engaged."

Everyone started clapping and stamping their feet and catcalling. Except for Libby and Bernie. They were in shock.

"This is not going to turn out well," Libby predicted when she got her voice back.

But Bernie hadn't heard what Libby was saying because she was looking at her dad. Was it her imagination, or did he seem to be in shock too? Or was that just wishful thinking on her part?

"We have to do something," Libby whispered in Bernie's ear.

"Yes, we do," Bernie replied.

The question was what.

RECIPES

I have three recipes for you. I thought I'd have four, but making clotted cream turned out to be much more difficult than I imagined. I'm going to give you the recipe anyway, though, because it is the traditional adjunct to scones and strawberry jam in an English tea, and because maybe you'll have better luck than I did. Also, clotted cream is delicious, and you can always whip the cream if worse comes to worst.

The recipe is simplicity itself. Take two pints of heavy (not ultra-pasteurized) cream, then put a filter in a coffee basket, put the basket in a strainer, put the strainer in a bowl, and pour the cream into the filter in the basket. Put the bowl with the strainer in the fridge for six hours, and scrape down the sides of the filter with a spatula every once in a while. The whey will separate from the cream, and what is left in the strainer will be clotted cream. At least that's the theory. Only, as I said, it didn't work for me. I'm not sure why. If you want to have a go, please feel free and write me if you're successful. I'd love to know what I'm doing wrong.

CHINESE MARBLED EGGS

In keeping with the tea theme, the next recipe is for Chinese marbled eggs, basically hard-boiled eggs with their shells cracked and marinated in soy sauce, tea, and spices. This recipe uses black tea, which can either be loose or in bags. The eggs are easy to make, they're a great snack, they look cool, and kids seem to love them. It's one of those recipes that you can tinker with.

6 large eggs
1 or 2 tablespoons or 1 or 2 tea bags of black
  tea
½ to ¾ of a cup of soy sauce
2 tablespoons of Chinese five-spice powder
  or two-star anise
1 cinnamon stick
1 teaspoon of sugar
A couple of strips of dried tangerine peel

Bring water to a boil, put in the 6 large eggs, and let them cook for 3 to 5 minutes. Then take the pot off the burner, take the eggs out, allow them to cool, and carefully crack the shells. You can do this with the back of a spoon or by rolling them around on the counter. The deeper the cracks, the more the marbling. Then add to a pan with boiling water the black tea, the soy sauce, the Chinese five-spice powder or two-star anise, the cinnamon stick, and the sugar. You can also add a couple of strips of dried tangerine peel if you have that on hand. Put the eggs back into the pot and bring the water to a boil. Then turn the heat down to a low simmer, cover the pan, and let the eggs cook for 30 minutes or so. Remove from heat and let them steep for anywhere from 2 hours to overnight in the fridge.

The next recipe has nothing to do with tea, but it is delicious, so I'm including it anyway. This recipe comes from Dino Centra, who is a truly excellent cook.

GNOCCHI ALLA ROMANA

This is what Dino has to say about the origins of this recipe. Unlike the better-known gnocchi, which are made from potato, these are made from semolina, a durum wheat flour. Long before ships brought native crops from the Americas to Europe, Italy was a land without red sauce, corn polenta, or potato gnocchi. But even without the potato, gnocchi still existed in the form of the classic gnocchi alla Romana, a custardy, oven-baked version made with semolina, egg, cheese, and butter. You could say these are the OG: the original gnocchi.

6 cups of milk
Kosher salt
1½ cups of semolina flour
8 tablespoons of unsalted butter, divided in half, plus more for greasing the pan
1 cup of grated Parmigiano-Reggiano, plus more for grating right before baking and at the table
3 egg yolks

Preheat oven to 450 degrees. In a large saucepan, heat the milk over medium-high heat, whisking occasionally to prevent scorching, until it is steaming. Season well with salt. While whisking constantly, sprinkle in semolina in a fine shower to prevent lumps: the mixture will thicken and become difficult to whisk. Once all the semolina is added, lower the heat to medium-low, switch to a rubber spatula or wooden spoon, and cook over medium-low heat, stirring constantly for 10 to 15 minutes, until a sticky, dough-like mass forms and begins to pull away from the sides of the saucepan; make sure to stir deep into corners and all over the bottom of saucepan to prevent scorching. Remove from heat.

Stir in 4 tablespoons of butter until melted and thoroughly incorporated. Stir in the grated cheese until melted and thoroughly incorporated. Scrape in the egg yolks and stir until thoroughly incorporated.

Scrape the semolina dough into a buttered, rimmed baking sheet. Using a wet rubber spatula or wet, clean hands, and rewetting frequently to prevent sticking, press and smooth the semolina dough into an even layer about ½-inch thick. It's okay if the dough does not fully reach all edges of the baking pan, as long as it's even throughout. Press plastic wrap against the surface, and refrigerate until set, at least 40 minutes and as long as overnight.

Using a 3-inch round cookie cutter or similarly sized glass, cut the semolina dough into rounds. The rounds can be refrigerated for up to 3 days covered with plastic wrap before topping with butter and cheese and baking. Scraps can be saved and refrigerated for up to 4 days: deep fry in oil for a snack or assemble in a smaller baking dish to make a mini version of this dish.

To bake, grease a large baking dish or oven-proof skillet with butter. Using a thin metal spatula, scrape each semolina round from the baking sheet and arrange them in an overlapping pattern in the prepared skillet or dish.

Melt the remaining 4 tablespoons of butter and drizzle all over the semolina gnocchi. Grate more Parmigiano-Reggiano generously all over. Bake until the gnocchi are hot and brown on top, about 15 minutes.

Serve, passing more grated cheese at the table.

TRIPLE GINGER LOAF

This last recipe comes from an old friend of mine, Linda Nielson, and is worth repeating. It is extremely versatile. This cake goes well with tea or coffee. You can serve it as a snack, put it in a lunch box, or serve it as a dessert. It is tasty and, as my grandmother used to say, a good keeper. What more do you need? Also, ginger is good if you are having digestive issues.

⅔ cup of flour
1 teaspoon of ground ginger
1 teaspoon of ground cinnamon
1 teaspoon of baking powder
½ teaspoon of cardamom
½ teaspoon of salt
2 tablespoons of peeled, grated, fresh ginger
½ cup of brown sugar
½ cup of white sugar
½ cup of applesauce or ½ cup of vegetable oil
4 egg whites, or 4 ounces of egg substitute,
  or 2 eggs

½ cup of buttermilk or sour milk or fat-free
   yogurt
6 tablespoons of minced, crystallized ginger

Preheat oven to 350 degrees. Sift the dry
ingredients, mix the wet ingredients, combine,
add the crystallized ginger, and mix. Butter an
8-inch loaf pan. Bake for 50 minutes, and let
cool in pan. You can double this recipe and
bake in a Bundt pan, if you would like.

Center Point Large Print
600 Brooks Road / PO Box 1
Thorndike, ME 04986-0001 USA

(207) 568-3717

US & Canada:
1 800 929-9108
www.centerpointlargeprint.com